8-25-23

D0113747

3 -

The
Untelling

Also by Tayari Jones

Leaving Atlanta

The Untelling

TAYARI JONES

WARNER BOOKS

NEW YORK   BOSTON

Copyright © 2005 by Tayari Jones
All rights reserved.

Warner Books

Time Warner Book Group
1271 Avenue of the Americas, New York, NY 10020
Visit our Web site at www.twbookmark.com.

Printed in the United States of America

ISBN 0-446-53246-0

this is for doug

Acknowledgments

My parents and siblings are extremely good people. I am lucky.

Thanks to Sally Keith, who "gets" me, and Bryn "Pie" Chancellor, who scours all drafts. Anne Warner nudges me toward what is right. Camille Dungy is bright as a horn.

Major love to my friends who lent their eyes to any of the six major incarnations of this novel. These folks helped me see what was good but told me how to fix what needed fixing: Barbara Ann Posey Jones, Deanna Bryant, Ginney Fowler, João Costa Vargas, Chad Unrein, Maxine Kennedy, Jafari Allen, David Van Fossen, Kiyana Sakena Horton, John W. Holman, Aisha Moon, June Aldridge, and Eric Beaumont.

Linda Eldridge is everything a bartender should be. Scott Vaughn taught me to relax. Renee Simms helps me

viiiAcknowledgments

understand perspective. Jewell Parker Rhodes, Crystal Wilkinson, Merrill Fietell, Monique Truong, and Suji Kwok Kim are the counterargument to all the snarky things people say about writers. Deirdre McNamer was an inspiration even before we met.

Mr. Ron Carlson helped me at the start of this project; you will find his fingerprints everywhere. Ms. Pearl Cleage is one smart colored woman.

I want to acknowledge the generous assistance of the MacDowell Colony, the Family and Friends of Gerald Freund, the Corporation of Yaddo, John and Joan Jakobson, the LEF Foundation, Arizona Commission on the Arts, the Ledig House International Writers Colony, Le Chateau de Lavigny International Writers Colony, Bread Loaf Writers' Conference, Wesleyan Summer Writers Conference, East Tennessee State University, and the G.E. Foundation.

Jane Dystel is a shrewd agent, loyal advocate, and extremely kind human being. Caryn Karmatz Rudy is my editor and friend.

The
Untelling

Prologue

Ariadne, my given name, the one that's on my driver's license, is the sort of name that you're supposed to grow into. It was my mother's idea. Her parents underestimated her when they called her Eloise, a name that had strained at the seams before she was old enough to spell it. Our mother's gifts to the three of us were lush, extravagant, roomy names. Names that fit us like oversized coats, trimmed in seed pearls, gold braid, and the hides of baby seals. My father had wanted us to have family names, with at least one of us girls named after his mother, Lula. My mother, who indulged my father in many things, could not give him this. Why, she wondered, would someone in this day and age give a child a name that was so *Mississippi*? "That is not what Dr. King died for."

People shook their heads with each pink birth announcement; teachers squinted at class rolls and said, "Who ever heard of black people with names like that? Those kids are going to be *confused*."

Mama never forgave us for not appreciating our names. When my older sister, Hermione, came home from first grade and announced that she wanted to be called Sonja, Mama had said, "Why do you have to be so ungrateful? Your name is from *Shakespeare*." My name, Ariadne, is taken from the Greek. Mama explained that I was named for a princess. My tenth-grade English book gave me the rest of the story. Ariadne was a Greek princess; this much is true—my mother is not the type to lie. The princess Ariadne saved her lover's life with a length of string which he used to wind his way out of a deadly maze. To show his gratitude, he married her. After only a few weeks he dumped her on a rocky island and sailed off. When I confronted my mother with this story, she insisted that there was a happier ending, that Ariadne ended up marrying the god of wine, but for me the story ends when she is sitting on the island watching the black-sailed boat churn away.

My other sister, the baby, Mama's miracle child, the one who got born despite the tied tubes, her name was Genevieve, for the patron saint of Paris.

Nicknames were forbidden.

I was there when Daddy said Genevieve was too much name for a baby. Couldn't we at least call her Jenny? Mama sighed and waved her hand, one of her elegant gestures that let everyone know that she was more than just an Eloise.

I was nine, sitting on the floor between Mama's knees

while she threaded clear plastic beads onto my braids. I felt hot prickles of jealousy over my lip. Why hadn't Daddy stuck up for me and my name? "Ariadne" was obviously the worst of the lot. Genevieve, who had the best name, a name that someone had at least heard of, she lay on a white receiving blanket and chewed on her toes.

I looked up and met my father's eyes, and turned my face to the orange carpet before they could accuse me of listening to grown folks' conversations.

Mama said, "Lincoln, maybe it *is* too much name for a baby. But Genevieve will not be a baby forever."

I looked up again, fast this time. Mama lost her grip on my braid; heart-shaped beads fell on the floor and rolled under the couch. We were all still for the duration of three heartbeats. This had been one of those Greek myth moments, when you could just hear the gods look up from their newspapers and raise their eyebrows.

On the Saturday before Easter 1978, Genevieve was six months old, teething and blowing spit bubbles, when the whole family piled into our burgundy Buick. I liked her. Hermione often told people that I was jealous of the baby because of her soft hair and bleached pine bedroom set. But I wasn't jealous. Genevieve was a beautiful thing, all curves and folds of flesh, smelling of rose water and drool. This is what I remember and this is the truth.

We were on our way to the spring performance at the YWCA, where I took ballet, tap, and jazz. The recital was to be held in a large gymnasium that smelled of Pine-Sol and feet, but all of us were dressed up and looking good. Daddy wore a white shirt with "creases sharp enough to shave with," he'd said, running his fingers down his stiff sleeve. According to Mama, Hermione's pants were too tight, but they looked good; on her the snugness seemed deliberate, a taunt. My mother out-dressed us all, but that was her way. She wore a butter-colored suit and matching pumps. Genevieve was just a little brown face in a nest of aquamarine lace and ruffles. I'd put on a green jumper over my pink leotard and white tights. This was my favorite dress, worn at least once a week, pulled hot from the dryer each time. I liked it because it covered the raised outline of my training bra, the first of anyone in beginning tap dance. When I wore it, I seemed to be like any other girl with my tight plaits and heart-shaped beads.

Hermione hadn't wanted to go. She was almost fif-teen and would have rather stayed home alone, staring at the phone and wondering why boys didn't call her. It was because she was fat. I knew this because I had read her red clothbound diary. *Must lose weight*, she had scrawled. *Orthodontia—expensive. Necessary?* I was glad that she was there, even gladder that she hadn't wanted to be. Staring sullen out of the window, she was making a "sacrifice," a word we'd talked about last week in Sun-day school.

Why hadn't we taken a photo of ourselves before pil-ing into the car? Just a Polaroid, or a quick snap with Hermione's 126 camera, creating something that I could use to compare with the images in my head, so that I could be sure exactly what was remembered and what was invented or just wished for.

I scooted closer to Hermione, breathing big gulps of her honeysuckle perfume. I lifted the red velvet cake from her lap. It was a big one, three layers, and dusted on top with chopped pecans. This lovely cake, slightly extravagant, was our family's contribution to the recital reception.

I was happy. I do remember this.

I had been telling the story of the dogwood trees, raising my voice over Hermione, who sang along with the staticky car radio.

"I'm trying to talk," I said.

"I'm trying to sing."

Daddy turned down the radio. Mama bounced Genevieve on her lap and said, "Shh, sweetie," to the baby and "Go on, honey," to me.

"Before Jesus," I told them, projecting from my diaphragm, like my Sunday school teacher had taught me, "the dogwood was as tall and mighty as the oak and pine."

"Please tell me that's not your Easter speech," Hermione said. "You know that's just a myth, don't you?"

"You don't even know what I was going to say. You didn't let me finish."

Hermione shrugged her heavy shoulders. "You were about to say that they used the dogwood to make the cross and now the tree is so shamed that it grows all little and hunched up."

"That's a good story," Daddy said. His eyes smiled at me in the rearview mirror.

"And," I said, "there's the part about the flowers. On

every one of the petals is a little red spot. That's the blood
so nobody could forget about Jesus."

"Daddy," Hermione said, "can you turn the radio
back up? Did they even *have* dogwood trees where Jesus
grew up, in Bethlehem or wherever?"

I know what happened next, although I didn't see it.
My eyes were on the nut-crusted sides of the red velvet
cake when a blue El Dorado barreled down the left side
of Hunter Street, just after Mosely Park. I'd snuck my
finger under the cellophane for a taste of icing and was
trying to silently work my thumb to my mouth when
Daddy said, "Jesus," and I thought we were still talking
about dogwoods. Then the car lunged to the right, to the
left, and back again.

I ruined the cake when our car crumpled against the
bark of a hundred-year-old magnolia. I hugged it to me,
grinding the white icing and red meat of the cake into
the bib of my jumper. When the car stopped moving, I
didn't look up right away. I stared at my lap and the mess
I'd made, dark red like watermelon, busted and overripe.
Then, Mama wailed and Genevieve stayed quiet. Daddy
barked, "Wait!" and Hermione cursed softly, enunciating
each filthy word while I stuffed a handful of cake into my
mouth, choking on its buttery sweetness.

Then the women came, some streaming, some tumbling, from frame houses built among the dogwoods.
They ducked under blooming branches, using the flats of
their hands to keep sheer scarves on their heads. They
hurried toward me and my family, screaming at children
to call the ambulance. These were the sort of women
who could stop cars by placing their bodies in the roads.

They hustled across the street without looking and the cars did stop. They ran to help us while speaking the name of God.

I watched all of this through the lined rear windshield of the Buick. On the radio the Commodores sang, "I'm easy like Sunday morning." I wasn't hurt. Later I bit my finger until it bled, but when the metal bumper connected with the hundred-year-old bark, I was fine. I regarded it all with slight disbelief, like I was watching a movie with bad actors. My mother bolted from the car, holding Genevieve, who was silent and impossibly bent. When Mama sprang from the car, Hermione clambered out behind her. I scooted toward the open car door, but my sister turned. "You stay here with Daddy," she said, pushing me down onto the ruined cake. I said, "Okay," mashing the metal plates of my tap shoes into red velvet sludge.

Daddy was slumped but not silent against the leather-covered steering wheel, taking in the stinking air with jagged breaths. I dug old french fries from crevices in the car seat and ate them.

A light-skinned lady wearing pink hair rollers tapped on the window. I cranked it open, letting in a sweet whiff of magnolia and daffodil. She pushed her face into the car, blocking my breeze.

"You all right in there?"

"Yes, ma'am," I said.

"What about everybody else?"

"I'm stuck," Daddy grunted. "I'm hurt some."

"Don't move, then," the lady said. "You're not supposed to move when you're hurt."

"I want to get out and see my mama. I got icing on my shoe. The cake got mashed." I reached down for a handful of oily red cake and held it out to her.

The lady looked at my hands and then turned to where Mama was. "Jesus," she said. "Go on and stay where you are, sweetheart. Help be here in a minute. Everybody's tending to your mama. She got your sister there with her. Holler if you need something."

In the backseat I wiped my hands on my tights and then twisted the button on the pocket of my jumper until it came loose. Then I popped the pearlized plastic in my mouth, chewing with the stale french fries until a pain in my jaw reached my ears and I could almost cry. I wanted to leave the car and escape my father's groaning, but that would have been the sort of cruelty that could never be forgiven.

"You hurt, Daddy?"

"Yes."

"Want me to climb up there?"

"No. Stay where you are."

"But I'm by myself."

"No, you're not. I'm here."

"It's hot in here."

"Spring," he said.

Daddy smelled bad, like sweat and something hotter and thicker. "What about the cake?" he said with words that were more air than voice. I felt something swelling inside me, like what was supposed to happen if you swallowed watermelon seeds. The fruit would grow, crushing you to death from the inside.

"I think I'm going to die," I told him.

"No, baby. You're not going to die. Tell me about the cake."

I looked down at the chunks of moist red cake and off-white icing on the rubber floor mats. "It's ruined." I felt my face collapsing. I opened my mouth, but there was no air to cry with.

"Ariadne, baby," he said. "I'm so sorry."

He started to sob in gasps and coughs. I stuck my fingers in my ears and sang nursery rhymes. I sang about Georgie Porgie, Mary and her lamb, even nasty rhymes I had heard boys sing at school. With my hands tight over my ears I ignored my father, my good kind father with the space between his front teeth. My sweet daddy who gave me two-dollar bills for every A on my report card. To the only man who had ever loved me I said, "I'm not listening. I can't hear you."

Since we had no relatives, the police called Mr. Phinazee, my father's best friend. He was out of town, so his daughter, Colette, came to pick me up. She was only about nineteen, but she seemed like a woman to me. She wore the white barber's coat she wore to work at her father's shop.

"Come out," she said to me, opening the door.

I scooted to the other side of the car, pressing against the door. My hands were still sweet from cake and I pressed them to my mouth, nicking my skin on the edges of my teeth.

"Come on," she said, crawling in. A heart-shaped locket bounced at her throat.

She was close to me now. Colette's face was young,

as smooth as cardboard and the same color. Hands around my waist, she tugged me from the canal of the backseat into the spring day.

When the paramedics came to remove my father from the car, she held me to her and used one rough hand to press my face into her collarbone. "Don't look up," she said. Her other hand rubbed my back in slow, easy circles. I stiffened, worried that she would feel my bra through the armor of my jumper. But she just rocked me like an infant and hummed a quiet tune.

Many times since then, I've tried to identify the song that was on her lips that afternoon. Sometimes I am convinced that she hummed "Amazing Grace" while they strapped my father to the stretcher and hurried him away. But every now and again I will hear a scrap of music that pierces my heart and I will think that maybe this is the song she played in my ear, the song that separated me from my pain for a few moments on the worst day of my life.

"Aria," she said softly into my hair. "Shh, Aria."

I knew that she was talking to me, although no one had ever shortened my name.

"I like it when you call me that."

Aria wasn't a name that I needed to grow into, something I could appreciate later. It was a name I could use right then, leaning against a police sedan on the side of the road near a hundred-year-old magnolia. I slid into this new name, pulling it close around me like a donated blanket.

"Are my daddy and Genevieve going to die?" I asked Colette.

"That's up to God," she said, laying me down on the backseat of her father's Brougham.

As we pulled away, I looked back at the dogwood trees that lined the road, staring at the bloody blossoms clustered on the branches like a hundred dying butterflies.

Chapter One

I still live in Atlanta. All of us do—Mama, Hermione, and me. Mama still lives on Willow Street, in the house we moved to after losing the split-level on Bunnybrooke Drive. She stays there out of spite, I think. This way no one can forget the cruelty that life has done her. Hermione and her family live in a suburb called Lawrenceville, halfway to Athens, which is as far away as you can get without actually leaving town. I can picture my sister leaving us for good, moving to France, doing a Josephine Baker, wearing a dress made of fruit. She can likely envision such scenarios for herself as well. But she stays here in Georgia because of her husband, Mr. Phinazee, who is far too old to learn any new tricks.

I make my home in the West End. Little plaques affixed to the street signs insist that it is "The Historic West End," a designation secured by real estate interests. For the last twenty years people have predicted that this area was on the rise. They point to Grant Park, which has become a Victorian oasis, smack in the center of town. It's only a matter of time, they say, urging yuppies and buppies alike, until gentrification elevates the West End, the *historic* West End, too. I hope they are right. I only rent my house, so I have no real financial stake in the prospect, but I like the idea of imminent transformation and appreciation.

The West End is a hard place to wrap your mind around. My house is off People Street, not too far from the Wren's Nest—where, depending on your take on things, Joel Chandler Harris either wrote or plagiarized the Uncle Remus stories. Just over a mile away is Spelman College, my alma mater, built where there were once Civil War barracks. And across the street from Spelman are some of the meanest housing projects in the South. I guess the only really consistent variable in the West End is that nearly everyone within a five-mile radius is black. From the bourgie girls I went to college with, all of whom seemed to be doctors' daughters or professors' kids, to my neighbors, cracked out and depressed, everybody is black. My landlord, crooked and mean, is every bit as black as the people who run the homeless shelter on the corner of Landrum and Cascade.

Lately white folks are moving into our neighborhood, one by one. I'm not bent out of shape about it. A gay couple, Jewish, according to my roommate, Rochelle, bought the pale yellow bungalow across the road, which has recently been restored to its turn-of-the-century splendor—wraparound porch and stained-glass panels in the mahogany door. Rochelle and I considered taking them a gift to welcome them to the neighborhood. She suggested baking cookies, but then we worried that they might not trust us enough to eat what we had prepared. The very idea of this offended us as though we had actually offered them the cookies and they'd refused. So we never introduced ourselves to them and they never introduced themselves to us.

Quiet as it's kept, the house where Rochelle and I live is identical to the showplace across the street. Ours is a fixer-upper that hasn't been fixed up yet. The paint flakes like green dandruff; underneath, the wood is dotted with termite tunnels. Inside, however, is much nicer. The wood floors might be paint-flecked and scarred, but you can still tell that it is good pine. In my bedroom there is a great old fireplace, but the mantels were stolen decades ago, when all the houses in the West End stood empty and abandoned. Still, the mantels can be replaced along with the crystal doorknobs and brass window cranks.

Last March, crackheads stole two potted ficus trees and a wrought-iron mailbox from the house across the street. The three of us—me, Rochelle, and my boyfriend, Dwayne—watched from my front porch. The porch is one of the best places in our house, despite the fact that it is not screened in. Our landlord let us keep the wicker patio furniture left by the previous tenants. There were two pieces, a love seat that could seat two people comfortably and three in a pinch and a high-backed throne that Rochelle called the Huey Newton Seat. At night we left the love seat on the porch, figuring that it was too bulky for crackheads to steal; but the Huey Newton Seat was stored in the living room when it wasn't in use. "It's a cultural antique," Rochelle insisted. I told her that most people didn't even remember who Huey Newton was, but she said that they would steal the chair anyway. It was like stealing a rare coin not because it's rare, but because it's a coin. It was a pain to haul the chair in at night—it was over five feet tall and the wicker was brittle with age. But Rochelle does what she wants.

Winter had just ended when my neighbor Cynthia and her cousin stole the Jewish guys' mailbox and ficus trees. Dwayne and I had sat close and cozy on the love seat and Rochelle used the Huey Newton Seat. The day was cool, but the sun warmed our foreheads. It was the sort of afternoon that is hot and cold at the same time, letting us know that spring was ahead of us, but not quite allowing us to forget the winter behind. Rochelle and Dwayne had laughed as Cynthia, who lived three doors down, and her cousin dragged the dainty trees and their glazed pots down the repaved driveway. Dwayne said, "Remember the Alamo," and this made us laugh. The mailbox was harder to steal. Together they tugged at the white post until it gave way, like a stubborn hunk of crabgrass. We laughed some more, now rooting against the taming and gentrification of our neighborhood. We delighted in the hardheaded nature of poverty, of a block that didn't welcome change. We drank to Cynthia and her cousin, clicking the rims of plastic tumblers of lemonade, vodka, and ice.

So I'm not sure why I was stunned when I came

home one May afternoon to find deep ruts in the soft wood around the dead bolt on my front door, the door itself hanging open just a bit, the way you do when you know company is coming and you don't want them to bother to knock. Why did I stagger backward, a step or two from the opening, frightened and disbelieving at the same time, my eyes scanning the quiet road for a face that could explain things to me, straighten this whole thing out? Of course I knew that this wasn't the safest of neighborhoods. My mother, who lives less than ten miles away but never visits, sends me news clippings snipped from the back pages of the *Journal-Constitution*, little news articles about rapes, murders, and drug busts in the West End. She keeps me informed so I will always be aware of how safe I am not. It wasn't that I doubted the accuracy of the articles. Lying in bed, I often heard gun-shots as distant as thunder and close as lightning. But I didn't imagine that someone would one day dig out the locks on my door, rifle through my belongings, taking what they wanted, leaving the rest. This wasn't supposed to happen to Rochelle and me.

We often joked that no one bothered us because everyone knew what we did for a living: nonprofit work at the Literacy Action and Resource Center. Even crack-heads knew that there was no money in nonprofit. We'd borrowed this quip from Lawrence, our boss, who used the same rationale to explain why the Literacy Center—three miles away in Vine City—had never been vandal-ized, burglarized, or otherwise defaced. This, despite the fact that four homes on the block were boarded up, housing drug addicts and other vagrants. We really did believe that we were exempt from the crime in the area due to our vocation. Not because of our low wages, but because our neighbors understood that we were here trying to do something good. We taught people to read. Wasn't that something that just about anyone could see was an honorable and decent way to spend one's time?

I set my hand on the brass-plated doorknob, worn down to nickel from so many hands, too many twists. Then I curled my fingers back. What if someone was still inside? I tripped down the three crumbling stairs, dislodging clumps of old cement, and took a few steps to the jagged sidewalk. Where was the nearest pay phone? On the corner was a stump where a phone used to be. Across the street the Jewish men had installed a black iron fence with curlicues and other flourishes that kept people off their property. Along the border were knee-high hedges which, over time, would grow as high as the fence. It made sense to knock on their door, ask to use their phone, but somehow I didn't want to admit to them what had happened.

Summer had come early this year. It was only the middle of May, but temperatures were in the high eighties and, if the weatherman could be believed, the humidity was seventy-four percent. My neighbor Cynthia sort of materialized in the thick air and moved toward me. She carried a canvas sack, the strap diagonal across her flat chest.

"What's wrong with you?" Cynthia wanted to know when she reached me.

"Somebody broke in." I worked to keep the whine out of my voice. No matter what had been going on inside my house, I knew that Cynthia had likely seen a lot worse. She was thin in the way that all crackheads are when they have been doing it a long time. Her forehead, blooming with white-topped acne, managed to be oily and ashen at the same time.

"You went in yet to see what all is missing? You called the police?"

"I didn't want to go in. What if somebody is still in there?"

Cynthia said, "Don't worry. They been gone."

"You saw them?"

She nodded. "It was two men."

"What did they look like?"

"Sort of regular," she said.

I scanned her face to see if she was telling me the truth, but how was I to know what the truth looked like? My eyes kept drifting up from her yellowish eyes to her hair. It was straightened, held in place by hair gel that dried in great white flakes. But just over her ear, where Billie Holiday had pinned her gardenia, was a silver clip studded with pink and white rhinestones.

"That's pretty," I said. "Your barrette."

"You want it?" she said, pulling it free.

I stared at it lying across the dark creases of her hand. Up close it wasn't so nice. Many of the stones were missing, leaving dead rusty sockets.

"I'll give it to you," said Cynthia. "For two dollars."

I patted my pockets. "I just have one dollar."

"That will work," she said. "You can give me the other one next time I see you."

I held the dollar out to her, but she made no move to

take it. The barrette bounced slightly in her vibrating palm. I plucked it from her hand. She, in her fast, noiseless way, covered my other hand in hers, almost caressing it before she slid the dollar bill from between my fingers.

"That's a real nice hair bow," she said. "Don't forget about the rest of my money." She raised her eyebrows and gave me a sympathy smile, just turning up the corners of her mouth without showing teeth. I looked back at my house, the front door still slightly ajar. From where I stood I could see that our two umbrellas were still stashed in the wire basket by the door. I slipped the heavy barrette into the pocket of my skirt and moved in the direction that Cynthia had gone. When I found a pay phone, I'd call Rochelle and tell her to come home. I'd call the police so they could write up a report. Then I'd call Dwayne and ask him to make things safe again.

Rochelle arrived first, having the shortest distance to travel. She'd been at work, bringing all the files up to date. She swung into the driveway, causing the gravel to jump like popcorn.

She hopped out of the car and trotted to where I sat on the curb. I almost gasped at the sight of her. Rochelle and I had been roommates for three years and we'd known each other since we were both eighteen. You'd think I'd be immune to her odd beauty, but her fantastic coloring—hair gone so gray that it was almost magnolia cream white and her deep brown skin—this was the sort of thing that you kept noticing over and over. My boyfriend, Dwayne, says Rochelle would be pretty if she weren't so weird-looking, but I think that she wouldn't be so pretty were she not so unusual.

"It wasn't Cynthia," I said.

"No," Rochelle said, settling beside me on the hot curb. "Cynthia wouldn't break into our house."

"They say that the best way not to get robbed is to know your neighbors. People don't rob people they know."

Rochelle nodded, but we were both just parroting what we'd read in pamphlets about urban renewal. This was the kind of thing that we told our parents.

My mother had said, "Even if you form a relationship with the people on your street and they decide not to rape and murder you, what about the people on the next block over? They would slit your throat over a cup of purple Kool-Aid."

"We can't tell our parents," I said.

"Depends on what's missing," Rochelle said. "Depending on what's missing, we might have to tell them anyway."

She was thinking of all the things she'd already bought in preparation for her wedding, namely her wedding dress—a voluminous crepe lisse affair, lush with gold thread and lace—which cost about as much as a decent used car. There were other items, the Baccarat bud vases and the china place settings that had already started arriving although the wedding was more than six months away.

"They wouldn't take the dress. Burglars don't steal clothes. They want electronics."

"Aria," Rochelle said, "we saw Cynthia and her cousin steal a goddamned mailbox."

"I know," I said, hoping to soothe her. "That was different. And anyway, Cynthia didn't have anything to do with this."

"Did you call the police?"

"Yeah."

"Nine one one?"

"Yeah."

"You know what Public Enemy said?" Rochelle asked with a smile.

"Nine one one is a joke?"

"No," Rochelle said. "Crack killed applejack."

"That wasn't Public Enemy."

"Well, whoever said it. That was way back when we were in high school. Do you think it's getting any better?"

"I hope so," I said.

The police came next. One guy in a blue and white Crown Vic. He instructed Rochelle and me to wait where we were while he made sure there was no one inside the house. I told him that Cynthia had seen two men leave. He wanted to know why Cynthia hadn't called the police. "A neighborhood watch is supposed to do more than watch," he said.

I shrugged, thinking of the afternoon that Rochelle, Dwayne, and I had just watched what happened to the home across the street.

It took less than ten minutes for the policeman to determine that the house was vacant.

"Is it in real bad shape?" Rochelle wanted to know.

"Is that your real hair color?" he said, reaching out to touch one of her silver dreadlocks.

Rochelle recoiled just slightly. I knew she didn't like it when strangers felt licensed to touch her just because of her difference. The officer paused, but squeezed a hank of her hair between his fingers anyway.

"My hair's been gray since I was a teenager," she said.

"That's a trip," said the officer.

"What about the house?" I asked him.

"It looked okay to me," he said. "Of course you are going to have to do a thorough look-see to know if anything is missing. But as far as I can tell, things seem undisturbed."

A voice squawked out of his receiver, reminding me of the day of the accident. There were dogwood trees in our yard, but this time of year they just stood there leafy and benign.

We sat with him on the porch while he filled out paperwork. Rochelle signed on various dotted lines. As the policeman handed me the pink copy of the triplicate form, he stopped.

"You know who you look like?"

"Yeah," I said. "I know."

"Penny, from *Good Times*. You look like Janet Jackson would look if she was a regular person."

"Is that all?" Rochelle said, holding her hand out for the form.

He shrugged, moving all of his heavy equipment with his big shoulders. "You can go through and see what's missing if you want. But really—your TV and stuff was all in there. Did you have more jewelry?"

He was looking at Rochelle's engagement ring. It was somewhat smaller than a dime but plenty large enough to sparkle like a disco ball. She put her left hand behind her. "It's just costume jewelry."

The policeman chuckled. "You can save that lie for the crackheads."

I gave him a careful smile and waited for him to leave.

Rochelle and I held hands as we crossed our threshold. The officer had been right. It didn't look like anything was missing. The red, white, and blue Priority Mail boxes containing various wedding implements were still stacked against the living room walls. The small television still rested in the particleboard entertainment set, the VCR still attached.

"Do you want to look in your room first, or mine?" Rochelle said.

"Yours," I said, understanding that there was much more at stake here for her than for me.

Her room was disorderly, but Rochelle was just that sort of person. I couldn't say for sure if some burglar had left the drawers hanging open or if Rochelle herself had dumped the contents of her jewelry box onto her unmade bed. Rochelle regarded the tangle of silver necklaces and gold bracelets without reacting.

"Let's open the closet," she whispered.

"I'm sure it's still there," I said, although my heart was suddenly knocking in my throat. Of course it was still

there. What I said earlier was true. No one forces their
way into a house just to steal a wedding dress. And Cynthia had said expressly that the robbers were men. Only
a woman would know the value of a wedding gown.

We stood in front of the door, still holding hands like
girls on a field trip. "It's there," I said again.

"What if it's not?" Rochelle said.

"It *is*," I said, pulling open the door to the shallow
closet.

When the doorknob cracked against the wall behind
it, we both jumped.

"I see it," I said to Rochelle. "It's still there."

She let go of my hand to touch a fold of creamy
white silk. "Thank God. I was so scared."

Moisture gathered in the corners of Rochelle's eyes,
but she rubbed it away with her shoulder. "I can't believe
I am crying about this." She laughed a little bit. "It's just
a dress."

I stretched my hand to stroke the dress too. I had
been there with Rochelle and her mother when they
found this gown, the one dress that satisfied them both.
Opulent enough to suit Rochelle's mother's agenda,
with the signature of Amsale, the Ethiopian designer, to
calm Rochelle's opposition to spending so much when
people around us had so little. I was pleased enough to
tag along, as a member of her wedding, the only brides-
maid. I'd been moved by each of the dresses that
Rochelle tried on, whether they were strapless or high-
necked, floor-dragging or tea-length. To me every wedding dress was gorgeous with promise.

I wasn't jealous. This is true. I had regarded

Rochelle's wedding preparation as a sort of apprentice-ship for myself. Hands-on training for my eventual jaunt down the aisle. I never believed then that it wouldn't happen to me. There were some things that were prom-ised to a person. Some things were your birthright. I was just waiting my turn.

"They came in here," I said to Rochelle as soon as we stepped into my bedroom.

"Maybe not," Rochelle said, taking her turn to re-assure me. "I bet nothing is missing."

"That's not the point," I said, feeling suddenly ill. The nausea left me unsteady, like an overfull bowl of soup.

I didn't own much that was of value to me, or to any-one else. What I do care about I keep in the top drawer of my nightstand. Seventeen monogrammed handker-chiefs, cheap cotton purchased at Zayre or Woolworth, one of those stores that have long since gone out of busi-ness. These were my father's. The day after the accident, my mother gathered all his handkerchiefs in a basket for mourners to use and take away as souvenirs. Like per-sonalized matchbooks from a wedding reception. I'd emptied the basket, stuffing them into the pockets of my gray wool coat. Also among my keepsakes was a mangy dust rag. Years ago, I'd been oiling my mother's buffet when I noticed that the ragged scrap in my hand was a baby's diaper. Maybe it had been mine, maybe Hermione's, but I hope it was Genevieve's. Under these items was the most personal of everything I'd saved: a cache of unsent letters I wrote to Hermione after watch-ing *The Color Purple* three times in a single afternoon. The nightstand drawer was shut crooked on its tracks.

Someone had opened it, fondled all my best things, and hadn't found them to be worth stealing.

"I'm sick," I said.

"Nothing's missing," Rochelle said. "Nothing's missing."

I sat carefully on my bed and willed myself to be completely still. I imagined the contents of my stomach roiling in waves, then settling, like water after a struggling swimmer has finally drowned. Rochelle's hand was smooth and cool against my cheek.

Whoever had broken in had not bothered anything in the kitchen or bathroom. Rochelle's prescriptions—some of which could be used recreationally, I supposed—were still in the medicine cabinet in their orange containers. The beer bottles still lined the refrigerator doors; the blue jug of vodka lay on its side in the freezer. Nothing was missing from my room either, though the drawers had been opened and the comforter pulled from the bed and heaped on the floor.

"It's freaky," Rochelle said. "Like they broke in just to look around."

"It wasn't Cynthia," I said.

"No," Rochelle said. "Nobody ever heard of crackheads breaking in without stealing anything."

Without discussion we headed back onto the porch. I was a little bit scared, but more than that, I just didn't like being in the room so recently occupied by a curious intruder. Despite Cynthia's eyewitness account, the burglar in my mind's eye was a woman, opening the jars and creams on the bathroom counter, sniffing, making a face. Mocking my choices and Rochelle's. I thought that I could still smell her, that I caught a whiff of magnolia perfume.

"Sometimes I wonder what we were thinking when we moved in here," Rochelle said, settling her narrow hips onto the Huey Newton Seat. "We're not like these people, you know."

"Maybe you're not like them," I said.

"Come on, Aria," she said. "This isn't a value judgment. Just an observation. You're not like these people either. You didn't grow up in a neighborhood like this."

She was right. While I did grow up in Southwest Atlanta, this wasn't my corner of that corner. My folks didn't have money like Rochelle's family, but I didn't grow up in shouting distance of drug addicts. We had burglar bars on our windows, but they were the fancy kind, as much for decoration as for safety. The bars on windows here were metal and ugly, like braces on teeth. The house on Willow Street, the one we moved to after losing Daddy and the house on Bunnybrooke, didn't have central air and there was no garage for our car, but the neighborhood was stable. People didn't get killed. When someone broke a windowpane, they replaced it with new glass. No one taped plastic film over the hole, waiting for payday. But here on our block, entire houses stood empty, the windows secured with plywood, "No Trespassing" spray-painted in orange.

"I want a drink," Rochelle said.

"We have vodka in the house."

"If I don't come out in five minutes," she said, "come in and get me."

She moved through the door in the way that she did

things. She was unafraid, no matter what she had just said to me. Her kindness was like that. She didn't want me to feel bad for feeling the way that I did. My sister Hermione had been that way when we were little. We had gone to the zoo together with our parents, each of us wearing yellow balloons looped to our wrists with cotton string. Somehow mine came untethered and floated upward, over the monkey house and the bird-cages. When I began to cry, Hermione bit through her string, releasing her balloon as well. "Don't cry," she'd said. "I don't have one either."

Dwayne arrived just as Rochelle emerged from the house carrying a plastic pitcher of fruit punch and the frozen bottle of vodka. I was embarrassed at how pleased I was to see him. I hadn't gone to Spelman just to grow into the sort of woman who feels all the tension drain from her body at the sight of her boyfriend's car. It would have been better if I could have been more like Rochelle. She and Rod were in love definitely. Theirs was the sort of engagement of which everyone approved. Even Dwayne, who didn't care too much for Rod, agreed they were made for each other. But Rochelle didn't seem exactly grateful for Rod, the way I thanked God for Dwayne. My boyfriend was a large man, six feet four and solid in his oversized clothes. He was the type of man that made you just want to climb up and hide in his branches.

Rochelle seemed surprised to see Dwayne's car at the curb.

"I called him," I said. "You didn't call Rod?"

She shrugged.

"It is sort of Dwayne's line of work," I said, reminding her that there was a practical reason for him to be here. Dwayne is a locksmith and someone had just pried open our front door. Rochelle's Rod was a nice guy, a dentist, the sort of man that any mother would embrace as a son-in-law. But he was only useful if you had a problem that originated inside your own mouth.

In a way, you could say that Dwayne is my first boyfriend. Not my first lover; I've slept with more men than I will easily admit. But Dwayne is the only man who had really *claimed* me. We'd only been going out for a month when he started referring to me as his "woman." Rochelle laughed at this, saying it all seemed so "retro"; she and Rod called each other partners. But she couldn't know what it means to me to be acknowledged in public like that. It's been nearly a year and Dwayne has never come out and said that he loves me, but he doesn't have to. More than one man has whispered those words to me, but none of them were telling the truth. When I speak, Dwayne stoops a little, angling his head downward, showing the world that he's listening, that he cares what I have to say.

Climbing onto the porch, Dwayne gave me a quick kiss before looking at the damaged door or even saying hello to Rochelle. I smiled despite the situation as he knelt before the violated threshold.

"Shit," Dwayne said. This was not the first time he had made a professional call to our house. Less than a month after I'd met him, I locked myself out of this same front door and he opened it with metal gadgets he stored in his glove compartment. He was so confident and competent inserting the silver prods, moving them this way and that, sweet-talking the door the way a farmer might murmur to a skittish cow. He talked to the lock, moving his fingers until it yielded.

On that day he had been pleased to be of service— our romance was still fairly new; we were still trying to impress one another, each of us eager to prove to the other that we could be *useful*. But now he seemed agitated. "It looks like somebody just got in here with a screwdriver. You can't blame the lock. It's a Baldwin." At this he glanced over his shoulder at me.

I nodded. Dwayne had installed the brass-faced dead bolt himself.

"It's the wood," he explained. "A lock can't be no better than the door you set it in. When is your lease up?"

"February," Rochelle said. "Right after my wedding."

"I can install you a four-inch dead bolt," Dwayne said. "Maybe that'll hold you over until then. February is what? Eight months away?"

I felt my pulse flutter at the very idea of measuring time in months, for there were dynamics to this situation of which Rochelle and Dwayne were unaware. Namely, that by February my own life would be different, my body too. I was almost three weeks late and had thrown up three times in four days. A person didn't have to be an ob-gyn to know what that meant.

As I watched Dwayne rummage through his toolbox, I imagined myself telling him that we'd soon be parents. His face would be sober and serious, but then he'd look at me, searching my face for his cue. I'd give him a smile to let him know that it was okay to be happy, that this was a good thing. He might not say, right then, that he was excited, that he loved me, but there is more to life than what you do and don't say to one another.

Dwayne removed the lock, leaving a clean hole in the door. "Rochelle, why don't you just go and stay with Rod? He's got a nice house." Now Dwayne made eye contact with me. "And my apartment isn't all that big, but I got a Medeco Grade One on my front door. Nobody can get past that."

Again I felt my pulse move like something eager and excited.

"Is this a private moment?" Rochelle said. "I could go inside."

"No, no," Dwayne said. "I'm not trying to run you off. I'm just thinking aloud." He slipped his screwdriver inside his collar to scratch his back. "I'm just talking. I know you two are determined to tough it out over here."

I nodded yes and Dwayne turned his hurt face back to his work. I rose from the love seat and knelt beside him, my ring finger tracing the downy hairs at the base of his neck. When the time was right, once I had all the details from my doctor, I'd tell him my plan—I wanted to live here in the West End with Dwayne and the child that we would have by spring. He was convinced that our home had been broken into because of the neighborhood, but I knew the reason was that we were two women living alone. But if he lived here with me no one would force the lock, no matter how curious they were about what we kept in our drawers, no matter how much they thought they could get for our television set. We could live here and make a difference, be the kind of family profiled in the Sunday paper. Atlanta from the ashes and all of that.

Chapter Two

People often ask **Rochelle** and me how we met. In this, best friends are a lot like married couples: people want to know how this union got its start. We tell them that we met in college, freshman year, which is true. In those days I was still struggling to meet all of the goals on my twenty-point list for self-improvement. Although I had only traveled about eight miles across town to go to Spelman, I considered it a fresh start. Distance was more than a matter of city blocks; because I had accepted my brother-in-law's offer to pay my tuition, my mother spoke to me only twice during my first semester of school. It was as though I was three time zones away.

The list was jotted on a sheet of lined paper ripped from a spiral notebook. My years of living with a snooping mother had taught me that the best way to keep something private was to make it look unimportant. A leather-bound diary with a brass lock was an open invitation for invasion. No one would ever think to unfold the sloppy sheet of paper on which I'd inked everything I wanted in the world.

The items on my list were abstract and conceptual. When I met Rochelle, I was concentrating on item seven: *Be known for something decent.* Toward this end I had decided to run for freshman class office—nothing as extravagant as president, but I planned to make a bid for the post of recording secretary. When I wrote on my list that I wanted to be known for something decent, I had in mind something academic. I considered myself to be a basically smart person. Not a genius, but my test scores had always shown me to be a little above average. But I was only at Spelman a week before I realized that here the average was a little bit brighter than the averages at any of the high schools I'd attended. These were worldly girls who knew things, had taken lessons. Calinda, my roommate, was sleep-deprived and haggard as a result of staying up all night to whisper to her boyfriend, a real Italian, who lived in Naples.

The dean's office was crowded with ambitious freshmen. This was the term I still used even though a large bulletin board in the hallway said "Welcome Fresh-*women*!" I couldn't get my mouth to say the word; it sounded a little vulgar and more than a little awkward. The dean's secretary looked up at me and gestured to a stack of half-sheets of green paper.

"You have to fill that out to be put on the ballot."

There were at least twenty-five girls in the office, all clutching green forms. I wondered how many of them were running for recording secretary. I took my form and sat on the carpet next to a girl who wore her gym uniform—navy-blue shorts and a white T-shirt knotted behind her to show off her slim waist. Smelling of sweat and baby powder, she inked her answers in the blanks fast, without worrying the end of her pen or scrunching her brow. I sat beside her with my own form, trolling through my canvas bag. I finally found a green felt-tip dented with toothmarks. The girl had finished her application by then and offered me her ceramic roller-point. It was a good pen, probably a graduation gift.

"Do you need this?" she said.

After I shook my head no, she stabbed the pen into her hair like a chignon stick.

"I'm Rochelle Satterwhite," she said, holding out her hand. "As class president I'm going to do something about the athletic department. I turned down a volleyball scholarship to UMass to come here. And we don't even have intramurals!"

I looked at her yellow-white palm for a second too long. Who knew that people could get scholarships for volleyball? When I didn't make a move for her hand, she stretched her arm a little farther and caught me in her dry, snug grip.

"It's more serious than you think," she said. "Girls at white schools are playing all kinds of sports. We don't even have field hockey."

"I'll vote for you, but I'm uncoordinated."

"I think I know you," Rochelle said.

"From the ice cream social?"

"You're Calinda's roommate, right?"

"Yeah."

"She's running for recording secretary." Rochelle swiveled her head, surveying the crowd in the room. "She was in here a minute ago."

One of the things that I prided myself on was my ability to conceal my thoughts. For example, Rochelle had no idea that I had never even heard of field hockey or intramural sports. I had just looked her in the face and made myself a mirror, frowning when she frowned, raising my eyebrows just seconds after she'd raised hers. But Rochelle noticed the change in me when she told me about Calinda's candidacy.

"What's wrong?" she asked.

"Nothing," I said. "I just didn't know that Calinda had been in here yet. I was just getting her form for her. But I guess she doesn't need it now." I chuckled and mashed the green sheet into a hard tight ball.

"Okay," said Rochelle. "If you say so." She stood up and looked down at me. "You sure you're okay?"

I nodded.

"Okay," she said again, and turned to walk toward the door.

"I'll vote for you," I called after her.

The motion in the room stopped for a second. I heard someone say, "That's not fair. Campaigning isn't supposed to start until tomorrow."

I tucked my lips under and raised my eyebrows in a silent mea culpa, but Rochelle didn't really mind. She grinned at me over her shoulder as she stepped into the breezeway. I watched her reading the flyers posted on the bulletin board outside of the dining hall. She snatched one down and slipped it into her backpack. I thought about my list, hoping I had just accomplished goal number four. *Make friends with someone you admire.*

Steagall's, a cross between a snack bar and corner store, was Rochelle's unofficial campaign headquarters. She and five of her friends ordered chicken wings and wheat bread before settling at one of the plywood and cinder-block structures that passed for tables and benches. I ate there often, since cafeteria food didn't agree with me and other restaurants didn't agree with my budget. Besides, Steagall's was close enough to campus that a person didn't need a car to get there.

Rochelle and her friends went there nearly every evening to plan their strategies. I sat nearby with my order of wing-on-white, hoping that they might ask me to join them. I marveled at the six of them exchanging ideas in a quiet huddle in the noisy back of the restaurant. How had they bonded so quickly? I hadn't even managed to connect with my roommate, who took her meals with her own peer group—a gaggle of girls who cursed their parents for not allowing them to go to Harvard.

Rochelle's committee stayed at the restaurant late, until eleven-forty, when they all packed up to make it back to campus before midnight curfew. I packed up then too and tried to mingle with them as they walked back to Spelman at a quick clip, working hard to avoid eye contact with the neighborhood men we passed. The girls always allowed me to travel with them. I was not their friend, but I was their Spelman Sister and this was not the sort of neighborhood where young ladies like us walked alone.

I lived in the Howard Harrell Hall, the busiest dorm on campus. It wasn't new like the Living Learning Center, where the honor students lived, nor was it charming and bright-shuttered like Abby Hall, named after one of the Rockefeller wives. Howard Harrell was a brick box sectioned into small, uncomfortable rooms, teeming with intent young women. The halls reeked of wild-cherry air freshener, butter-flavored popcorn, and singed hair. Every stereo in all 133 rooms seemed to be playing the sound track to *School Daze*, the newest Spike Lee film. The movie had been shot across the street from our campus; our dorm mother had worked as an extra.

I often closed myself into a narrow bathroom stall for a few moments of privacy; there, on the back side of the door, was a bright square of paper urging me to select someone named Renee Abernathy for class president. I snatched the flyer down and stuffed it into the napkin disposal. I moved to another stall; finding Rochelle's flyer, I made myself comfortable. Stumbling upon her campaign materials made me feel like this was a place that I should be, that Rochelle had anticipated my being there and left the flyer as a personal greeting.

The morning of the campaign speeches, I walked over to Sisters Chapel early, before the dining hall opened for breakfast. This was something I found myself doing about three mornings a week, although this was not on my list of life-improving goals. As a matter of fact, it went against item number seventeen: *Stop being so weird.* And eighteen: *Grow up.* I tried to will myself to sleep in, to be like other people. But I slid out of my twin bed anyway, pulling on sweatpants under my nightshirt and creeping toward the chapel so early that the red brick housing projects on three sides of us were silent.

During public events it was easy to forget that Sisters Chapel was actually a chapel and not just an unusually ornate auditorium. When sophomore girls in high heels modeled leather dresses on this stage or successful alumnae stood in front of the microphone attempting to inspire us, even I almost forgot the sacredness of the building. At those times the wooden pews were just seats, the stained glass only windows. The pipe organ just an instrument.

But in the mornings, when I went there alone, I could feel God in that space. It wasn't the sort of thing that I went around talking about, but its power danced along my skin, nudging my sluggish blood.

I tiptoed across the parquet wood floor of the stage, lowering myself at the edge, dangling my legs. Beside my hip was a small pewter plaque in memory of Dr. Martin Luther King, Jr., who lay in state in Sisters Chapel for one week in 1968. My parents and Hermione stood in line for three and a half hours on a damp April morning to see Dr. King's body. Hermione was barely three years old, but she claims to remember it. She says that my father cried great, heaving sobs.

Mother says that Hermione can't possibly remember, not in the way you remember most things. They took Hermione so that she would have at least seen the man, that the memory would implant itself inside the chambers of her heart and the spongy part of her bones, but she couldn't possibly recall it in the way that she professes to. And, besides, my father didn't cry. He paid his respects and his heart was certainly heavy, but he didn't actually cry. He wasn't a crying sort of man. My mother says this with authority.

In those early days of my college life I still hoped that I would glimpse my father's spirit there in Sisters Chapel. There was something that I wanted to tell him, some things I wanted to explain. At times I imagined that he existed just inside my peripheral vision. When I faced the stained glass, my father was there near the organ pipes. As long as I was satisfied with this blurry, shadowy vision of him, he would stay there. If I turned my head to really see, like Orpheus, I'd lose everything.

I know now that life and death don't quite work that way. But I felt something while sitting alone in the chapel so early in the mornings. In that quiet space, there was the possibility of safety and forgiveness.

Just after seven a.m. the back door scraped open. My heart flopped in my chest. I took deep breaths and tried to calm myself. I wasn't doing anything wrong, was I? The back door had been unlocked, and there were no signs saying that a person couldn't enter the chapel whenever she liked. I thought about my list. *Stop being so weird*. This was weird, hanging out in an empty chapel at the butt-crack of dawn. And it probably wasn't so safe after all.

"Hello? Is someone there?" I called.

"I'm sorry," said a voice that could have been anybody's. High-pitched but uninflected like a newscaster's. "Is it okay for me to be in here?"

"It's not for me to say," I called back into the darkness behind the stage.

Rochelle emerged from the wings, like an actress. Like me, she wore a nightgown tucked into sweatpants. Her hair was wrapped around big green plastic rollers, held in place by metal clips.

"Are you doing something personal?" she asked me. "I can go. I just wanted to see how the chapel was set up. I'm running for office and we have to give our speeches today."

Stung, I smiled anyway. "I know. I'm Calinda's roommate. Remember?"

She covered her mouth with her hands. "Shit. I'm sorry. Of course I remember. I'm just not awake yet."

"I'm Aria."

"That's your real name?"

"My real name is Ariadne."

"Where's your string? I could use it." She raised her eyebrows and looked satisfied, the way people do when they've said something smart.

"Are you nervous?"

She sat down beside me on the edge of the stage. When she spoke, the pins in her hair touched each other with a soft clicking. This time she smelled of cocoa butter and rubbing alcohol. "I'd really like to win something. I played sports in high school, you know."

I nodded.

"You don't care about sports, do you?"

I shrugged.

"Then what *do* you care about?"

I shrugged again.

"I mean," she said, "out of all the colleges in the world, why did you come here?"

"My mom went here. This is where my parents met. I was thinking maybe the same thing could happen to me."

"My dad went to Morehouse," she said. "But I came here because Alice Walker went here."

"She did? I read *The Color Purple* in high school. I saw the movie too."

"She hated it here," Rochelle said. "But that's not the point."

"You know who else went here," I said. "Esther Rolle."

"Damn, damn, damn," Rochelle said.

We laughed together, and while laughing it was easy to forget that Sisters Chapel was a sacred place.

"I need to go back to my room and get some sleep," she said. "I was up all night. See you later, Ariadne."

"Aria," I told her. "People call me Aria."

She cocked her head. "You know who you look like?"

"Nobody," I said.

"You look like Penny, on *Good Times*. That should be your nickname."

"Aria is my nickname."

"That's not a nickname. That's just a short version of your regular name. A nickname is something that your friends think up to call you."

I felt something warm spread to my face. She had said it. I didn't. We were friends. She'd given me a nickname.

"Well, Penny," she said, "I really have to go to sleep." She reached her hand quick to the neckline of my gown and gave a tug, snapping a loose thread. "Look," she said. "It's your string."

There was a decent showing for the speeches, but the chapel was not nearly full. Just a week before at the Fall Fashion Show, the pews had been stuffed with students. We Spelman women were all there, but guys from More-house had come too. For that event I'd sat at the end of the pew, squashed against the armrest. But this time I sat in the middle of the fifth row, a comfortable distance away from the young lady seated to my right. On her lap was a placard bearing one word: Renee.

Rochelle made her way down the aisle to the stage looking fierce and determined, glancing neither left nor right. When she brushed by me, I could see that she hadn't completely ironed the white cotton shirt which she wore under her dark blue suit. The cuffs and collar were pressed stiff, but the areas almost hidden by her jacket were rough-dried and wrinkled. I worried for her, hoped that the others wouldn't notice this shortcut in grooming, that it wouldn't cost her crucial votes.

At the podium she set her jaw before producing a sheet of notebook paper folded down to the size of a playing card. The crackle of the paper was intensified by the microphone as she carefully restored the page to its full size. With a shaky voice she promised to represent our interests with the dean of women. She mentioned

Title IX. She also pledged to improve cafeteria food, hinting that fresh fruit would be added to the salad bar. Rochelle gestured as she spoke, holding her hands in front of her, unfurling her fingers like a magician producing a mockingbird out of thin air. I looked up into her face, trying to catch her eye to let her know that the speech was going just fine. Rochelle finished her talk the way all the candidates would, thanking us for our time and our support. She smiled.

I jumped to my feet before I thought about it, before I had a chance to worry what I might look like. I clapped with my hands over my head, banging my palms together before I realized that the people around me gave polite applause, for we were basically a courteous group of people. A chuckle emanated from the middle pews, a laugh that I sensed was a laugh at me. I slapped my hands together twice more before I sank back down onto the wooden pew.

The second candidate came to the microphone. She was a tall, brassy girl from Washington, D.C. "Divas!" she called to the crowd, who hollered back at her. The girl seated beside me held up her placard and waved it around, shrieking like white girls in that old footage of the Beatles.

I looked at Rochelle, frozen there onstage in an ornate high-backed chair. The bottom of her face was stretched into a smile, but I could tell that she knew what I knew. Candidate number two was going to win the election. I shifted in my seat and looked behind me at clusters of freshmen wearing buttons that indicated that DIVA was some sort of acronym. Devastating, Innovative, Vivacious, Audacious. Once again I looked at Rochelle, my new friend, trying to make eye contact. Don't worry, I wanted to tell her.

Rochelle didn't win, despite my vote. It wasn't even close, according to Calinda, who was so angry at her own defeat that she demanded an exact accounting of the ballots from the dean of women.

Rochelle and I didn't speak again until the following spring. And this is the part that we have never told anyone:

That March I had landed a pretty nice telemarketing job to supplement my pay from the newsstand at Lenox Square. My sister's husband sent a check to Spelman each term to cover my tuition plus room and board, but the rest was up to me. The newsstand job was a decent gig—fifty cents over minimum wage—but I needed extra money that month. Having inherited my mother's life-long fear of credit, I'd selected a word processor at Sears and put it on layaway. It was a compact Smith-Corona with a screen that let you look at up to ten lines of text as you typed. The sociology major required that a person write a lot of papers and I wasn't much of a typist. This word processor would beep when I screwed up and allow me to make corrections.

And if word got around that I was a good typist, it could be a way to meet people. Guys were always looking for girls to help them whip their assignments into shape. And the girls pledging sororities were always looking for someone to help them with their schoolwork while they jumped through hoops for their big sisters. I would make myself useful. It would only be a matter of time before at least one person returned the favor.

The cost of the machine, $500, was almost five times the cost of a six-week typing class. This my mother pointed out when I'd hinted that a word processor would be a great Christmas gift. So far I'd put down $275. I needed to pay off the balance by Friday, or my beautiful machine would be put back on the shelf and I'd lose my deposit.

The position at TelePolls was a temporary job, lasting just two weeks. All I had to do was contact random Georgians to ask their opinions about the upcoming gubernatorial race. The flyer promised that you could make up to fifteen dollars an hour. I had worked enough to know that nobody earned the "up to" wage, but I figured that I would make eight or even nine. The headquarters, a large warehouse space across from the Fulton County jail, was divided into fifty cubicles, each furnished with a telephone and a computer. The atmosphere in the room was cool and watery from the air-conditioning and smelled of antifreeze.

I didn't mind telemarketing, but the work space wasn't exactly inspiring. Temp work was better when I was the only one working short-term. In those cases, the other workers' desks would be festooned with greeting cards, glass figurines, and family photos in plastic frames. Sometimes I was even given a desk decorated with the missing secretary's memorabilia. But all of us at TelePolls were short-timers. Our cubicles were bare but for our useless tape dispensers and staplers.

I knew better than to use the script the company

provided, a silly little monologue which explained to the person that this was his chance to make his voice heard. Instead, I assured the person, just after "Hello," that this wasn't going to cost them anything. After that, I explained that I was a college student who really needed this job and if they would take just a few minutes to answer my questions, I could avoid being fired for another day. Most people had worked shitty jobs at some point in their lives and were willing to cooperate. The point of the polls was to find out their opinions about affirmative action, the death penalty, and abortion. I asked them if they thought that the families of murder victims should be allowed to participate in executions. I thanked them for their time. If they asked me if I was black, I told them that I wasn't.

Rochelle arrived two days into the second week, halfway through the project. I didn't so much see her as hear her as she offered her name to our boss. I took temp work quite often and was not accustomed to seeing my classmates. Most of the workers were women in their thirties who used lots of gel to hold their hair slick against their heads. Sometimes there were other college students, but they mostly went to Clark, Morris Brown, or Georgia State. Rochelle and girls like her, the well-off ones without accents, didn't do temp work.

I peeped around the edge of my cubicle as the boss led her to a cube two spaces over from mine. None of us liked this supervisor; he was what my mother would call "mighty familiar." As he showed Rochelle how to work the computer, his stubby fingers made slow circles on the nape of her neck, just below the baseball cap she wore.

From where I sat I could see her simple but expensive leather purse hanging from the back of her chair.

The boss must have felt me watching because he glanced at me over his shoulder, smiling with his big teeth. I turned my attention to my keyboard, pressing the button that caused the phone to dial. Just before it started ringing, I heard Rochelle ask when we got paid.

"End of the week."

"Thanks," she said quietly.

She was different here, not the same girl I often saw in the student union on dress-up Fridays, crossing and recrossing her muscular legs, pretending not to know that she was being watched. There, she was what I wanted to be, what I had come to college hoping to become. Whenever I saw her leaning against the back gate sipping Diet Coke, she reminded me of photos of my mother, pretty and fit, stylish and sure-seeming. I had hoped Spelman would work its magic on me, turning me into a lady, the kind of girl that employers would want to hire, the kind of girl that boys would want to marry. It was already the second semester, but I was still myself. I bought the same makeup as the other girls, filed my nails into ovals, and learned not to switch my hips so much when I walked, but I never looked like a girl on the verge of something great. In pictures of myself I always looked too anxious, too easy. Too cheap.

Here at TelePolls Rochelle seemed small and out of place. Despite the way she was dressed—in close-fitting, dirty jeans and an overly large baseball cap parked just over her eyebrows—she didn't blend in with those of us in the cubicles. Maxine, who occupied the cube across from mine, gave me a playful kick in the shin. Although I didn't return the kick, I saw Rochelle as the others saw her—useless, like a cut-crystal Christmas ornament. Although she was everything I wanted to be, here I was embarrassed to know her.

Freshman year was nearly over, but I was still trying to realize the goals on my twenty-point list. Some were easier than others. Number two: *Don't get pregnant and ruin your life.* All this took was one tiny pill swallowed down just after I brushed my teeth. There was a "family planning" clinic right on campus, just behind the dining hall. I went to the desk, gave my name, and just like that, was given a dial pack of twenty-eight pills. The lady dispensing them didn't even look up or volunteer to counsel me. I was still trying to be known for something decent, but it was just too difficult to stand out at Spelman. I had managed not to make a reputation for myself, which was an improvement over high school; but there was still work to do.

The break room at TelePolls looked like the waiting room in a mechanic's shop. Gray walls, six wire-framed chairs with thin, worn padding in the seat. Along the perimeter were vending machines dispensing off-brand snacks. I slid three quarters in the machine and watched a metal coil wind backward until my cheese and crackers fell into a tray. I was alone in the break room, since all the others liked to take their free time on the parking ramp, despite the smell of exhaust fumes and pee. On the ramp, people could get away from the oppressive airconditioning of the office and they were free to smoke their cigarettes.

With a tiny plastic spatula I dug hardened cheese spread from the little cup as Rochelle entered the break room. We hadn't spoken since she started working two days before.

"Hey," I said. "How you doing?"

She turned to face me. "Ariadne, I thought that was you. But you're always in your cube, I couldn't tell."

"It's me."

She looked at the snacks in the machine. "I know I need to eat. But I don't feel like it." She sat down, crossing her arms hard over her chest. "It's so cold in here."

"You could go out to the ramp with everybody else."

"I'll throw up if I go out there. The smell, you know."

I held out a cracker that I had spackled with cheese stuff. "Have some of this."

"If I eat that, I'll throw up too." She pulled the powder-blue baseball cap down so low that I could no longer see her eyes. Using her fingernails, which were long and unpolished, she prodded the cluster of pimples on her chin. One of them burst; a spot of dark blood bloomed against her chalky brown skin. She took a napkin from the empty chair beside her and pressed it to her face. "I'm so gross."

"Are you okay? You look a little peaky."

"I don't feel good, that's all," she said. "Do you know when we get paid?"

"At the end of the week."

"Do you know if they are going to take money out for taxes and everything?"

I leaned in and looked at her more closely. Rochelle was not the sort of person who I would have figured to be strung out on drugs, not with all her talk about field hockey and exercise, but I had heard rumors that there were girls at Spelman who took all their parents' money and sucked it right up their pampered noses. This was the story I heard from the girls I worked with at the newsstand. They had never seen this in action, but they had heard it from reliable sources. They'd looked at me to confirm or deny, but I wasn't the right person to ask. If my classmates were doing things like that, they would have kept it secret, and no one shared their secrets with me.

"Yeah, they take the taxes out. They always do."

She nodded. "I figured they would."

"Are you sure you don't want a cracker?" I said to her. "You can have the last one."

She licked her lips. "I'll eat when I get back to campus."

We went back into the office and found our places in our cubicles. I put on my headset and pushed the button, thinking about Rochelle as I waited for someone to answer the phone. I didn't know much about drug addicts. I knew a few guys who smoked a lot of weed, but they weren't drug addicts, exactly. When they ran out of smoke, they were irritated but not desperate. But Rochelle was a changed person from the one she'd been when I met her in the dean's office, just six months ago. Her ponytail was heavy and dirty, hanging lank through the vent in the back of her baseball cap. Her face was all broken out and her cuticles looked like she'd been chewing on them. And I could tell that she really needed the money.

On the days that followed I avoided her in the break room, snatching my crackers out of the machine and heading to the parking ramp with everyone else. I could feel her eyes following me as I gave a casual hello, breezing past her and heading outside. I knew she wouldn't follow me. She had said that the smell of the urine and exhaust made her ill, but I knew that she was too afraid to try and socialize where she so obviously didn't fit in. I did feel a little sorry for her, but I didn't want to associate with drug addicts. I had seen *Lady Sings the Blues*. I couldn't afford to be friends with someone who would drag me down any lower than I already was. I complimented myself on keeping my sympathy in check and letting my good sense prevail as I ignored her, sitting shivering in her cubicle.

Out on the parking ramp I leaned on the concrete railing and looked out over the city. Maxine, whom I knew from working seasonal gift wrap at Rich's, stood beside me. She was just twenty-five but seemed much older. She lit a menthol cigarette.

"Smoke bother you?" she asked.

"No," I said.

She sucked on the cigarette with a little popping sound. "Are you getting a lot of surveys done?"

"Enough," I said. "Not a lot, but enough."

Maxine said, "It's hard to stay cool. Calling white people in Dahlonega and shit asking what they think about race relations. Then they hang up and you lose your commission."

I shrugged. "I hate having to ask them about abortion."

Maxine exhaled smoke as she talked. "Fifteen dollars an hour, my ass. You got sixty cents? I want to get a Coke."

I handed her my can. "I only took one sip."

She took it from me and drank. "What's up with your girl?"

"That's not my girl. I know her from school, that's all."

"Her cube is right next to mine. She's not getting any surveys done. I wouldn't be surprised at all if they let her go. I can hear her." Maxine raised her voice in pitch to imitate Rochelle's. " 'Hello, I'm calling from the TelePoll Research group.' I hear her saying it over and over, so I know that she is having to make new calls because nobody is talking to her." Maxine chuckled. "That's what she gets."

"You don't have to laugh," I said. "I sort of feel sorry for her."

"You work every day; do you think she feels sorry for you?"

"But she looks so bad," I said. "And she's nice, most of the time. I've seen her around at school."

"Well, she looks like shit on a soda cracker right now," Maxine said, looking behind her and twisting out the cigarette on the heel of her sneaker. "Not that I look much better."

Payday rolled around finally. I had to call the people at Sears and beg them not to restock my word processor before I could get to the store on Saturday morning. On the last day of the job, we all organized our tools in our work areas, like second graders straightening up their cubbies. Earphones had to be wiped down with alcohol pads and then cords twined tight around. The keyboard was to be square in front of the monitor and the stapler and tape accounted for as well. Our boss took a look in each person's cube, surveying the contents before handing over our pay. I made my body stiff and still as the boss grunted over my shoulder. "Yep, yep, yep," he said as though crossing off items on an invisible list. He paused before letting out a final yep and handed me my check. It was one of those cardboard deals where you have to tear off the edges and unfold the whole thing to see how much you made. I suppose it's how the company saves on having to buy a whole separate envelope for each person. An old lady that I temped with last Christmas ripped her check down the middle trying to get those edges off. She taped it back up, but the bank wouldn't take it.

I owed $250 on the word processor. That included taxes and everything. My check was only $232, but I could come up with the rest. I'd worked twenty-seven hours over the two weeks. Base pay about six dollars an hour, but I got an extra dollar for every survey I'd finished. Uncle Sam got his part right off the top, but all in all it wasn't too bad. I slipped it into the flap on my backpack and waved good-bye to Maxine.

"How'd you do?" she asked me.

"Good enough," I said.

Maxine tipped her head toward Rochelle, who hadn't left her cube. "Be grateful, girl, everybody ain't able."

To get out of the door, I had to pass Rochelle. I tried

to tarry, adjusting the straps on my backpack, pulling my socks up, but Rochelle just sat there. Our boss bent over his desk writing something on a clipboard.

"Y'all hurry up, hear?" he said.

"I'm headed out," I said.

"Me too," Rochelle said.

I walked toward the door at a fast pace, planning to just blow by her. Make my way without looking. This girl was in trouble and I didn't need trouble. Doing drugs was like shoplifting. When I was in high school, my friend Yolanda used to steal Super Glue and eyeliner from the SupeRx at Greenbriar Mall. When she got caught, both our mothers were called, although I hadn't stolen a thing. I'll never forget Yolanda's glossy mouth cursing at the security guard as he dumped the contents of her fake Gucci on the counter. Drugs worked the same way. If I had a friend strung out on cocaine or whatever Rochelle was on, nobody would believe that I wasn't doing it too.

When I reached her cube, Rochelle called my name. Not my given name, but the name she had given me in the chapel six months before. "Penny. Wait up."

I stopped and waited up. I told myself that I was being a sucker. That she never called me Penny in Manley Hall on a Friday afternoon when she milled about trying to make weekend plans. But I waited on her. Maybe it was the sound of her voice pleading and pretty. Or it could have been the name itself, Penny, the orphan girl who found a new mother and somehow grew up to be Janet Jackson.

Rochelle gripped my wrist as we left the office and tugged me into the break room down the hall. She shut

the door with a click and leaned herself against it, blocking my way. Her face, what I could see of it under the
bill of the cap, was strained and ashen. I felt my hands go
cold, the way they did when I was scared.

"How much did you get paid?" she asked me.

"Not that much," I said.

She moved from the door, letting herself fall onto
one of the dirty-cushioned chairs, and covered her face
with the palms of her hands. "I only made thirty-two
dollars."

"That's because you were only here half a week."

"I didn't find out about the job until late. I would
have been here the whole time if I had known." She bent
at the waist, resting her head on her knees. "I really need
the money."

"What for?" I asked, testing to see if she would tell
me, if she would let me into this secret world that was
happening right there in my dormitory, this world that
was so secret that I lived there and didn't see it.

"I have only forty-five dollars to my name," Rochelle
said, raising herself enough to pull off her baseball cap
and toss it across the room. The hair underneath was
shoulder-length and stiff. I touched my own hair, short
but soft and delicate, like spider's silk.

"Can't you get the money from your parents?"

"No." Rochelle pulled a ballpoint pen from her book
bag, drove it through her coarse hair, separating it into
halves. She grabbed a hank of hair in each hand. "You
want to know how I got the forty-five dollars that I
have? I didn't get my hair done." She leaned forward,
showing the groove where she'd split her hair apart with

the pen. The part, marked with blue ink, was flanked by Rochelle's new growth; her real hair was kinky in texture and the soft gray color of old roads.

"My hair started going gray in middle school."

"Does it run in your family?"

"I don't know," she said. "I'm adopted." Rochelle stood up, her eyes darting around the room until she spotted her cap. She picked it up from the floor, covering her hair even before she stood back up, and returned to her chair beside me.

"It's okay," I told her, eager to assure her that I could be trusted. "I'm not going to tell anybody. About your hair or this whole thing with the money." I couldn't bring myself to tell her that I knew why she was so fraught for cash, that her need and distress were written all over her. How could I? In just a moment she had offered me what I needed, what made me desperate. She'd told me her secret, something that other girls didn't know.

"So I had this idea," Rochelle said. "I would let people charge things on my gas card and give me the cash. I would offer a discount, you know?"

"That's a good idea," I said.

"But my mom had already cut my card off. I shouldn't have told her I needed the money, then she wouldn't have known to cut the card off."

"Your mother sounds like my mother," I said.

"Do you know what my mom said when I told her? She said, 'At least you know you're fertile.'" Rochelle looked into my face and gave a little smile as the meaning of her words made its way into my brain. "You didn't know that part, did you?"

I shook my head. "I thought that you were on drugs."

She sighed and worried the bumps on her chin. "I wish that was all it was."

"What about your boyfriend?"

"I didn't tell him."

"Why not?" I asked, thinking of the thin, bookish upperclassman I'd once seen her kissing at the back gate, just before curfew. "He seems nice."

"He *is* nice," she said. "Nice enough to want to get married or something like that."

"Really?" I said, thinking how romantic it would be to be engaged. "Is he a senior? It wouldn't be a shotgun wedding if it's his idea."

Rochelle threw the powder-blue baseball cap on the floor. "I don't want to be married. I want to be on student government."

The right thing to do would be to sit beside her and hug her the way her mother should have, with her head just below my collarbone and my arms around her waist. I would rock back and forth a little bit and make shushing sounds. But I knew that if I did, I'd have to give her the money. Rochelle looked at me with expectant eyes; she knew that I was deciding whether or not to help her. To her credit she didn't try to convince me. She had told me her truth and shown me her hair and it was now up to me.

This was not my first experience with a girl in trouble. When I was in high school, a pretty girl named Lee-sha Anderson had come to me to find out where she could get help. She figured that I was the kind of person who knew about such things, since I was famous for things that weren't decent. I'd helped Leesha get what she needed and she'd promised me an invitation to the Sweethearts Ball—a dress-up affair, admit-cards only. After I'd dropped Leesha at the clinic, I'd gone to Rich's to choose my dress, a lavender drop-waist that I really couldn't afford. She never sent the invitation. Now I see that I wouldn't have had a good time anyway. An invitation wouldn't have made anyone accept me. People would have whispered and laughed at my hair, at my date who was much too old to attend high school functions. But I didn't know this then and I had opened my locker each day waiting for the printed invitation with its gold lettering.

But Rochelle Satterwhite was no Leesha Anderson. I remembered Rochelle's campaign speech, so earnest and out of touch. And then I thought about my twenty-point list. When I got back to my dormitory, I would revise it. Item seven would be changed to *DO something decent*.

"How much do you need?" I said to Rochelle.

She crossed the small break room and knelt before me, pressing her face into my abdomen. "Thank you. Thank you."

I patted her head through the dirty canvas cap. "It will be okay."

I think back to times like that and it's as though I am watching a movie about myself. It makes me feel like I am getting old, because I can now look at my younger self like she was a different person from who I am now.

I often find myself wanting to go back and whisper into my own ear, explaining the things that once confused me. I wish I could have told myself how things were going to turn out.

There are many ways to get old, to ripen. Hermione was just past eighteen when she got married, and she became a grown woman in less than a week. I saw her just three days after she'd run away, and she was older already; her extra weight didn't seem like plump tight baby fat anymore. She looked like a woman who had had two or three kids. She had that look like her body had been used for something.

I've aged just this month. In a single morning that I retched over the toilet and realized that I was pregnant. It's not the pregnancy itself that was the milestone, but how pleased and satisfied I was to realize it. The news zipped through me like something fast and shiny. I'd spent the last decade worrying about the possibility of a baby taking root in my body. Maybe the fact that I can say I've been doing *anything* for a decade says something too, about aging. Every month when my period arrived, I gave a quick thanks to God. Other girls complained about the possibility of ruining white pants or having to postpone certain types of rendezvous, but I'd always just turned my face upward and murmured my gratitude. One of my missions had been to prove my mother wrong. I wasn't going to get pregnant and ruin my life. This was not what Dr. King died for. And on this my mother and I agreed.

But now I was a grown woman. More than a fourth of my life was gone, assuming that I would live a normal life span. When my father was my age, his life was three-quarters gone. I was ready to start my own life, have my own family. After this baby, when people asked, "Do you have a family?" I would say yes and tell them about Dwayne and the baby. I would not mention my mother, my sister, or the ones who were dead. I could answer without acknowledging any of them and this would not be a lie.

Chapter Three

I don't think that anyone would have guessed that I would grow up to be a teacher. It wasn't my calling or my dream. As a kid I never cared much for school, sitting in hot classrooms trying to learn on demand. I didn't admire my teachers, any of them—not the young pretty ones who forced shy boys to ask us to dance or the old ladies who were obsessed with penmanship. I didn't hate it enough to dedicate my life to changing the system, however a person would go about doing such a thing. In third grade a guest speaker asked all the girls if they would rather be nurses or teachers; I said that I wanted to be a hairdresser and spend my life helping people look better. As soon as I got old enough to understand obvious things, I set my goal as getting into a good college. At Spelman I had chosen sociology because it seemed like something a regular person could do well in. A subject in which I could earn Bs or As if I just did my homework and went to the library. Rochelle had majored in English because she is supposed to have a gift for language. Dwayne didn't go to college at all, but went into locksmithing because even when he was little, locks loved him. When his baby sister had trapped herself in the bathroom, Dwayne was the one who got her out. His daddy was outside on a ladder trying to force the window, and five-year-old Dwayne just goosed the handle and the door swung open. I don't have a special gift, not one that I have noticed anyway. But I do fine in the classroom.

Before meeting my boss, Lawrence, at a job fair, I'd worked at the Institute for the Blind, where my mother manages the front office. She is a force in that place, well dressed and stern. Mama is the secretary that runs the entire operation. When I finished college and couldn't find a job on my own, she found something for me at the Institute.

My job was to read aloud. I sat at my desk in a tight, windowless room and read any papers that the clients brought in. Sometimes I read letters from family members or important official documents. These I read carefully, using phonetics to pronounce Latin legal terms. Sometimes the clients would ask me for interpretations. "So what does that mean? Am I going to lose my house?" I would tell them that I didn't know the answers, that I only read aloud, and then referred them to Legal Aid. My other responsibility had been to read the newspaper, each word, to whoever chose to assemble in the lounge every day at noon. I didn't mind reading the articles and features, but the advertisements threw me. I wasn't sure if I should inflect to convey the exclamation points and bright colors. I felt dumb bellowing, *Huge clearance! Everything must go!* Many of the people I read to didn't seem to have a preference. They just sat around me like a circle of kindergartners, leaning on their canes or stroking their big dogs. A reel-to-reel recorder made a record for those who might want to listen later.

Working at the Institute had shown me that my mother and I had things in common after all. We were the best-dressed women there. Makeup and hose, even though most of the clientele couldn't appreciate our efforts. I think we both knew it was silly, but we couldn't help ourselves. We never spoke of it, but we dressed the way we did because we spent most of our day around white people and we didn't want to give them any reason to think they were better than us. Mother had come by this insecurity quite honestly—she'd grown up during Jim Crow—but I learned it from her and from whatever had come twined into my DNA.

Drew Alexander had been blind only three or so months when I met him. Some sort of congenital problem, he'd explained to me. His eyesight just got worse and worse and now he couldn't see at all. He was young, less than thirty, and angry.

"Bum genes," he said. "Something passed down from my father. I never met him, but he left me something to remember him by, didn't he?" His accent was sugary, southern white. Whenever I heard someone speak that way, the words so lazy they seemed to be lying down, it

made me feel like only white people were really south-
erners. That the rest of us were just squatters.

Drew Alexander laughed with good-looking teeth,
blue-white and shiny. He was a living endorsement for
his designer jeans. Slim, cornflake blond, masculine, but
leaning toward androgyny. He smelled nice, like
spearmint and lemon zest.

"Did you want me to read something for you?" I
said. "I read for people."

"How do you get a dog? That's what I want. A big
German shepherd."

"I can refer you to someone. You'll probably get a
yellow Lab. I see a lot of Labs."

"I don't care what you see."

I became very quiet. This was how you made yourself invisible to blind people.

"Don't do that," he said. "I'm sorry. I don't mean to
be rude."

"Not at all," I said. "Would you like me to read something to you? I can read a book if you like, a magazine.
We have some here; or maybe you brought something
with you?"

"Are you pretty?" he said. "What do you look like? I
can tell from the way you talk that you're African American. I don't mean any offense by that. But y'all talk different than white people."

I nodded, though he couldn't see me.

"So what do you look like? Are you sexy? Do you
have big tits?"

"Mr. Alexander," I said, "this is not appropriate."

"I know, I know," he said. "Mea culpa. I just keep getting out of hand. I don't mean you no harm. It's hard not being able to see things. Waiting for somebody to tell you what's in front of your face. It's hard. But I do have something I need to get read to me. Let me just pull it out of my bag."

He bent down to rummage through his sack and I noticed that his hair was dyed blond. The roots were dark as dirt. I wondered who colored it for him. Did they assure him that it looked good, that it brought out the green of his eyes?

He placed a worn magazine on my desk. Pornography. The real stuff. Not *Playboy*. This was hard-core. I rolled my chair away from my desk and started toward the door, but Drew Alexander blocked my way. He reached for me, holding me around the waist. He took his shades off and showed me his eyes, hazel and empty. His lips were against my cheek; he spoke, scraping my skin with his tongue. "Don't be so mean. Don't be scared. It don't matter if you're ugly."

I struggled to get away from him and he held me harder, pressing me against the wall. The light switch gouged my shoulder blade.

"Help," I screamed, hoping my voice would carry through the shut door. "Fire!"

"Don't be so mean," he said, squirming against me. It didn't matter how quiet I made myself now. He was touching me. "Be nice."

I pitched my voice louder. "Help!"

My mother opened the door. "What is the problem?"

Drew Alexander released me. My impulse was to run

to my mother, receive the hug that should have been her impulse to offer.

"Mama," I said, returning to my desk and handing her the magazine. "He brought this in and then he grabbed me."

My mother glanced at the magazine and rolled it into a club. "Mr. Alexander, I believe you were banned from the Institute a month ago? I am asking you to leave. Or do I have to call security?"

"Where's my cane?" he said. "I can't see to get out without my cane."

I took it from the arm of his chair and gave it to him. He tapped out with a delicate noise.

I sat down on the sharp edge of my desk and buried my face in my hands.

"That was awful," I said to my mother. "He attacked me."

"It's you," Mother said. "Only you could almost be raped by a blind man in a public place. Is this what Dr. King died for?"

The next week, I noticed a newspaper ad for a job fair sponsored by the Urban League. When I read this notice aloud, the enthusiasm in my voice was real.

The job fair was held in a huge conference center, crammed with business-suited black people scuttling around rows of tables decorated with various corporate logos. I pulled my résumé from my leather portfolio several times, to assure myself that it was still there and that it looked good. It listed anything I thought would make me more attractive to employers, including a bulleted list of "personal traits": self-starter, creative, great people skills, mature. I'd spent more than three hours checking it for errors, consulting the real dictionary when I doubted the accuracy of my word processor's spell-check. As an extra flourish I'd spent an additional ten cents a page for heavy paper the color of pigeons.

The recruiters reclined in their chairs, waiting for an irresistible candidate to show herself. They all had that slightly bored, cocky attitude like obviously rich or handsome men in nightclubs. They spoke to each other with knowing looks as they sipped soft drinks. I handed a lady from Coca-Cola my résumé; she nodded, put it on the bottom of a stack of other people's histories, and shoved a red and white brochure in my direction. I repeated this scenario at a few other tables—Georgia Power, Delta Airlines, BellSouth. *Hi, my name is Aria Jackson. Here's my résumé; I look forward to hearing from you.* And, true to the nightclub model, they all promised to call.

Walking toward the back of the room to get one of the free Cokes chilling in a humming cooler, I ran into a chubby man wearing a wool suit; it wasn't a great suit, but it was decent. He was older than most of the other job seekers. I put him at about forty-two. Maybe he'd been laid off and was now looking for a second career. I felt a little sorry for him, but he seemed to be in a grand mood, winking at me as he reached into the cooler.

"Having much luck?" He handed me a caffeine-free Diet Coke.

I shrugged. "Okay, I guess. Nobody flat-out refused to take my résumé."

"What kind of work are you looking for?"

"I don't know for sure," I said. "I was thinking maybe I'd like to get into advertising or PR."

"How come?"

"I want a job that's positive. Upbeat."

"What have you been doing till now?"

I shrugged. "This and that."

He took the can from me and opened it with a gadget on his key chain. "I hope I'm not being too forward, but I think you would squander your talents in advertising. What would you do all day working for Georgia Power? Get people to use sixty-watt bulbs? That's a waste of time. I can promise you, people are going to burn electricity with or without you." He took a slurp of Cherry Coke before handing me a business card, a flimsy one, obviously run off on his laser printer. "Do you have any experience working with special populations?"

"I won't work with blind people," I said.

"I can guarantee you that there are no blind people in my organization. We do literacy, and not in braille. Think about it. Call me."

Two weeks after the job fair none of the employers had contacted me for an interview. I called Lawrence on Friday. He asked me if I could come in Monday morning for training. My mother was furious with me for leaving the Institute on such short notice, but I was glad to get away before I had to read the Sunday paper with all its coupons and comics.

Literacy Action and Resource Center is a lot of name for an organization that consists of three people: Lawrence, Rochelle, and me. Rochelle came on board about two years ago to replace this guy named Khafre who quit working at LARC in order to go to law school. Rochelle had just dropped out of Emory University, where she was working toward a Ph.D. in English. "It was just so esoteric," she had told Lawrence when she met him at the NAACP job fair. They'd run into each other at the blood pressure machine. Later I found out that Lawrence went to the fairs but didn't pay to set up a table. Instead, when he needed someone, he roamed the venue looking for the kind of person he wanted.

Lawrence hired Rochelle that very day; he liked that she used the word "esoteric." After he decided she was too valuable to be cooped up in the classroom all day, Rochelle was named "development coordinator," but she taught one section of general literacy every other year. Her job was a little better than mine. Same pay but more prestige. She was the one who represented LARC at fund-raising luncheons. Rochelle made conversation with the donors, laughing at their esoteric jokes and making smart comments beginning with "actually," while Lawrence and I listened politely and tried not to draw attention to ourselves or mispronounce anything. Rochelle was kind enough to never mention this invisible caste system, not even in jest.

On Mondays, Wednesdays, and Fridays I teach GED prep to twelve teenage girls who are "under the supervision of the Fulton County Court." This twist in the clientele is due to Rochelle's flair for grant writing. She's always proposing new classes in order to tap new sources. This prison thing has been a bonanza all the way around. Lawrence teaches two sections a week at the federal prison in Reidsville, sleeping over in a Days Inn in nearby Vidalia. Of course this means that some of our general literacy sections have been put on hiatus, but our numbers are up. This year we've accommodated thirteen percent more students than the year before.

At first I had been a little apprehensive about taking on juvenile offenders. It wasn't the offender dimension that upset me so much as the juvie part. After walking through the fire at six high schools in four years, I didn't want to be even a *spectator* to adolescence. But here I was, three times a week in front of an eclectic class of unlucky girls. The youngest ones were fifteen, and the old ladies of the group were nearly twenty. Knowing how it feels not to be the teacher's pet, I tried to treat each of my students equally. But I was partial to Keisha Evers—seventeen and just a tiny bit pregnant.

Usually it takes about three weeks for the classroom dynamic to jell, but this term we had all found our places on the very first day. As usual I started class by asking each girl to give her name, age, and something that made her unique. Keisha did as she was told, then blurted, "It wasn't like they said it was. He told me I could use his Discover to get me some clothes and everything. Then when the bill came, he let his wife call the law, saying I stole it when he was supposed to be mentoring me."

I looked at the roll to remember her name, then said,

"LaKeisha, that is a little more information than I asked for."

"Well," she said, "it's what everybody wants to know. Don't nobody care who in here is double-jointed." She touched the knee of the young woman beside her, who had offered her deformed elbows as proof of her unique-ness. "No offense," she said before going on. "I'm just saying that we should get to tell our side of the story. That's all people want anyway."

"That may be," I said, looking at the bookmarks I'd planned to give as prizes to the students who could re-member all their classmates' names and quirks. "But I don't want to invade anyone's privacy."

"It's not like that," Keisha said, turning again to her double-jointed neighbor. "Why you in here? What's your name again?"

"Angelina," she said, picking orange polish from her cuticle. "They found drugs in my apartment. It wasn't a lot and it wasn't all for me."

And so they had gone around the room. Some girls spun elaborate tales involving boyfriends, addictions, abuse, and misunderstandings. They talked about their kids. Two or three just mumbled a charge and an apol-ogy. Many of the stories were as thin and translucent as rice paper, but a few weighed in with the thick heft of truth.

Keisha watched her classmates as they spoke, nodding earnestly and rubbing gentle circles on her bulb of a stomach. She made sympathetic comments where there were pauses: "That wasn't nothing but racism" or "That right there was just your lawyer's fault." She pointed at each girl when it was time for her to speak.

When each person in the tight circle of metal desk chairs had introduced and explained herself, Keisha turned to me. "So, miss," she said, "what about you?"

I fingered the orange and green bookmarks and said, "Well, I'm originally from here. Got my degree at Spelman. I've been teaching literacy for four and a half years."

She rolled her eyes a little and glanced at her classmates. "Not résumé stuff. We want to know what's really up with you."

I thought about Lawrence and his warning about "boundaries." He'd lectured me during my orientation meeting: *Do not socialize with your clients; it's inappropriate and counterproductive. And some of the people who will come through these doors are master con artists. The rest just want you to save them. Either way, it's bad news and it's the reason why you need to have clear and firm boundaries.*

I had tried to do it Lawrence's way at first—avoiding lingering eye contact, offering no details about my personal life. If someone had asked me my zodiac sign, I'd have refused to reply. But then I had been working nights, teaching older students who just wanted to learn. They weren't curious about my personal narrative and weren't interested in sharing theirs. They just wanted to read well enough to get their GEDs or driver's licenses. At Christmas they all chipped in to buy me a silver-plated desk set, and that was about as intimate as it got.

But on the first day of this term, I'd been in the center of a ring of girls, their faces wide-open like ceramic bowls. The twelve of them had stared at me with almost tangible anticipation.

"I don't know," I said. "There's really nothing to tell."

"Oh, come on," Keisha said with the grit of annoyance and the sugar of pleading. "Tell us *something*. How old are you? Are you married?"

"This is a little inappropriate," I said in a voice that I hoped was clear and firm.

The dozen young women had sighed in disappointed unison and had opened their textbooks.

Now we were five weeks into a fifteen-week term and I'd thought back on that moment several times. There were only eight girls left out of our original twelve. Tomeika got caught smoking crack, just down the block from my house. As our in-class writing assignment we wrote letters to her. I didn't know what to write, so I sent her copies of our reading assignments, poetry by Sonia Sanchez and Nikki Giovanni. I hoped it might help somehow. Double-jointed Angelina and pretty Benita just disappeared. Lani said she was bored and dropped out.

Each time I whited out a name from my roll book, I remembered that moment and their open faces and I wondered how much blame I should heap onto my plate.

Lawrence tells me not to mourn. At least nobody died. Two people up in Reidsville had passed away on him already. On the first day of the term he had warned me that I should expect a few to recidivate, a few to vanish, and at least one to die. Some days, when my girls were quiet and hunched over their workbooks, I wondered which of them it would be.

After class today, when I'd gathered all my things and left the building, I found Keisha sitting on the porch swing. She didn't pretend not to be waiting for me. She used to do that at first, rummaging through her large purse, looking for keys, although she always rode the bus to class. Now she sat openly, whipping her eyes toward the door when it opened. Rocking in the wood swing, she chipped layers of paint with her airbrushed finger-nails. Her pooch of a belly protruded just farther than her apple-sized breasts.

"Hey," she said, patting the space on the swing beside her. "Be careful. It's hot."

I eased down and felt the heat through my slacks. I sat next to her, rocking back and forth in the heavy air. From the porch I could see the roof of the Phillis Wheatley YWCA—my family's destination on the day of the accident. I think that I like being so close to the place where everything changed. It's a sort of daily explanation of why things are as they are. It's like keeping a picture of Sir Isaac Newton on your desk to keep from forgetting about the fundamental nature of gravity.

My mother thinks this is perverse, and allegedly this is why she never comes to visit me. She and I agree that the past is alive and thriving in Southwest Atlanta. Mama believes that the intensity of pain is directly related to proximity. This is why she likes living where she does—close enough to ache but too far to actually bleed. She will never come to my house, and, sometimes, this pleases me. Hermione has never visited either, and this snub breaks my heart. She can't blame it on my zip code. As far as my sister is concerned, the past has passed. Mama and I need to just move on. At least this is what she says. I find it hard to believe that someone as bright as Hermione would not see what is so obvious. The past is a dark vast lake and we just tread on its delicate skin.

"What's wrong, Miss Aria?" Keisha said.

"Nothing," I said. "Just hot, that's all. I can't believe it's only the last week of May."

"I always pick the worst times to get pregnant," she pouted.

"I thought this was your first baby."

She shook her head. "I told you I got a little boy. He is in Oklahoma with my aunt. His name is Dante? Remember I told you that?"

I shook my head. "This is the first time I'm hearing this."

She made a smacking sound and crossed her arms over her chest. "See, Miss Aria. You ain't right. You act like you care about us and everything, but then as soon as people finish talking, poof, you forget whatever we told you."

I was pretty sure Keisha had never mentioned another child. My memory wasn't as good as Rochelle's, but I would have remembered something like that. I mentally scrolled through our previous conversations. It was hard to keep track of all the confidences she shared. I knew I wasn't supposed to be so intertwined with a student, but Keisha looped me in with the stories of her life and held me fast.

She must know how affected I am by secrets, confessions. Before the first week of class was over, she helped me carry my belongings to my car. Before I'd even opened the trunk, she told me that the man who had accused her of credit card fraud was the father of her child.

"Now, that's a secret, Miss Aria. He doesn't even know himself."

Secrets flattered me, the idea that someone, even Keisha, would trust me with something so private. She told me something new each week, it seemed, until I began to think of myself as her confidante. When I listened, sometimes I pretended that I was the young girl pouring my heart out to a woman that was not old, but older than me. Wise enough to give decent counsel. When I talked to Keisha, I tried to tell her things that I wished someone had told me. Not that I would have followed any sensible advice. When I was a teenager, I wasn't interested in things that were good for me. But I think that I would be a happier adult if I could look back on my teen years and remember that there was someone there who cared enough to try and give me a few words by which to live.

"Keisha, you didn't tell me about Dante. I wouldn't have forgotten about something like that."

"Whatever," she sniffed.

"What's wrong?"

"Nothing."

"Hungry?"

"Hungry for Taco Bell."

"Let's walk over there," I said, glad to see her smile.

"Taco Bell is too far to walk," she huffed, not rising from the swing.

"It's just up the street," I said. "Not even half a mile. Walking is good exercise."

"I'm not trying to lose weight." She stretched her T-shirt around her, emphasizing the small pouch of a belly. "I'm *pregnant.*"

Lawrence walked out onto the porch then, looking relaxed and slightly disheveled in a wrinkled T-shirt and pressed pants. Keisha scooted up off the swing.

"How are things going, Aria?"

"Good," I said. "Gearing up for the GED."

"And you, young lady?" he said. "When is the blessed event?"

Keisha placed a hand on each side of her stomach. "October."

She looked at her yellow sneakers; Lawrence looked at me; I stared out at the boarded-up bungalow across the street.

"Well," Lawrence said after standing almost a minute in the murky silence of an interrupted conversation. "I'm going back in. If Eric comes by, tell him I'm out back."

"Okay."

As soon as the front door shut Lawrence in the building, Keisha said, "Eric's his boyfriend?"

"His partner," I corrected. "They've been together six years."

"They want a baby, don't they?"

"I don't know," I lied.

"He asked me about my baby. He asked me if I was going to keep it."

I raised my eyebrows.

"I'm not lying," she said. "I went in his office to do some paperwork and he started asking me all these questions about the baby. Who is the daddy, did I feel that I would be able to raise it right, and what did I think about adoption and everything like that."

I shook my head and shrugged. I knew that Lawrence and Eric were interested in having kids, but I was surprised to know he had been quizzing Keisha. If it was inappropriate for me to take a student to lunch, certainly adopting their babies would be a breach of boundaries as well.

Rochelle and I had attended Lawrence and Eric's "commitment ceremony" two years ago. It was supposed to be the same as a wedding, but it didn't feel like one. It wasn't just that there were two men standing before the preacher in matching linen suits. There was something about the vibe of the gathering that didn't feel quite official. Maybe it was because it wasn't in a church, or maybe it was because there were not enough relatives there. Out of the four parents, only Lawrence's mother was present. Rochelle says that they are as married as anybody and I suppose that she is right.

"So what did you say to Lawrence when he asked about your plans?"

"I told him that I was keeping my baby. My mama's sister in Oklahoma got Dante. That was different; I was fifteen then. She couldn't have kids and she promised that she would take good care of him. But I am keeping this baby; I'll be eighteen by the time it gets born. And if

I *was* looking for someone to adopt, I would give it to a regular family to raise."

"You told him that part about the 'regular family'?"

"No, I just told him that I was keeping it."

Keisha whined until I agreed to drive her to Taco Bell. She slid into the passenger side and ejected the cassette tape before I could even get the car started. She fiddled with the radio, quickly locating her favorite hip-hop station. The car filled with the voice of a young man waxing about bitches and Bentleys. I looked at my worn Anita Baker tape that rested in the cup holder and wondered if I was getting old.

At the restaurant I handed Keisha a clean twenty-dollar bill, not expecting her to spend the whole thing. It would take some doing to blow twenty dollars when the most costly thing on the menu was $1.19. But she managed, giving me less than a dollar in change when she came back to the car carrying four white bags stuffed with burritos (supreme and regular), tacos (hard and soft), and a couple of tostadas. There was an extra-large Mountain Dew that we would share.

"I got a lot." Keisha grinned. "Because I'm eating for two."

She got in the car, infusing the vehicle with the smell of greasy meat and imitation cheese. I had reinserted the Anita Baker tape and she didn't complain. She twirled a blond braid around her finger and looked out the window. "I've lived in the same apartment my whole entire life," she said. "Me and my mama."

"That's okay," I said.

I swerved to avoid potholes and bottle glass in the

parking area of her apartment complex. I angled toward a space.

"Don't park there. Go around the side so we can keep an eye on your car from the window." She spoke with her eyes focused on the bags of food. "Not that this car is all of that, but you never know what people want to steal."

I followed her up the concrete steps to her second-floor apartment. The door was covered with red foil and bore an oddly shaped wooden sign that said "God Bless Our Home."

"My mama made that," she said. "You know how that vocational stuff is. When I did vo-tech, I learned how to do calligraphy."

She opened the front door and we pushed into her living room. "You not allergic to plants, are you?" she asked me, as she asked me every time I came to visit. The tidy apartment was jammed with houseplants. Yellow and white kalanchoes bloomed in clay pots in the windows. Spider plants hanging from ceiling hooks grew and drooped. A robust shoot of ivy climbed up a makeshift trellis, completely obscuring the north wall.

"I like plants," I said.

"Me too, but my mama is crazy for anything that can grow. She got the ivy from a social worker when I was born. It was just one little leaf sitting in a cheap pot. Now look at it." She went to the window, swiveled open the blinds. "That's better."

I followed her into the kitchen and watched as she spread the food on a metal mesh table that looked like part of a patio set. "You want a tostada?"

Sitting on a metal chair felt like I was settling into the foliage. It seemed that we should spread a blanket over the worn carpet and have a picnic. "Just one taco, please."

She unwrapped a taco, the orange oil pooling in the crease. My stomach lurched, sending me stumbling in the direction of the bathroom. I emptied my stomach, closed the toilet, and rested my face on the carpet-covered lid.

"Damn, Miss Aria," Keisha said from the doorway. "I'm the one that's pregnant."

"Me too," I said. The words slipped from between my teeth easily, like oiled melon seeds. It was a dumb thing to do. I knew this before I finished my sentence, just like you know that you've locked your keys in the car even before the door slams, but there is nothing you can do but watch.

Keisha lowered herself beside me on the bathroom tile. "For real, Miss Aria? You're pregnant? I didn't even know you had a man." She leaned toward me, one of her synthetic curls grazing my cheek. "You not going to have an abortion, are you? I don't believe in that."

She waited for me to answer her questions, but I closed my eyes beside her, silent and horrified with myself. Keisha went on, still close enough to kiss me. "I guess I don't really know anything about you. You won't tell anybody where you live, how old you are, nothing like that. That's one thing I can't stand about social workers. Y'all know everybody else's story, but you don't let anybody get even a sniff of your business." Her breath was cool on my sweaty neck.

I squeezed my eyes tighter, hoping the tears would run back into their ducts. This was another of life's

Greek myth moments. When you're pregnant, it matters who you tell first. It shows where your heart is, where your priorities are. Dwayne should have been the first person to know. There should have been a moment when this news was only ours. I put my hand in my hair, twirling my twists until they strained at the roots and hurt.

"How many weeks are you?" Keisha wanted to know. "Six or something like that? Who's the daddy?"

"Oh, come on," she said when I didn't respond. "You can't tell me that you're pregnant and then decide it's not my business. Come on, Miss Aria, you know everything about me."

And she was right. I knew more about her than I knew what to do with. Over the course of the term, Keisha had shown me her archives of pain. In March she'd missed a week of class. I'd dialed her phone number and gotten the polite message that the number I'd reached had been disconnected. Lawrence had just shrugged. These things happened. Teaching was contribution enough. No one expected us to roam the street rounding up truants. But I had gone to find her anyway, using a city map that my mother had given me years ago, when I first got my driver's license.

The moment my knuckles had touched the foil-covered door, I struggled with the urge to bolt. Who knew if this was Keisha's real address? It occurred to me that I didn't know who she lived with and under what circumstances. Spring was still young enough that the evenings were cool. I could hear the noises of televisions wafting from the open windows of the apartments around me. It seemed as if everyone was tuned in to the same station. The artificial cheeriness of a sitcom laugh track came through in bursts and starts. After several seconds had passed, I made up my mind to leave. I'd done my best. Then Keisha had opened the door, bleary-eyed; her braids, gathered in a rubber band, were slack like filthy yellow ribbons. Her skin was grayish, as though she had been dusted all over with flour. Yawning, she rubbed the blanket print crisscrossing her cheek. She paused for a moment, as if processing who I was, and then invited me in, asking if I was allergic to plants.

"I tried to call," I explained.

"It'll be back on soon," she said.

From the living room I could see the sink piled high with dishes that stank of sour milk and rotting food.

"My mama is in the hospital. Her blood pressure is too high for them to send her home." She shrugged inside of a baggy T-shirt. She touched the sides of her belly as if to steady it. "Our money is funny. It's always funny, but Mama hasn't been to work in three weeks and I haven't been working either, trying to see about her."

"Can I turn on the light?" I asked her.

"Go ahead."

I turned the knob on the base of a plastic lamp, igniting a low-wattage bulb. The light seemed to bounce off the gloom, never penetrating it, like headlights in fog.

She sat on the couch and stripped the leaves from a potted gardenia. "Too bad we can't sell some of these damn plants." She gathered the leaves in her hands and tossed them up like confetti.

I sat on the edge of the sofa, ignoring the dead-animal smell of the kitchen. I slapped at something inching its way up my neck before I realized that it was just a leaf. "It will work out."

"I've been on some hard times. I've done some things for money. My mama too." She rubbed her stomach like a crystal ball. "Everybody has, I guess."

"The credit card situation?"

"That, and other stuff too. And I didn't steal that credit card. He gave it to me. I earned it, you know?"

I nodded.

She began to rock herself and worried a keloid on the underside of her ear. "I never told this to anyone before," she said. "Not even my mama, because we don't really talk about things. But it wasn't turning tricks. Sometimes you have to get a man to help you out. It's hard out here. When I tried to use the credit card and they told me to wait, I didn't think nothing about it. He had gave me the card to use. Promised me before anything even happened between us. So I was just standing there while the saleslady went in the back and called the police. When the security people came and got me, I didn't even tell them how I had permission to use the card, how me and him had been together and everything. Because I felt like I deserved what I got. Like I had crossed a line, backed up, and crossed it all over again."

When I nodded, she gave me a smirk. "You don't know nothing about this here."

But I did know. Not about having sex for money, but I knew about doing things that made you feel nasty, that made you feel like you deserved whatever you got. I didn't argue with her, though. I didn't want Keisha to know all the things I've done or the shame I've felt. "I brought your assignments," I said.

She took the sheaf of paper and set it on the coffee table. "My boyfriend, Omar, said he was going to help us out when he gets paid, but that's not for another week."

I nodded again, thinking about my mother, how she gently corrected anyone who called her a "single mother." She was a *widow*, she explained again and again. Keisha didn't even have any pretty language to fall back on. "Single mother" was what people would call her when they wanted to be polite.

Keisha and I never talked about my visit to her apartment. She returned to class in less than a week, pretty and clean, her hair rebraided and fresh. After school, she had given me directions, as though I had never been to her home. But still, her disclosures were between us, making our relationship lopsided.

"I don't know nothing about you, Miss Aria," she said again.

"I'm not trying to be secretive," I told her. "I am still thinking it out. I haven't even told Dwayne yet."

"That's your boyfriend's name? Dwayne? You didn't tell him yet? How long y'all been together? I'm the first one you told?"

"Yes," I said.

"How many weeks are you?" Keisha asked again.

"I'm not sure. Haven't been to the doctor yet. Five weeks maybe."

I put my face in my hand and breathed in the rose-water scent of my hand lotion.

"Lay down on the couch, Miss Aria," Keisha said.

I followed her to the gray couch. I stretched out on the cracked vinyl, although I really wasn't tired and no longer wanted to be there. The ceiling was scarred with brownish water marks. Keisha knelt before me and slid off my cloth loafers. Kneading my feet through my stockings, she said, "When you're pregnant, you have to take good care of your feet. It's like everything that's on your mind gets trapped in your feet."

I closed my eyes and enjoyed the feel of her hands. I tried to banish my superstitions. It wouldn't matter that I had opened my mouth when I shouldn't have. Keisha rubbed the base of my foot with her knuckles. This was going to be the best part of being pregnant, the way people tried to anticipate your needs. Rochelle would host my baby shower and think of intelligent party games for the guests. Maybe Dwayne would propose without me having to ask him to. And my mother would be pleased, a son-in-law and grandbaby, all within the space of a year.

Lying on Keisha's sofa, I wished for Hermione. When I was a teeny little girl, before the accident, she was the one I ran to with my stories of grade school trauma. When I was thirteen, she washed her hands of me, marrying Mr. Phinazee, our father's friend, the summer she finished high school. They moved to Lawrenceville, thirty miles north. When I tell people these days that my sister lives in Lawrenceville, they don't react. But Lawrenceville is a lot closer to Atlanta now than it was ten years ago. Then it was as though Hermione had moved to a distant unsettled land, as though she had moved to live on a ranch in Wyoming. Now Lawrenceville is just another suburb. People drive all the way out there just to shop.

When she first married, I used to call her up, hoping that she'd put clean sheets on the fold-out bed and invite me for a sleepover. She had always been polite enough when I'd call, hinting that I wouldn't mind the drive, but she claimed that the house was too junky, or she and Earl needed some alone time, or something like that. Now she pretends to want to save me the hassle of struggling with northbound traffic. "You don't want to drive way out here. I-85 will be constipated at this time of day."

I tell her that I don't mind driving. You would think that cars would terrify me, that I'd cry at the very idea of four-wheeled transportation. This is how these things worked on television. But I never understood the car to be the cause of my family's misfortunes. I blame the magnolia we hit and the dogwoods that watched. The sight of them each spring causes my body to tremble, just below the skin where no one can see, but I can feel it.

"See," Keisha said, stroking the sole of my foot with her acrylic nails. "It's not the end of the world. People get pregnant every day."

When I made it back home from Keisha's apartment, I found Cynthia in the driveway, kneeling in the gravel. I watched her for a while as she rooted around in the dirt. I called her name and walked toward her. She stood when I came near; in the golden light I noticed the tiny rocks embedded in the skin of her bare skinny knees. She wiped her forehead with the tail of her T-shirt, flashing her abdomen, striped with stretch marks.

"Miss," she said, "can you help me?"

"I don't have money," I said, patting my empty pockets.

"You owe me a dollar. For that hair bow."

"I can go in the house and bring the barrette back to you."

"Then I would owe you your dollar back. Keep the bow," she said. "I don't need it." She dropped herself again to the driveway, collapsing suddenly like she had lost use of her legs. "Are you going to help me?"

"Help you what?"

She looked up from the dirt and pebbles sifting through her fingers. Her skin was gray with dust. "I dropped something out here this morning."

"What?"

She didn't tell me; she just took another handful of gravel and examined each pebble.

"When did you drop it?"

"Ten o'clock. While you was at work." She grabbed two handfuls of driveway gravel and held them to her face, urgently scanning the contents. She plucked a pill-sized rock and put it in her mouth and quickly spat it out. "Damn," she said. "I thought that was it."

I stepped back and she spat out another dirty pebble. "Cynthia, you're not going to find it."

"Could you turn on the light?" Her eyes were on me as a halo of gnats circled over her cornrows, which were caked with dandruff and dirt. "Could you at least cut on the light for me? I'm not asking you for no money or nothing like that."

I went into the house and fastened all the locks on

the door. They were good locks, Dwayne's four-inch dead bolts. I leaned on the door with my heart knocking against my collarbone. I wasn't shutting the door against Cynthia herself. She was just a dried husk of a woman. She may have been a thief, but she had never struck me as a violent person. I shut my door and locked it against the intensity of her need. Pressing my stomach with the flat of my hands, I swallowed back sadness and bile.

I checked the locks once more before dragging the phone from the living room into my bedroom. The air conditioner still hadn't been fixed; the air in my bedroom was murky and dense. But still, I crawled under the limp sheets of my bed and even pulled the store-bought quilt over me before dialing my sister's number. The machine picked up—"You have reached the Phinazees . . ."—and I didn't leave a message.

Still thinking of my sister and of dogwoods, I returned to the living room and from the safety of the window, watched Cynthia bowed in the gravel. Small clouds of dust bloomed around her fast-moving hands. Watching her, I thought about Keisha and the way she traced words with her fingers when she read.

I flipped the switch, washing the driveway in harsh white light. Cynthia looked to the house with a wave and a little smile. I sat in the window until I didn't want to watch her any longer.

Chapter Four

I have never been good at playing hard to get, that faked indifference that is supposed to make everyone love you. In romance it wasn't a matter of promiscuity, no matter what my mother may have said. I've never slept with any man just for the thrill of it, just because I was curious about how he might move, how it might make me feel. It was more that I was desperate and optimistic at the same time. When a decent-seeming man asked me to lunch or to dinner, or just asked for my phone number, my optimism said that he could be the one. My desperation is what made me cooperative, wriggling out of my clothes after only a few kisses.

In a manner that is both different and identical, I am the same way with Hermione, constantly offering myself to her, in the form of cookies baked to honor some greeting card holiday or volunteering to babysit, although she always refuses. Sometimes she will come home from work to find me sitting on her porch with my back propped against her oak front door. I smile as she drives up, holding out her mail. Today I sat on her step, jittery with coffee and worry. When I was little, Hermione was the person I went to when I was in trouble, when I'd done wrong. Today I drove all the way to Lawrenceville not to tell her about the baby, but to tell her that I hadn't told Dwayne. I wanted her to show me what I could do to right that wrong, to set things back on their proper course.

Dwayne would love Hermione's neighborhood, the deliberate order of it, the newness of the houses, the inky asphalt road. Hermione and her family lived in a pinkish-white house, three stories, stucco front. Five or so shrubs, lollipop round, framed the front steps, while an orderly arrangement of crepe myrtles marked the perimeter. This was a new subdivision. No dogwoods or magnolias that took hundreds of years to grow.

The heat had broken for the evening, leaving behind sluggish humidity and hungry mosquitoes. Slapping them dead against my grimy neck, I waited for my sister to come home. I peeked into the stained-glass door pane, looking for mobile shadows that would tell me that she was inside, just ignoring me. Through the blue glass I saw only the carpeted staircase rendered in kaleidoscope, and nothing more. I mashed the bell again, listened to the chimes play Beethoven, and squinted through the glass. Finally I sat down again, nearly convinced that there was no one home.

Once, when I was eleven and Hermione sixteen, our mother locked us out of the house. At the time, we had lived on Willow Street only eight months and were still smarting over the loss of the house on Bunnybrooke Drive. I was in sixth grade.

The elementary school let out an hour earlier than the high school. I could have walked home right afterward, when the other kids from our block made their way to their houses, where their cheerful, normal mothers either waited on them or left sandwiches in their stead. The kids used to wait for me—no doubt their parents had told them to be nice to me, the poor thing who'd watched half her family die. They would linger, fastening their jackets extra slow, waiting for me to gather my books and follow. But day after day I gently dismissed them, explaining that I was waiting on my sister. They would nod their heads and leave quietly, assuming quite correctly that this had something to do with my father being dead and my mother being crazy.

I waited on Hermione on the stone porch that spanned the entire length of the elementary school. Sometimes she would be prompt, showing up just after I'd finished my math homework. On other occasions she'd appear after five o'clock when all the teachers had gone home, leaving me by myself with only the custodian, Mr. Henry, to look after me. These were my favorite days.

"You still out here?" Mr. Henry would ask me when he came outside to empty his mop bucket into the vacant parking lot.

"Yes, sir."

"You want me to let you in the building so you can call your mama?" Mr. Henry would smile down at me. His face was brown and crinkled like a grocery bag that had been reused. I liked him.

"No, sir."

"You sure?" He would pat his pocket with a clank. "I got keys to all the offices, you know. I ain't supposed to let anybody in, but they ain't supposed to leave little children all alone. Wasn't even last year that someone was snatching kids right around here."

"No, sir," I said again. "I don't have anyone to call. But my sister is on her way."

"When you get ready to go, tell me, so I can know you safe, hear?"

"Yes, sir." I'd give him a solemn nod, knowing I'd no intention of knocking, setting his mind at ease. When I spotted Hermione rounding the corner, I would creep away, purposely leaving something of mine behind. Once, I'd left my ballerina pencil box, scattering the pencils and denting the case with my heel. The next day the case was waiting for me in the lost and found and Mr. Henry peeped into my homeroom to make sure that I was alive and safe. I waved the case at him, mouthing the words "thank you." He couldn't have been more relieved had I really been his pretty little daughter.

Mama locked us out on Halloween. Hermione showed up at the school well after six, wearing her regular clothes, but pale yellow bunny ears jutted from her straightened hair. I'd gone to school that day dressed as a robot in a costume I'd made myself: a large box covering my clothes, with holes cut out to accommodate my head and arms. A second small box served as a helmet, with holes cut out for my eyes. The costume won me a flashlight and a certificate that read "Most Creative."

Mr. Henry congratulated me on my award. "You come up with that idea all by yourself?"

"Yes," I said, hearing my voice echo inside my cardboard headdress.

"You're a smart one. Make sure you let me know when your sister comes to get you. Last time, you scared me half to death. Don't do an old man like that. You got a jacket up under them boxes? There's plenty sweaters in lost and found. Nobody would notice if you put one on."

I would have liked to borrow a sweater. The October wind easily permeated the boxes and the leotard I wore underneath. But I didn't want to take the boxes off in order to put on warmer clothes. I'd chosen this costume because it hid my body, the heavy curves that made everyone stare at me. "I got on clothes enough under here already."

When Hermione finally arrived, I searched my bag for something to leave behind. My canvas pack held only generic items—plastic pens, chewed pencils, rubber coin purse—that could have belonged to any girl at my school. I turned on my award flashlight, for one last look at the glowing red bulb, before smashing it against one of the white pillars in front of the school. I scattered the broken glass, leaving my mangled prize for Mr. Henry to find.

In those days my sister was plump and sexy. In the

year since the accident she seemed to celebrate her ripe figure, favoring push-up bras and wide belts that emphasized her thick hourglass. On this evening she wasn't feeling so pretty and was in a terrible mood. I could tell even before she clomped over to where I kneeled struggling to repack my book bag. The cardboard costume had rubbed my underarms raw.

"Hurry up," she snapped.

"I'm trying," I whispered. "It's hard with this thing on."

"Why don't you just take it off and throw it away? Halloween is over."

"But we didn't trick-or-treat yet."

"Do you really think Mama is going to let you out of the house?"

"She might," I said, feeling tears gathering behind my eyes. "I won a prize for my costume. I want to keep it."

"I don't care what you do with it," Hermione said. "I just want to get home. It's six-thirty."

I didn't ask her where she had been for the last three hours. Her white turtleneck was grimy with makeup that she used to hide blue-red scars on her neck; she had told me these were called passion marks.

"Do you ever wish you were dead?" she asked me once we had left school grounds.

I shook my head. "Not really."

"Not wishing you were dead enough to do anything about it. But do you just wish someone would pull the plug on you?"

I turned toward her, but I couldn't catch a look at her face through the small eyeholes in my costume. In the yellow streetlight, making out the shape of her, all I could think was how much I loved my sister. "If you were dead, who would take care of me?"

"Maybe your mother?" Hermione laughed. "Don't freak out. I am not going to kill myself. I might kill somebody else, but I am not going to kill myself." She laughed and I tried to laugh with her.

She punched the cardboard box I wore on my head. "Take this thing off. It's weird to talk when I can't see your face."

"I don't want to." Lately my forehead had erupted in a crop of pimples hidden under my fluffy bangs. Precocious acne, my mother called it, using one of her favorite words. Several mornings a week she looked at me just before I went to school and said, "Precocious puberty. Help me, Jesus."

A gaggle of boys dressed as superheroes charged by us, smelling of sweat and bubble gum.

Hermione said, "There is so much stuff that you think matters that turns out to be nothing. Just bullshit."

"Like what?"

"Good grades. Virginity."

"What's that?"

"Absolutely nothing."

I didn't have to look at her to see that she was irritated. I walked beside her, working hard to match her pace despite my bulky costume. I didn't mean to be so stupid. "Like the Virgin Mary?"

"A virgin is a woman who hasn't known a man in the way that a woman knows a man." Hermione laughed and chucked a mini candy bar at a parked car. "It's all bullshit, bullshit, bullshit."

"I know," I said, eager to agree.

"You don't know," she said.

"I'm sorry."

"We may be the sorriest family on the planet," Hermione said. "There should be a Gallup poll."

I stayed quiet. My sister enjoyed teasing me, talking way over my head, watching me jump, like the smallest kid in a game of keep-away. The night was very cold. I knew that beneath this cardboard my nipples were standing up—"headlights," as Hermione would say.

"So what do you think about Earl?" she asked me.

"Mr. Phinazee? He's nice. Makes me think about Daddy."

"Air makes you think about Daddy," Hermione said.

I turned my head to see if she was being mean, but the night and the cardboard conspired against me again.

"What if he wanted to marry Mama?"

"He would be our stepdad," I said. "And we could be sort of a normal family."

"As long as Eloise is our mother, we will never be normal. Lord have mercy. I am so high." My sister laughed loud, beautiful, and mysterious into the night.

I saw the pumpkins first, dozens of them lining the driveway, framing the porch like track lighting. The jack-o'-lanterns were fabulous, complicated faces, glowing with ritual candles.

"I know I am not *that* high," Hermione said.

I stopped and lowered myself beside one of the

driveway pumpkins. Its eyebrows hunched together with worry. Mother had carved narrow, suspicious eyes.

"Get away from those things before you set your boxes on fire. Now, *that* would be really fucked up."

I stood in the middle of the driveway while Hermione inspected the other carvings. She examined three or four and returned to where I stood. She snatched the cardboard box off my head, causing me to squint against the cold. Hermione before me was large and pretty, her cleavage puckered with chill bumps. "Oh, Ariadne," she said. "Don't you wish we had someplace else to go?"

"I like the pumpkins," I said. "They are the best on the block."

"Aria," she said, "look how many of them she made. It's the whole goddamned pumpkin patch."

A clutch of children crossed in front of our house. "Why don't they come here to trick-or-treat?"

"Because they can tell," Hermione said.

I took my sister's hand and we went to the front door. Hermione slid her key into the top lock and then the bottom. She turned the handle, but the door opened only a few degrees before it stopped, secured by the safety chain.

"Mama," Hermione called, "we're locked out." She punched the doorbell a couple of times.

Hermione pressed her face in the open space between the door and the jamb. Her makeup was chalky in the white light spilling out from the house. "She's in there," Hermione said. "I'm looking at her."

"Maybe she didn't hear us ringing."

"Aria, she hears us right now. She's sitting in the dining room pulling the guts out of more motherfucking pumpkins."

"Did we do something to make her mad?" I tried to recall the details of the morning. Had I remembered to put my gown in the hamper? Had I rinsed my cereal bowl and put it in the dishwasher?

"It's Earl," Hermione said. "I know this has to do with Earl."

Hermione took a couple of steps back and then hurled herself against the door. The yellow bunny ears flipped and flopped with her effort. The door groaned, but the chain stayed firmly attached. "I *see* her," Hermione said again. "She is such a bitch."

"Don't break the door, Hermione," I begged. "You're going to make her mad."

"She's making *me* mad," Hermione said. "It's not right."

We sat on the porch. My sister was soft and lovely in the light of the jack-o'-lanterns. She wiped her eyes with the back of her hands. "What does she want from us? We were there, just like she was. She knows there wasn't nothing we could have done."

Hermione cried and I touched her hair. When she uncovered her face, she said, "See what I mean about wishing to be dead?"

"I don't want to die."

"Good," Hermione said. "I don't want you to." Standing up, she dusted off her broad bottom. She gave a chortling jack-o'-lantern a sharp kick and punted a scowling one half across the yard. It smashed against the trunk of the old hickory tree. "I need you to help me, Aria."

I struggled up and with a running start kicked a melancholy pumpkin into an azalea.

Hermione laughed. "Not with the pumpkins. Fuck the jack-o'-lanterns." She bent at her thick waist. "Lord have mercy," she said in between crests of laughter. "I must still be buzzing. I need you to help me push the door in."

"Okay."

"You have to take that box off."

I hesitated. It was dark out and there was no one in the yard but my sister and me, but the street was crowded with trick-or-treaters, many of them boys. "Can't I help in what I have on?"

"Shit, Aria," Hermione said. "It's cold."

I slid my arms through the holes in the box and crossed them over my chest. When Hermione pulled my costume over my head, I closed my eyes.

"You must be freezing," she said, seeing that I wore only a long-sleeved leotard and tights. "You must be freezing to death." Hermione rubbed my arms and held me to her, and I pressed my face into her neck where the passion marks were. "Mama," Hermione sighed. "Why do you have to be such a bitch?" Squeezing me, she pressed her lips to the top of my head, and it was all worth it for that moment of closeness.

"On three. We are going to rush the door. Okay?"

I nodded, still warm and electric from her embrace.

"One, two."

I took a deep breath and readied myself.

"Hang on," Hermione said. "Tonight is an exception. Tonight the goal is to get into the house. But after this the goal is to get *out*. Okay?"

I nodded, naked and vulnerable in the October air.

"All right," said Hermione. "Ready, Freddy?"

I'll never forget my sister just as she was that night— busty and bad, high out of her mind, hurling herself again and again at the front door. We did it together until we tore the chain from its mounting. Tumbling into the living room, we tangled together like a heap of puppies. Mama was waiting for us in the dining room. With a paring knife, she hollowed out the eye of a smirking jack-o'-lantern. The too-warm house stank of pumpkin guts and damp newspapers.

"You will not have a car, Hermione. I will not allow it."

Hermione touched my shoulder. "Why didn't you come open the door for us?"

Mama said, "When I was young, they used to call me Iron Pants. I am forty-one years old and I can count the men I've known on one hand. One hand, Hermione Sophia Jackson. One hand and I still have fingers left."

Bewildered, I looked to my sister, who rolled her eyes.

"Mama, I can't believe you locked us out," Hermione said.

"Keep it up, Hermione. Just keep it up. No one is going to marry you."

Hermione pulled the bunny ears from her hair and let them drop on the pile of orange seeds and pulp. "We had to break the door."

Mother turned her attention back to her carving. "I knew you'd find your way in."

Two years later my sister found her way out. She married Mr. Phinazee, my dad's best friend. He gave her the car he'd promised her and a house too. A home of her own that she could get into or out of whenever she liked. When she was expecting Little Link, he bought her a new house, bigger and just a bit farther out of town. Now I sat on the steps of that house waiting for her, hoping to be invited inside.

I had been there more than an hour when the sun sank and the lawn sprinklers clicked on, spotting my jeans. I pushed myself up and headed for my car. I felt as though Hermione was standing me up deliberately, with this being just another reminder that she had her own life now. Yes, we were sisters, veterans of the same war, but that was then, this was now. I walked down her unmarked driveway to where my car waited, dribbling oil onto the cul-de-sac. I moved toward the curb in mincing baby steps, allowing my sister a few extra seconds to intercept me and welcome me into the beige rooms of her home.

I do believe she loves me. Hermione is my sister, my very first friend. She was simply living a different life, a matter of circumstances. When she left home, Mr. Phinazee had opened the trunk of his silver Brougham and she had tossed in only one hard-sided suitcase. Everything else she left behind, even thirteen-year-old me.

I tried to keep in mind that Hermione had only been eighteen, with the ink still wet on her diploma. To me she had been an adult, mature and fully formed. But really she had been just older than Keisha. I suppose any time would be a fine time to start a new life. Isn't that what we tell the girls at LARC?

I placed my hand over my still-flat stomach. A new life was just behind my palm. A busy cluster of dividing cells. I sat on the hood of my car and waited for Hermione. I would wait all night if I had to.

Mr. Phinazee drove up in the middle of the second sprinkler cycle. He pressed a gadget on the sun visor of the minivan and the garage door yawned open, showing the empty slot for Hermione's miniature Mercedes. My sister loved to drive. I used to fantasize that she and I would take a road trip together, drive to California in her Mercedes, me riding in the front seat, squinting at a map and saying, "Just go west. We'll get there if we keep going west." In my daydream she and I are in the car alone; Little Link, Mr. Phinazee, Mama, and all the other people we know are just outside of the frame, keeping themselves busy, not bothering us.

"Look who's here," Mr. Phinazee said, unstrapping my nephew from his filthy car seat. Little Link is one of those children that look like short, solemn adults. Did they jinx him naming him after my father? My nephew stared at me with interest but didn't say anything. Hopefully my child will be a baby of a more lively sort. A little girl that women in the grocery store will coo at. I'll have to teach her not to take gifts from strangers. I'll worry how to impart this without making her distrustful. My daughter will have big eyes and smile with pink gums.

"Hermione went to the gym," Mr. Phinazee said. "She said she might go out with some of the other girls for a smoothie." He said the last words as though pronouncing a foreign language. "Me and my boy here, we been to the barbershop."

I never knew quite what to say to Mr. Phinazee. For so long, I had thought of him as an uncle. His daughter, Colette, used to tell people that Hermione and I were her cousins. When our father died, my sister and I stayed at their house for four days. On the night before the funeral, Colette snuck us out to watch the midnight showing of *Saturday Night Fever*. I still like Colette even though she stopped being social with us after Hermione married her father.

"Wanna come in for a Coke?" he said. "Hermione will be back after a while." He set Little Link down on the garage floor. The boy took a couple of tentative steps. Mr. Phinazee smiled at his son. "I don't mind babysitting. Hermione needs to get out sometimes. She's young yet."

I followed him into the house. The whole place was infused with the chemical odor of the air fresheners jutting from the wall sockets. The cloying scent of magnolia tickled my throat and I coughed. The kitchen was very modern and white, the counter cluttered with graduated canisters, all clearly labeled: Rice, Cornmeal, Coffee.

Little Link plopped down and pushed a wooden train across the tile floor. I sat on the floor too and tried to make him smile.

"He's an old soul," Mr. Phinazee said, unscrewing the

Coke bottle with a hiss. He handed me a blue tumbler. Looking up at my sister's tired husband, I regretted having come over unannounced.

Mr. Phinazee seemed exhausted. Not the kind of tired that comes from a day of hard work, but the kind of weary that comes from what you've seen and done over a lifetime. His skin hung loose from his cheeks. The whites of his eyes were the same beige as the walls.

"Do people ever tell you how much you look like your daddy?"

I shook my head. "Mama says that Genevieve was the one that looked like him. I just look like myself."

"Lincoln was my best friend, you know that? When he went courting your mama for the first time, I lent him my shoes."

I nodded at this information I already knew. Mr. Phinazee's father had owned the barbershop where my daddy used to sweep the floor. I also knew that they fought once. Daddy knocked loose one of Mr. Phinazee's teeth. After that they were friends. That's how things were between men.

We drank Coke without talking. The only sounds in the room were the quiet hums of expensive appliances and the clicks as Little Link shoved his train.

"I was glad to send you to school," Mr. Phinazee said to me. "Glad to do it. Lincoln was my best friend. He was like a younger brother to me. You know that."

"Yes, sir."

"Don't call me sir," he said. "Call me Earl."

I nodded and didn't speak.

"I would have sent your sister to Spelman too, but

she wouldn't go. Said she already had her Morehouse Man." He laughed and poured more Coke, gulping it down like whiskey.

Little Link made a town of wooden blocks and knocked it over with his train. Squares of colored wood tumbled across the Mexican tile. Mr. Phinazee made as if to kneel, but I stopped him.

"If I get down there"—he smiled—"I might not be able to get back up."

"Don't say that," I said. "You're not old."

I put Little Link's blocks back into their canister. "I guess I should get going back home. It's a long way."

He held out his hand and I used it to pull up. His fingers were long and spindly, knuckles sprouting coarse white hairs. His skin felt as though it were merely draped over his bones and muscles.

"You got yourself a fella?" he asked me once I was standing. I could smell him—a male combination of bay rum and sweat.

I smiled. "His name is Dwayne."

"Serious?"

"Very serious." I knew that he would be pleased by my news, to know that I, like my sister, had found someone who would help me make a new start. Someone who would give me a fresh family, a fresh set of possibilities. But I kept myself quiet. To tell my sister's husband before telling my sister herself would compound the sin I'd already committed by being loose-lipped with Keisha. "Dwayne is a good one."

"How old is he?"

I liked these questions, the sort of thing that my father would have probably asked. It made me think of Mr. Henry. "He's twenty-eight."

"That's good. Don't marry an old man." He held up his shirtsleeve and showed me a nasty scrape, scabbed over with puckered pink skin. "Nothing is more pitiful than seeing an old buzzard bust his behind on the playground."

I could think of a thousand things more pitiful, but I didn't bother to list them. I turned myself toward Mr. Phinazee and hugged him hard around his fragile middle. I felt him stiffen; then he gave my back a few uneasy pats. I tried to memorize the feel of him.

"You were the one I always worried about," he said, gently unwinding himself from my greedy grasp.

Chapter Five

I wanted to give my daughter an invisible name—something that would neither offend nor delight. Something easy to pronounce. I was leaning toward Monica for a girl and Brian for a boy. Two ordinary names. Bad things don't happen to people named Monica and Brian. If my daughter grew up to be an actress and wanted to change her name to Cleopatra, that would be fine with me, but I wanted to give her a quiet start with a blank-slate sort of name.

I tried to explain this to Keisha, who suggested that I name my daughter Alexandra.

"Too much like a soap opera," I said.

"Alexandra is a successful-sounding name. And if things are in alphabetical order, she will always be first."

"People tend to alphabetize by last name," I reminded her.

Rochelle came into the classroom then, carrying two canvas tote bags and a laptop computer case. "I just wanted to say hello," she said. "I gotta go to the office and put this stuff down. Fulton County grant deadlines are this week."

She didn't say hello to Keisha, who seemed to be concentrating on wiping down the dry-erase board.

"Cool," I said.

"And I have bad news. The A/C went out again. Landlord is MIA. I called a repairman. Also, the fridge is really on the blink. When I came down this morning, there was enough water to swim in."

"Kill my landlord," I said.

She laughed. "See you at home."

After Rochelle had shuffled down the short hallway and closed the door to the office we shared, Keisha said, "She rubs me the wrong way."

"Really? Everybody likes Rochelle."

"I don't like the way she looks. Her hair all matted up like that, and then the whole thing has the nerve to be gray."

"Now, Keisha, that's not right. She can't help her hair color. I think it looks beautiful."

She waved her hand as though she was fanning imaginary smoke. "I know she can't help it, and if I liked her I wouldn't say anything about it. But she acts like I am invisible or something. She talks to you and she talks to your boss. That's it. Nobody else even exists to her."

"She's not like that," I told Keisha. "She's real down-to-earth. She's my best friend."

"Did you tell her yet?"

"Not yet," I admitted. "I wanted to tell Dwayne first. I'm telling him tonight. I'll tell Rochelle in the morning."

"I can't believe you waited this long. It's been almost a week."

"But I wanted to wait until I had been to the doctor so I could have a due date and one of those fetus snapshots."

"They don't do the sonogram until way later, Miss Aria. You watch too much TV."

"I can't get into the gynecologist for three weeks."

"Take a pee-in-a-cup test."

I sighed. "Peeing in a cup won't give me *details.*"

"Well," Keisha said, "Dwayne don't need to know exactly how pregnant you are. I bet he won't even ask about your weeks. He just wants to know the basic facts: you're having a baby and it's for him."

"Lower your voice," I said.

"Miss Aria, you act like we're having an affair or something. All this whispering. You don't want nobody to know we have lunch together and stuff. I'll be glad when I get my GED so we can be friends out in the open. Then you can give me a baby shower and I could give you one back."

"I just haven't decided how I want to handle everything. So I need to keep this low." It was getting warm in the closed classroom, but I didn't open the door. Lawrence and Rochelle were only two doors away.

"You nervous about telling Dwayne? I was already pregnant when I met Omar, but I didn't come right out and tell him. I just waited until he noticed. He got all mad at first, cussing and everything. Talking about how since it wasn't his he wasn't giving me no money or nothing like that. You know how they do." She dislodged a tuft of lint from her braid. "Then he got used to the idea. He got two kids already, you know? One is in Louisville with his baby's mother and the other one he don't know where it is. So you can see how he wasn't too excited." She put both hands on her stomach. "But now he's so good. Gave me money to take my GED."

Dwayne has a son, Dwayne III; they call him Trey. Ten years old. He stays in Anniston, Alabama, Dwayne's hometown. It's not a secret. He told me the night we met, at the Leopard Lounge in midtown.

We had been drinking. Vodka tonics for me; he'd been downing Crown and Cokes with his cousin Maurice, the one they call Head Cheese. Neither Dwayne nor I had been exactly drunk, but we were buzzed enough to be a little more flexible and tolerant than usual.

Rochelle, on the other hand, had crushed about a half dozen Kir Royales. They tasted like champagne spiked with Robitussin, but she seemed to be enjoying them and they seemed to be treating her right that evening.

This was in October, homecoming weekend. We had been out of college almost five years, but we still marked the date on our calendars. Someone in her complicated network of almost-friends had told Rochelle all the people who had come to town for the festivities would be at the Leopard Lounge. We'd been sitting long enough for her to get rip-roaring drunk and we hadn't seen one familiar face. Rochelle was disappointed; every few minutes she would look at the door and then call the name of a person I didn't remember. "I know that Joe Johnson said he was coming down for homecoming. He always comes. Him and Alex Fontenot both."

"I don't think I know him."

"You know Joe," she'd say. "People used to call him Joey. Econ major. From Grambling."

I'd shrug, feeling a little embarrassed not to know Joey or any of the other people she was looking for. It was nearly midnight and none of them had shown. I was glad. I never knew how to behave at these reunions at which I knew no one.

Rochelle ordered herself another drink and went to the bathroom. I thought that maybe I should go with her, provide some sort of supervision, but I didn't feel like getting up, and what if someone took our seats while I was gone? So I just sat at the bar, looking at my reflection in the mirror behind the bottles. I wore an outfit of Rochelle's, a close-fitting backless dress, and an expensive new lipstick, the color of pennies. Still, the mirror showed me to be plain as wax paper.

A man leaned toward me. "Your girl okay?" he asked, watching Rochelle wobble like a drunken angel on her chunky-heeled boots.

"She's all right. Feeling good, that's all." I had to raise my voice and lean toward him to make myself heard over the dull roar of voices. There was an occasional shriek of laughter, far too loud for the sophisticated decor.

"Well," he said, settling onto the tiger-striped

barstool that Rochelle had just vacated, "she's feeling good and you're looking good. Ain't nothing wrong with that."

He didn't have a well-deep voice, but it was male enough and flecked with good humor. I was glad to talk to him, pleased to have the attention. I don't really feel comfortable in any of the martini lounges that have sprouted up on the north side of town. It's not that the clientele is rude, color-struck, or anything like that, but the citrus smell of their expensive hair products makes me feel like I'm at least two fashion cycles behind. Rochelle doesn't care. She goes wherever she wants, wearing whatever moves her. Sometimes I pause a moment before going in and she takes my hand, tugging me across the threshold. "Fuck them if they can't take a joke." But that wasn't the problem. It seemed like there was a joke out there that *I* just couldn't seem to get. So usually I sat quiet as a fish, hoping to eventually catch on.

I took a good look at this man who turned out to be Dwayne. He seemed like every other brother in the room in his straight-hem silk shirt and neutral-colored slacks. I liked his shoes, cognac leather with side buckles.

He grinned and said, "You know what? You look familiar. I'm not just saying that, you actually look like somebody I know."

I shook my head.

"For real, though. You do."

I raised my eyebrows and let him look me over and think about it.

"Do you talk?" His front teeth tilted toward each other, just a bit. It wasn't enough to ruin his smile, but

enough to let me know he'd grown up without money
for braces and retainers.

"I talk sometimes."

"Just not tonight? Just not to me?"

"I was just being quiet so you can figure out who I
look like."

"It's somebody," he said. "Let me ask my cousin. Hey,
Cheese," he called, and another guy ambled over. He and
Dwayne looked alike, but Cheese was shorter, lighter,
and older. "Don't she look like somebody we know?
Maybe somebody from home?"

Cheese looked at me and cocked his head to the side,
squinted. "Janet Jackson. She looks just like Janet."

"Not Janet," I corrected him. "Penny."

"Damn," Dwayne said. "That's it."

Cheese laughed. "All you need now is a Band-Aid on
your forehead."

"All right, man," Dwayne said. "You can go on back
to where you were."

"It's like that?" Cheese said, backing up.

After Cheese had left, we were stuck together with
nothing else to say. I'm not so good at talking to
strangers, even on a Friday night, even when they are
good-looking. I hummed along with the music. Anita
Baker sang, "I'm missing you, baby." I rubbed my sticky
lips together. "Are you in town for homecoming?"

He looked a little puzzled and I was embarrassed for
bringing it up at all. Taking a second look at him, I could
tell that he wasn't a Morehouse Man. He didn't have that
air of being the beneficiary of something large and in-

visible. "It's homecoming for Morehouse. A lot of people are in town."

"You went there?"

"No," I said, becoming more embarrassed. "That's for the guys. I went to Spelman. The women's college."

"I knew that," he said. "I just had a little too much to drink."

"Yeah," I said. "And it's late."

"Late? It's just two. Things are just getting started. Me and my cousin are headed to Atlanta Nights after this. They stay open till five. You have a man?"

"No," I said, draining the last of the watery vodka from my glass. "No man. No drink either."

He leaned toward the bar and said, "Excuse me." He lowered his voice a notch, like he could see that the bartender was busy and he hated to add to her workload.

"Kids?" he said after apologetically placing his order.

"None."

He said, "That's cool. I don't have nothing against women with children. But when I meet them at a club or somewhere, I always wonder why they're not home with their kids." He laughed, showing his pleasant imperfect smile.

"So, you have children?"

"One," he said. "A boy."

"How come you're not reading *Peter Pan*?"

The bartender slid me my vodka and tonic; Dwayne peeled off seven one-dollar bills, then added an extra for tip.

"Thanks," I said.

"The reason is that he don't stay with me. He's in Alabama with his mother."

"That's where you're from?"

"Yeah."

"You miss him?"

"Who?"

"Your little boy."

"Trey? It's weird," Dwayne said. "It's hard to just come out and say that I miss him, because I only spend time with him two, maybe three times a year. But when I think about him, I feel something here." He spread his hand below the Africa pendant dangling from a silver chain. "It's like I swallowed a hot buttered golf ball. So I know I must be missing something."

I knew what it was to have a hole in your heart in the shape of someone you never really got a chance to know. Taking the damp napkin from under my drink, I cooled my forehead, listening to the soft jazz humming out from invisible speakers. Vodka was making me drowsy and reflective.

Dwayne fidgeted a little in his chair, rearranging himself on the barstool, peeking at his cousin a couple of times. Spotting Rochelle heading our way, he set his half-empty tumbler on the glass-topped bar. "This is how you know it's time to stop drinking. You start confiding your personal business to strangers."

"It's okay," I said, and it was. I usually made a point to avoid men with children, which had gotten more difficult after college. I did this because I regarded each man as a potential husband and a potential father of my own children. If he wasn't involved with his children, I didn't want to chance him abandoning me and mine. If he was involved, I'd be forced to negotiate the complications of a "blended family." I didn't find either of these scenarios to be particularly appealing. But meeting Dwayne that night seemed significant somehow; I was moved by his frankness about his pain and his loss. It felt fated. He, a father without his child, and me, a child without her father.

"It's all right," I'd said, fondling his silk sleeve. "Sometimes you just feel connected with someone like that."

Dwayne and I still talked easily, spending at least a half hour each night on the telephone dramatizing the details of our days. He'd noticed over the past week that I wasn't talking so much. How could I tell him about going to get my oil changed when what I really wanted to tell him was that I was having his baby? When he wanted to know what was wrong, I told him that I wasn't feeling so well, which was true. Rochelle and I both were under the weather. If I didn't know better, I would think that pregnancy was contagious.

On Saturday night we entertained Dwayne's cousin Head Cheese and Cheese's new girlfriend, Denise. I liked these get-togethers with other couples. They made me feel married. After we had shown Cheese and his date to the door, we showered and dressed in the pair of pajamas we shared. I used the green flannel top and he wore the drawstring pants.

"That was fun," he said.

"Yeah," I said, sliding onto what I considered to be my side of his bed. "I like Denise."

"Well," Dwayne said, "don't get too attached to her."

He was right. Cheese had introduced us to at least five "girlfriends" over the last seven months. Denise was just the latest and the youngest. Sweet Denise, twenty, round-faced, and pleasant. She reminded me of Keisha with her curving acrylic nails, improbable hairpieces, and frosted lipstick.

"She's bright," I said. "You can't play Scrabble if you're stupid."

"How bright can she be if she's hooked up with Head Cheese?"

I let that go. It's never smart to criticize other people's relatives. And besides, I liked Maurice. I agreed that he wasn't a good choice for a young lady who wanted something lasting, but I understood how Denise could have been persuaded to give it a shot.

Dwayne sat up in bed, propped against his pillows, fiddling with a brass lock he'd brought home from work. The key was probably in his jacket pocket, but Dwayne wanted to try and open it using only metal prods. "This lock—it's an ASSA—is supposed to be pick-proof."

"Well, is it?"

"ASSA is good. But I'm a Medeco man myself." He let out a low whistle between his teeth as he slid the strip of spring metal into the slot again. "What I am trying to do is reach in and lift the pins. But ASSA, their locks are sort of doubled up."

"Sleep on it," I said.

This had been my favorite sort of evening, when we

played house. I'd cooked dinner for the group, family food: fried chicken, mashed potatoes, and green bean casserole. Denise and I had washed dishes together while the guys drank Jack and Cokes while watching *Sports-Center*. Cheese's parade of dates served as a sort of personal abacus for Dwayne and me. Each girl a wooden bead, marking the length of time that Dwayne and I had been together.

Dwayne's apartment was at the front of the complex. The lights and sounds from Windy Hill Road kept the bedroom glowing with a gentle light and buzzing with a subtle roar. I didn't care much for this type of living. If I enjoyed spending time here, it was only because it all felt so Dwayne-like. The sheets on the sleigh bed smelled like him—a cozy combination of strawberry incense and foot powder. The gym schedule on the refrigerator was his. The bed was covered with a bear claw quilt hand-sewn by his favorite aunt.

Even so, I found the genericness of it all to be rather disconcerting. The walls were painted a blue-white that reminded me of skim milk. I was sure the floors in every single unit were covered with the same carpet, dead-mouse gray. And if you were to pull up the rugs here, you'd find only cheap foam padding and particleboard. The first thing Rochelle and I did when we moved into our house was get rid of the seventies-chic shag, rust-colored and matted. Underneath we found wonderful hardwood floors. Of course they still need some work to buff off the paint stains and old varnish, but the potential for elegance is there. Lawrence tapped on the wall in my bedroom and told me that he thinks there is another fireplace just behind the Sheetrock. But here, what you see is what you get. Two rooms, full bath, a kitchen. That's it. This apartment is no better than what it seems to be.

In bed I moved toward Dwayne and snuggled against his sleeping back. I bent my own knees to match the angle of his until it was as though he sat on my lap while lying down.

"Dwayne," I said into the smooth space between his jutting shoulder blades.

He didn't answer, so I snaked an arm under him and hugged him hard across his chest. "Wake up."

"What?" he said, turning over, knocking me in the chin with his shoulder. He touched my face. In the shine of the outside light I made out the outline of his crooked smile. "Is this your way of saying you need some attention?" He burrowed against my neck and draped his leg over my hip.

"I have something to tell you."

"Okay," he said, withdrawing his kisses and his weight. "Do you need me to turn on the light?"

"You don't have to. I can see fine. And anyway, I have something to *tell* you, not something to *show* you."

"Is it serious?"

"Yes."

"Bad news or good?"

"Good," I said. "Basically good. I think. In the long run, good for sure."

"This sounds like the kind of conversation that you need to have the light on for."

"No," I said. "Please." I felt braver in the dark, when we could hear each other, touch each other, but not quite see. "Did you mean it the other day when you said I could move in over here?"

"Yeah," he said. "I wouldn't have said it if I didn't mean it."

"I want us to live together," I told him. "But not over here. We're going to need a house."

Because of the streetlamps just outside of his window, Dwayne's bedroom was dim rather than dark. The greenish light reflected off his eyes as he spoke. "It takes a long time to get a house. You need a down payment. You have to get qualified."

"I know," I said.

"So let's just live here for a while, see where it goes."

"I know where it's going."

The light reflected on his eyes while he waited on me to continue.

"I'm pregnant."

He took two complete deep breaths and shut his eyes before hugging me, but this embrace didn't have the iron lining or red heat we'd shared a few minutes before. This was the physical expression of a sympathetic sigh. "Who all knows?"

"Nobody," I whispered. "Just you."

"Aria," he said, rocking me in the near dark. "Baby. What do you want to do?"

"Get married?"

He stopped breathing for a moment. Long enough

for me to blink twice and swallow. The pause was like a skipping CD. Just a moment of silence before the music continued to play, picking up just where it had left off.

"We could do that," he said.

"We would need to do it soon," I said. "Before I start showing. If I'm waddling down the aisle, my mother won't come."

"You don't mean like tomorrow, do you?"

"No. Maybe in like six weeks?"

"How many months are you?"

"I can't say for sure."

"So you aren't positive?"

"I know. I know my body. I'm throwing up left and right. I'm late, late, late. Remember I got off the pill in February? And remember what happened last month."

"Rubber broke," he sighed.

"We don't *have* to get married. My daddy is dead, so there's no one to hold a shotgun to your back." I turned away from him and faced the wall, taking in my air in shallow breaths, waiting for him to touch my shoulder, force me to face him so he could beg my pardon, explain that it was all just such a shock. Of course he'd marry me. Of course he would.

I waited.

I wiped my nose on the bear claw quilt and I waited.

One-Mississippi, two-Mississippi, to keep track of time. When I got to one hundred twenty, I was leaving. I wouldn't even take time to get dressed. I'd drive across town in his pajamas and my underwear and he would never see me again. He had only forty-two Mississippis to go.

Dwayne got out of bed and turned on the light at two hundred eighty Mississippis. He threw back the covers, heaved himself to his feet, and headed to the closet. I watched him retrieve a large shoebox, big enough to house a pair of size fourteen Nikes. He sat back on the bed with the box on his lap and patted the space beside him. We sat close enough that my bare calf touched his through the flannel pajamas.

"I hope this doesn't make you mad or make you feel cheap." He gave my goose-pimpled thigh a firm squeeze. "Cheese has a brother, Jay. A straight-up crackhead. He stole my wallet a couple years ago, on Christmas Eve, can you believe that? Everybody says I must have lost it, but I know what happened to it. It's jacked up because me and him were tight when we were young. When Cheese went to the service, I used to look out for Jay. But now I don't fuck with him. But my auntie, his mama, never wants to face facts about Jay. She acts like he's the baby Jesus or somebody.

"So one time I was home for Easter and I was in the barbershop and who come walking in but Jay. He got all kinda stuff he's trying to sell—an old raggedy VCR, two fitted sheets, and his mama's wedding band. I wasn't tripping about the VCR and the sheets, but when I saw Aunt Iola's ring, I just got up from the chair and snatched it out his hand. I should have punched him in his jaw."

"So what happened?"

"Nothing. He didn't weigh but a buck oh five before he got cracked out, so you know how skinny he is now. He just looked at me, bird chest twitching up under his shirt.

"So I went to my aunt's house to give her the ring back. I drove straight out there, didn't even wait for the barber to line me up. And when I got to the house and told her what all had happened, she looked me square in the face and told me that wasn't her ring.

"I'm sitting there looking at the reverse suntan on her finger where the ring used to be and she's looking me in the face telling me that lie. So I got pissed, put it in my pocket, and left. I figure she knows where to find me if she wants it back."

He took the top off of the shoebox and poured the contents on the bed. There, along with his stiff new passport, a dead carnation, and three snapshots of Trey, was his aunt Iola's stolen ring.

"Cheese don't even know about that," Dwayne said, turning his face, not exactly kissing me, but pressing his lips to my jawline, my temples.

"You're sweating," he said.

"I'm so nervous."

"Don't be." He held his aunt Iola's ring out to me. "You can wear this, to have something on your hand, until we can get you the real thing."

Looking at the ring, I could picture his aunt Iola, the type of woman who would order a piece of jewelry from a catalog, seduced by the little banner that promised payments as low as ten dollars a month. I could even imagine the description, a short paragraph under a photo that had been "enlarged to show detail." *A cluster of diamond accents sets this ring aglow with 1/2 carat TW of sparkling elegance. The 10K gold nugget setting gives a modern look to this time-honored classic.* The half carat of diamond accents was made up of about six tiny stones, arranged to look like a three-carat solitaire. I forced it over my chubby knuckle. The tip of my finger tingled with the loss of circulation.

"Thank you," I said, looking at my hand.

"Okay."

We sat together on the side of the bed thinking our separate thoughts. "We don't have to," I said finally.

"No," he said. "It's a good idea. I mean, we weren't really at the marrying stage, but we were sort of headed in that direction."

"Rochelle is moving out in January. We could take over the lease."

He shook his head. "I can't live around all those crackheads."

I wanted to explain to him about the hidden fireplaces, how workmen could be hired to raise the ceilings, restore the wraparound porch, but he'd heard all this before. "The neighborhood is really up-and-coming," I said.

"Well," Dwayne said, "we can live there once it has up and came. Don't fight me on this one, Aria. You don't want our kids to be on a first-name basis with drug addicts, do you?"

I thought of Cynthia but didn't argue with him. "Please smile," I said. "I need you to be happy."

He did smile for me, a pained expression. Lawrence once told me that it takes forty-two muscles to smile. Watching Dwayne, I could see the strain in every single one of them.

Finally he turned off the light and lay back on his oily pillowcase. "Come here, girl," he said, pulling me up on his chest. "Let me show you why they call it making love."

I left the next morning after Dwayne had left for the gym to play basketball with Cheese and some other friends. I envisioned him on the court, telling everyone he saw, accepting claps on the back, claiming me and the baby both. He probably wouldn't play very well, missing easy layups, because he'd be distracted by thoughts of the long run. I knew the kind of man Dwayne was. He would spend the next seven months or so figuring the best way to save for a college education. He'd wonder what sort of grandfather he'd be.

I, on the other hand, was consumed by my visions of the short run. There was no way we could plan an elaborate ceremony like Rochelle's; we hadn't the time or the money. And even if we had been from well-off families, we would need to save to support the baby. I looked forward to declining social invitations, pleading poverty. I had to do that often enough now. Just last week Rochelle invited me to do a spa day with her and her mother. I didn't have the money to go; I'd been honest about it and it was a little embarrassing. But now, when I explained that my priorities had changed, it would give my lack of discretionary income a sort of moral clout.

Hopefully we could have the ceremony as soon as possible. I didn't want to run over to the justice of the peace, but I wanted to be Mrs. Upshaw long before my body changed. It was vanity, mostly. I was a grown woman—certainly no one thought I was a virgin—but there was something shameful about being pregnant out of wedlock, no matter how times have changed. I know that there are women out there who are single moms by choice, who never considered living as part of a family of three; I have read about these women in magazines. But personally I have never met a single mother who wouldn't rather have a partner.

I made it home, ran into the living room with the soles of my sandals smacking on the wood floors, calling Rochelle's name with my left hand held in front of me. She'd be happy for me. Hadn't I been happy for her when she announced her engagement in February? It was my turn for hugs, kisses, and oh-my-Gods. She'd be a good sport about me beating her to the altar. We weren't in a competition, and even if we were, she'd win hands down. I might be getting married first, but she was the one with the crepe lisse, the reception at the Egyptian Ball Room, and the five-hundred-person guest list.

Only Kitten was home to greet me. On the oak table was the evidence of Rochelle's breakfast, chunks of milk-soaked granola and grapefruit skins. Disappointed, I poured kibble into Kitten's ceramic bowl and replaced the batteries in his water filter. I ate an overripe banana and watched the cat chew a few mouthfuls. When he was done, I scratched him between his pointy ears. Good news and nobody to tell it to was more frustrating than all dressed up and no place to go.

I scooped Kitten onto my shoulder, stroking him like a baby. Dwayne doesn't like cats, so we wouldn't have a kitty of our own once we got married. Giving up Kitten was such a paltry sacrifice in exchange for the life I would be leading, I didn't know why I even thought about it. And besides, Kitten belonged to Rochelle, like everything around here worth having.

The telephone rang, startling me and Kitten too. Following the sound of the electronic ring, I found myself standing in the middle of Rochelle's disorderly bedroom.

Rochelle's room was larger than mine by two or three paces in each direction, but it seemed smaller because of all the stuff she had strewn around. Standing in front of her dresser, waiting for the phone to ring again, I smelled the gardenia and soap scent of the dozen sachets she had made for herself last winter. The ringing seemed to be coming from her upper left dresser drawer. I let it ring once again before easing my hand into the open drawer, telling myself that this was not really an invasion of privacy. If I were to slide open one of the drawers of the vanity just for the sake of looking, *that* would be beyond the pale. But this was simply a practical matter. This drawer was stuffed with soft and pretty things, most with the price tags still on. The phone rang again, from somewhere nearby. I moved my hand in order to look someplace else, behind the dresser maybe, but the machine picked up. "Breathe," said the outgoing message, "and you will know peace." Breathing, I held a sage-colored chemise, silk, against my chest. It would look better than the lace and nylon teddies that Dwayne favored. I put the nightie back in the drawer, stifling my urge to fold it carefully or even wrap it in tissue. Next I pulled out the satin gloves, which Rochelle thought were "too much" but her mother believed were "exactly right, perfect!"

I imagined myself following in the footsteps of our

housebreaker. It was hard to believe that less than a month had passed since then. I slid the glove over my right hand and up my arm nearly to the shoulder. I did the same on the left except I took my ring off and pushed it back on over the white satin. When I held my hand far from my face, the cluster of diamonds looked like a dime-sized solitaire. Dwayne would have to open a thousand locks to buy me something like that.

I admired my arms for a few moments more before sitting on Rochelle's unmade bed. For some reason her sheets smelled of purple lollipops. Lying back on her pillows, looking at the mosquito netting draped from the ceiling, I rubbed my satin-covered fingers together and almost cried. If I had time to plan, time to save, I could be a really beautiful bride. If I had more time, I could have done things right. Sent my picture to *Jet* magazine, invited people. I wouldn't complain if my mother made me wear pretty gloves.

Kitten crawled over me, kneading my stomach with his paws. I rubbed his black and white head until he purred like a lawn mower. I hugged him close, enjoying the warmth of his body and the softness of his fur. Even if I wasn't getting married, Kitten wouldn't be in my life forever. Even if Rochelle wasn't taking him as part of her trousseau. People live longer than cats. Relationships are temporary, Hermione liked to say. Even if love lasts forever, it's just a matter of time before one person dies on the other one.

I stretched in order to clear my head. This was not a time to be thinking about people dying or pets dying. This was the happiest day of my life. And I was happy. I

felt a swirl of emotions that day, the pleasant feelings flavored with sadness. It was probably just the side effects of
some sort of hormonal brew. I was happy. This I knew.

I got up and stood in front of Rochelle's gaping
closet door. Under the weight of the many dresses, coats,
jackets, and blouses, the wooden rod curved like a bow.
In between her suede jacket and gray tweed suit peeked
a fold of white silk studded with seed pearls. I mashed
the clothes to one side and pulled it free. I felt like a magician, pulling endless scarves from my sleeve. The dress
was enormous and light at the same time. Yards of
creamy fabric that seemed to weigh nothing.

I knew the gown would fit me. I'd known this since
the first time I helped Rochelle zip herself into it. Once,
when we were in this room together, drinking wine and
looking at color swatches, I almost asked her if I could
try it on. The words were in my mouth, trapped behind
my teeth. I think she would have said yes; my best friend
is a generous person. I shook my head and clucked my
tongue; she never even bothered storing it properly. She
just shoved this magnificent dress into her tight dark
closet. A gown like this has to breathe. All the bride's
magazines tell you that. Don't smother your silks.

I would be a beautiful bride if I could just have a
chance.

It's said that you can feel a stare before you even
know that someone is looking at you, but I don't know
how long Rochelle stood in the doorway of her bedroom watching me wearing her satin gloves, admiring
her wedding gown. I do know that I didn't feel a thing.

I looked toward the doorway only because the beauty of
the dress was suffocating. I'd lifted my head only for air.

"Why are you in my room?" she said, leaning against
the doorjamb. Hand on left hip.

Her tone was not exactly hostile, but it was more suspicious than curious. I wasn't sure how to answer the
question. She'd caught me unmasked, displaying the full
extent of my desire. I focused my attention on my upper
arms where the gloves pinched the skin. "I just wanted
to look at your dress."

"Aria," Rochelle said, "are you all right?"

"I'm pregnant," I said. "I'm having a baby."

She grew silent. "What did you say?"

"I'm pregnant."

"Oh shit, Aria." Rochelle touched her lips with the
tips of her fingers. "Are you freaked out? Don't get
freaked out. This can be handled. I'll be there for you just
like you were there for me."

"No," I said. "This is a good thing. I'm keeping it. I'm
going to marry Dwayne." I held out my hand to her. The
ring looked big and gaudy atop the slick white glove. I
worked it off and tossed it to Rochelle.

She caught it easily and walked over, sitting beside
me on the unmade bed. "So you told him about the
baby?"

I nodded.

"And he proposed?"

"Basically."

Rochelle scrutinized the ring on her palm like it was
an interesting insect. "Is this what you want?"

"Yes," I said. I didn't like how she sounded like a

schoolteacher who has only your own good in mind. "There's nothing wrong with Dwayne."

"No," Rochelle said. "I don't mean anything like that. I was just thinking about timing, that's all."

"He's got a better job than we do."

"This isn't about money," Rochelle said. "You should know me better than that."

"It's all about money," I said, wriggling out of the satin gloves. I shouldn't have tossed my engagement ring across the room. I should have invited her to look at it on my hand. Let her squint at it from the doorway; from that distance the clustered diamond chips looked like a three-carat solitaire. I wiggled my fingers, already missing the weight of the ring below my knuckle.

Rochelle held it between her thumb and forefinger, her own diamonds winking like flashbulbs. "Was this his mother's ring or something?"

"It's been in his family," I said.

"How long?" She raised her brows. "Since the eighties?" Rochelle laughed but stopped when I didn't join her. "It's a joke."

I knew it was a joke and last week it would have been all right. Rochelle teased me about Dwayne all the time. She laughed at his leather pants, at his cousin's nickname. But now none of it was funny.

"So when is the big day?" she said.

"In a few weeks, I think. Soon. I don't want to waddle down the aisle."

"Well," she said, "this is good, if it's what you want." Her voice seemed strained, her good humor forced. "So why did you come in here in the first place?"

"I just wanted to look close at your dress. I didn't go through your drawers or anything like that. I don't know how I am going to find a dress and everything in time." I touched the clean white fabric and looked up at her.

"You don't want to wear my dress, do you? I can't get married in a used gown."

"Never mind," I said. "I don't want to wear your dress."

"What exactly is it that you want?" Rochelle looped her arm around my shoulder and pulled me toward her. I squirmed out of her embrace.

"I want exactly what I have."

"And what is that?" Rochelle said.

I'd never been in a fight before. I'd never struck another human being, but I wanted to slap Rochelle hard and sharp across her cheek, surprise spreading across her face like blood. It would end our relationship completely, I knew this, but maybe it would be worth it to rub that satisfied expression from her face.

"I want what everybody wants. I'm not so different from you." I pointed to the cardboard boxes lining the wall and the bridal magazines heaped in the corner. "Your wedding will last for just one day and after that you won't have anything more than what I have. It will be you and your husband sitting in a room, just like it will be me and Dwayne. And you want to be happy and that's all that I want."

"Penny," she said, "I don't mean to hurt your feelings." She reached for my hand, the one I was preparing to send into her face. She took it, kissing the palm. "I really am happy for you."

I pulled my hand back, smearing her lipstick from her mouth to her chin.

Chapter Six

I had planned for Dwayne to meet my family way back in December. We had been dating for about three months, long enough for me to be sure that this was more than an extended one-night stand. My mother had invited me to the house for dinner on the first Sunday of the month. I'd accepted her invitation and told her that I'd be bringing a friend.

"A young man?" she wanted to know.

I was relieved to say yes.

The weather had been cool enough for me to wear my leather jacket. I liked to wear heavy clothes when I saw my mother; the jacket completely concealed my body and made me look slim. A supple suit of armor. Dwayne had worn leather too: black pants and a bright yellow sweater. I wished he had worn khaki or even tweed. A blazer maybe.

I had known that it was only right that I warn him, prepare him in some way for the scene at 739 Willow Street. But what should I have told him? I'd been dodging my mother's uppercut personality for most of my life, yet I was never really prepared. And besides, this could have been a good day. Mama might have welcomed him with a firm embrace and peck on the cheek. With my mother you never knew what you were going to get.

"Dwayne," I said, "if my mother is a little weird, don't take it the wrong way."

He said, "Weird how?"

"It's hard to explain."

"Well, give me an example. Is she weird like she might ask me to help bathe the dog, or weird like she might try to kill me?"

"Put your blinker on," I said. "Your turn is coming up."

"Don't ignore my question," Dwayne said over the click of the turn signal. "Crazy like what? Like a fox? Like Son of Sam?"

Using my teeth, I scraped flavored gloss off my lower lip while I let Dwayne pass my mother's house. I needed to tell him something, disclose the shape of my mother's madness, if not its magnitude.

"She does weird stuff when she's angry." I shrugged. "She's not a psychopath."

"For example?"

"Like one time she baked BBs into the corn bread when I was in high school."

"Because?"

"Because she was pissed. Me and my best friend went

to a college party at Morehouse and stayed out until seven in the morning. I spent two whole weeks waiting for her to punish me somehow. I came home every day expecting her to have smeared butter on my prom dress or something like that. Then one day I sat down for dinner and chomped down on hard metal. Tears came to my eyes and she was satisfied."

"That's deep," Dwayne said. "And we're about to go over there for *dinner*."

"No, no, no," I said. "It's not like that all the time." I felt hot shame spread from my chest to my face. "I mean, what I told you was true, but I don't think she's going to do anything freaky with the food."

Dwayne took one hand off the steering wheel and covered mine. "Did she do stuff like that to you a lot? When you were small?"

"Not when I was small; only after my father passed. We were fine before then."

This was an oversimplification, I knew. Hermione has told me a thousand times that things were not *fine* before the accident. They had not been as toxic as they became after Daddy and Genevieve died, but even before, our mother was not like other mothers. She'd had her quirks, insisting once that we drive all the way home from Callaway Gardens, more than fifty miles south, because she had forgotten to turn on the dishwasher. I have only fuzzy memories of these incidents, but Hermione tells me that before Daddy died, Mama was embarrassed by her personality, apologizing all the way back up I-85.

Daddy was annoyed. "Eloise, it doesn't matter if the

dishes are dirty when we get home. Don't spoil the kids' holiday."

"But there could be bugs," she said. "Lincoln, please just let me go back to turn on the machine."

And I had to agree with Hermione that this wasn't normal. But I also felt the need to point out that things were different before. Before, Mama may have been a little bit crazy, but she was never mean. I was never afraid of her.

Dwayne turned into the parking lot of a CME church, gravel popping under the wheels of the Crown Victoria, a retired police car that he'd bought at an auction. It was nearly three o'clock in the afternoon, but the parking lot was crowded. He eased the Crown between two black SUVs. He put in my favorite of his CDs, Wynton Marsalis and his daddy playing all the songs from the Snoopy cartoons, the sound track of a happy childhood. Pressing buttons on his armrest, he reclined our seats. Then he took my hand again and stroked my palm with the smooth skin of his thumb.

I told him about my dog, Vido. He was part Shar-Pei, but we didn't know that's what he was. We just called him a "wrinkle dog." I'd found him at Piedmont Park when I was twelve. Mama sent him to the pound when I was gone to Bluebird Camp.

Hermione had broken the news. She held me and rubbed my back as I cried. "I told her not to do it," she had said in a quiet voice.

Dwayne listened and warmed my hands between the two of his. I hadn't run out of things to say, but I stopped talking and squeezed Dwayne's fingers until my nails went white. "But I'm okay. I don't want you to think that I'm scarred for life or anything like that."

Dwayne didn't speak; he looked into my face with worried eyes while rubbing my hand in time with the cheerful jazz pouring from his speakers. I was unaccustomed to this sort of kindness.

I unfastened my seat belt and leaned toward him as it snapped back into place. I kissed Dwayne hard on his mouth, wanting to climb down his throat, find refuge in the warm pit of him.

He put one hand to the nape of my neck, fingering the tight curls there, and used his other hand to undo his own seat belt. I smiled into his mouth. In the privacy of my mind I whispered *IloveyouIloveyouIloveyou*.

He jerked away like he had heard me. "We're going to be late."

"We're already late," I said, pulling his face back to my own. "I don't care."

He turned to look at the clock on his dashboard. "Girl, you made me lose all track of time."

I leaned back in my seat and watched a woman walking through the parking lot. She moved with the rapid tick of high heels. The silver buttons on her trapeze coat were open, flashing a snug-fitting gray dress underneath. When she got within a few feet of our car, she shook her finger at us and laughed with a broad grin that crinkled her eyes shut.

"She reminds me of my mama," I told Dwayne.

"That's not how I pictured her."

"I mean, that's what she was like before."

"Before what?"

"Before everything."

He smiled. "Let my mama tell it; that's how she was too. She likes to pull out old pictures of herself looking all slim and everything and then she says to me and my sister, 'Look what you two did to me.' " He chuckled. "You need to meet my mama one day. She's a trip."

While he was talking, I watched the pretty lady in the side mirror. She climbed into her butter-colored luxury car and started the engine.

"Let's not go," I said to Dwayne, clutching at his meaty upper arm. "Can we just go back to my house? Rochelle is out of town until tomorrow. It could be just us. We can listen to CDs. Drink some wine."

"Make some love," he said with an open grin. "It don't matter to me, but won't it make your mama mad if we just don't show up? From what you said, I'm not trying to get on her bad side."

"Please," I said. "Please. I don't want to go. Let's just go back."

I hoped that my mother was not still angry about last December's no-show. That situation was compounded by the fact that Hermione and Mr. Phinazee hadn't made it to that particular dinner either. "But at least they called," Mother said. "I didn't know what had happened to you." I'd apologized again, not offering any explanation for myself. When I called last week to tell her I'd be coming to dinner with Dwayne, she said, "Am I to take you seriously this time?" I didn't explain that I was serious last time, that every interaction with her is serious for me. I just said that yes, ma'am, I would be there.

For the occasion Dwayne borrowed Head Cheese's burgundy Jetta. The repo man was looking for it, but it should be safe outside my mother's house for a couple of hours. An air freshener dangled from the windshield, filling the car with the Christmas scent of pine.

"Right here," I told him. "Don't pull in the driveway. Leave the car at the curb."

He sat in the car and looked. It wasn't a nice house. Before Daddy and Genevieve got killed, we lived in a nice split-level on Bunnybrooke Drive. It was red brick with optimistic yellow shutters on the windows and lime-green electric appliances inside. The backyard was big enough for a pool, and saving for this had always been an abstract family goal.

We moved into the Willow Street house after everyone had been in the ground for a few months, once Mama realized that the insurance wasn't going to be enough to subsidize our lifestyle. The house, 739 Willow Street, wasn't shabby, exactly. The split-level on Bunnybrooke was nicer, with its finished basement and extra bedroom for company, but the house on Willow Street was good enough for the three of us—two bedrooms, one bathroom, tiny closets, like all the others on the block. But my mother's house seemed steeped in sadness in a way that her neighbors' houses did not. Hermione blamed it on the sprawling hickory-nut tree in the middle of the yard.

"It sucks all the nutrients out of the soil. That's why we can't have flowers or even grass like regular people." She said this nearly every time we were in this house together. "And, Mother, what if there's an ice storm? One branch could tear a hole in the roof."

My mother always said the tree was fine. That it gave shade. Kept the electric bill down.

"It looks okay," Dwayne said. "The way you described it, I was expecting to see the Munster house. It's okay. Just needs some paint or something."

I knew that this was more a matter of simple maintenance. Just last summer Mama had hired workers to install aluminum siding.

"Maybe not paint," Dwayne said, staring out of the window. "But something to spruce the place up a little bit." He got out of the car and walked around to open the door for me. I hoped my mother was watching through the picture window as I took his hand and rose from the clean new car.

"Front door or side door?" Dwayne wanted to know.

"Front," I said. "No, side."

"That's your sister's minivan in the driveway?"

I nodded.

"Then she went in the side. Let's go in the way she went in. Front door is for company anyway."

We walked up the driveway with our pinkies locked. Hermione and Mr. Phinazee's van was filthy, as though they'd driven across the country, not just across town. Dead bugs studded the windshield and red dirt decorated the sides like painted-on flames.

Dwayne peeked in the window and said, "That's an upscale baby seat. How much do you think something like that costs?"

I turned and hugged him. "I'm so hot. I'm so scared.

I should have drunk some wine before we left, to take the edge off."

"No drinking for pregnant ladies." Dwayne kissed me quick on my forehead and pressed the bell. "Don't worry. It's all good."

My mother came to the door with a red-lipsticked smile. "Why did you come to the side door, Ariadne? We don't want to make the gentleman walk through the kitchen."

Dwayne smiled. "No trouble at all." Then, ignoring her extended hand, he dragged my mother into a confident embrace.

She raised her eyebrows in surprise and then she melted into the hug, closing her eyes and leaning into Dwayne's bulk. She looked as though she wanted to press her cheek to his, to raise one foot from the floor like a young girl greeting a returning soldier.

I watched her and I envied them both. I envied Dwayne the warmth of my mother's touch. I would have liked to ask him how she smelled. If she still wore L'Air du Temps. Were her arms thin? Was she developing a little pouch of a stomach?

And of course I envied her position inside his embrace. One of the few places where I felt protected and secure.

He released her and she smiled. "It's good to know you. I hope we'll be seeing a lot of you." She turned back toward the stove. "I'm still cooking. Take him into the den to meet everyone." As she waved us away, I noticed the engraved gold band, still on her left hand.

When we were in the hallway in front of a collection of my baby pictures and Hermione's, I said, "Was that okay?"

He shrugged. "I was just trying to come in smiling."

"I think it worked."

"But she didn't even say hello to you," he said. "I didn't appreciate that."

I squeezed his hand. "Welcome to my life."

We lingered in the corridor leading to the added-on den. The hallway was lined with photographs—studio portraits, framed snapshots, magazine prints. People we knew, people we didn't, us and celebrities, all clustered in this hallway. Captured in a cheap poster frame was a Sealtest ice cream box featuring two smiling sisters. The girls were not Hermione and me.

We'd met those girls in Piedmont Park the day that a photographer was scouting for little black girls. I was five and Hermione was ten. Daddy was there too, barbecuing. Steaks for himself and Mama. Hot dogs for the kids.

This was just after the playground had been renovated with the addition of a large spiral slide. Everyone wanted to ride. We stood in line, standing on fragrant wood chips, with about twenty other children. Then, fighting claustrophobia, we pushed into a column and climbed a twisty staircase that took us to the top of the barber pole slide. It gleamed like chrome and was griddle hot, burning the backs of our legs as we swirled down, squealing, ramming into a clog of boys and girls at the bottom. It was fun and I had run to my mother to tell her so.

"Stand up straight," she said. "There is a photographer here. He's taking pictures of girls to put on the ice cream box. Tell your sister."

I ran back to the slide, trying to stand up straight and trot at the same time. I whispered to Hermione, who smiled. She had been chubby even then, but didn't know yet that there was anything wrong with it. We smiled all afternoon, rode the swings together, clearly sisters, wearing identical red shirts and striped shorts. We hoped that the photographer would think we were cute.

When he realized that we were mooning for him, he'd returned our attention, aiming the barrel of his camera at us again and again. He called me "Daffodil" and he called Hermione "Gorgeous." He took our photo near the swings, holding hands, walking backward, smoothing the walls of a sand castle. When we left the park that afternoon, we were sure we'd be celebrities. Black Shirley Temples. We waited for several months, eagerly scanning the frozen food dessert case, but we never saw any black girls on Sealtest boxes. Daddy was dead by the time Mother saw the other girls. She recognized them, the second pair of sisters at the park. They hadn't worn cute identical outfits; their hair hadn't been oiled and ribboned. They had bad teeth. No one considered them to be competition. Mother fed us the ice cream in parfait glasses, saved the box, and hung it on the wall. To remind us, she said.

Dwayne put his finger on a framed snapshot of a snaggletoothed girl in a brown velvet dress. It was a department store portrait, complete with a pull-down holiday screen.

"Is that you?" he said. "My mama has the exact same picture of me."

I smiled and said that it was me, although I had no idea who was in that photo. The girl seemed to stare past the camera, so I figured that she was one of the children from the Institute. Mama liked the blind children, especially the ones that didn't cover their eyes, the ones who somehow pretended to see. "They don't complain," she said. "You would think they would have a lot to complain about, but they don't. They just wait their turn."

I touched a photo of Hermione and me wearing blue shirts with large white collars. "That's me and my sister."

He laughed. "I guess it was the seventies. When you meet my mama, she'll show you all my Afro pictures."

I took his hand and took him into the den, where Hermione sat on the brown shag carpet wearing a pistachio-colored pantsuit. The front was marked with nuggets of half-sucked candy. Little Link was sober and pensive, oblivious to Hermione's efforts to teach him the difference between a circle and a square. Mr. Phinazee read the Sunday funnies.

"Hey, everyone," I said. "This is Dwayne."

Hermione looked up and clambered to her feet. She tried to pluck the candy chunks from her jacket. "Mama didn't tell me you were coming."

"I came by your house the other day."

"I told her," Mr. Phinazee said. "It was nice visiting with you."

"I meant to call you," Hermione said.

"Don't worry about it."

My sister touched her hair. "I look like shit. And you brought somebody with you."

"Dwayne," I said, "this is my sister, Hermione." I picked Little Link up and put him on my hip. He was solid, real, and silent in my arms. "This is Lincoln, my nephew."

"I'm two," Link said, holding up three grimy fingers. He stretched his hands toward Dwayne, who took the little guy from my arms.

"And this," I said, gesturing to my sister's husband, "is Mr. Phinazee."

"Earl," he said gently. "Just Earl."

"Earl, I'm Dwayne."

"Nice to meet you, Dwayne. You've got a good haircut over there."

I wasn't fooled by my mother's red oven mitts. I knew the meal had been catered. I recognized the menu from Seretha's, the soul food restaurant near our church. Fried chicken, pecan candied yams, and three-cheese macaroni. The green beans, she probably poured from a can herself, but the coconut cake was definitely Seretha's.

At my mother's urging Dwayne said grace. He gave the standard prayers, thanking God for the food for the nourishment of our bodies, but he delivered it with a certain eloquence that made him seem like he could be a preacher if he wasn't so humble. While everyone said, "Amen," he squeezed my knee under the table.

I felt myself relaxing. My body temperature dropped and the water under my arms dried. It was as if Dwayne was some sort of antidote to my family's usual tensions.

Hermione laughed and Little Link scooped his vegetables with a rubber-tipped spoon.

I watched Dwayne flatter my mother, exclaiming over this bought meal. She grinned like a girl. I took a close look at my fiancé. He *did* look like a preacher with his fresh haircut and white shirt. Why had I never noticed this before?

"Earl," my mother said, "more sweet tea?"

I swung my eyes to my sister. Like me, Mama usually called him Mr. Phinazee. But for Mama this was not merely the force of habit. Before he started sleeping with Hermione, she'd always called him Earl. She called him *Mister* as a matter of spite.

Mr. Phinazee said, "That would be nice."

Hermione laughed and said, "Dwayne, we should invite you to join the family."

He grinned in return and showed his crooked, charming smile. I felt his leg press mine under the table. Of course I noticed the lead-in so perfect it seemed to be scripted. I pressed his leg back, silently pleading with him to let the opportunity go, to wait until there was a moment less symmetrical, not so choreographed. I wanted this to feel like real life, not like television.

"Actually," Dwayne said, setting his chicken leg on the good china and wiping his fingers on the linen napkin, "we're engaged."

"Praise God," my mother said.

I sat beside him with my mouth stretched into a smile that cracked the dry skin on my lips. I willed myself to feel happier. To let some of the joy infect me too. Mr. Phinazee stood and shook Dwayne's hand over the gravy boat. He pumped it up and down, repeating the word "congratulations." Hermione took my left hand and examined the ring. "Don't worry," she said as she hugged me. "You can always trade up."

Mother, from her place at the head of the table, tapped her glass with a salad fork. "When's the date?"

"June twenty-fifth."

"So soon?" Hermione said. "That's just a few weeks from now."

"I have a feeling," said Mr. Phinazee, "that there's more good news on the way."

Dwayne gave a sheepish little-boy smile and said, "What can I say?"

My family laughed and clapped like a studio audience. Mother rose and returned with champagne flutes, cloudy with neglect. My fiancé's name hovered on three pairs of lips, four if you counted Little Link, five if you counted the words uttered under my breath. What about me? I wanted to shout. I'm the one having the baby. It's me that's family. But I said nothing and raised my empty glass, trying to smile as everyone drank to Charming Dwayne.

When we climbed into the Jetta, I was so angry that my body burned with it. I pulled the neckline of my dress away from my sweaty skin and blew cool breath onto my cleavage.

"I think it went really well," Dwayne said. "It wasn't what I was expecting at all. They seem pretty cool." He cleaned one of his molars with his fingernail.

"They are not usually like that."

"Maybe they've changed," he said.

I turned the air-conditioning vents toward me and looked out the window. It was seven o'clock and the sun had just started to set.

"What?" Dwayne said, showing a little pique of his own. "Seems like you're disappointed that they didn't hate me. Like you were waiting for the shoot-out at the O.K. Corral."

"You have chicken grease on your lip."

"Maybe this is a mood swing or something, but you are definitely tripping."

"You don't know them," I said. "*My mother* gets so excited she breaks out a magnum of champagne? That's alcohol, you know. Eloise Jackson *kissed* you when we were leaving? Hermione says she'll call me? Don't you see why I'm pissed? They have never acted that way for just me. And stop being so impressed. My mother didn't cook that food. She bought it."

"So?" Dwayne said, merging onto I-20. "This isn't even our car. It's Head Cheese's."

"Just take me home," I said.

We drove on, listening to the radio. The evening had set upon us quickly. Dwayne turned on his lights and the DJ announced that he would be playing slow jams from now until midnight.

"Maybe I did try a little too hard," he said. "The co-conut cake was good, but it wasn't that good." He looked at me with a smile. "But I wanted them to like me. Make things easier for us and for the baby."

"I wanted them to like you too." I didn't turn away from the window. We were just past Ashby Street, the gateway to the West End. A tall desperate-looking man ran to our car and squirted the windshield with dirty dishwater. Dwayne fumbled to find the wiper controls and shooed the man away.

"Crackheads," he said. "I don't know how you stand it over here."

"I wanted them to like you too," I said again. "I just wasn't ready for them to love you."

Chapter Seven

The **Atlanta Women's Center** is part of a huge medical confederacy housed in a glass tower in the middle of downtown. When I got in the door, I told a pretty Latina my name and she handed me a manila folder. I took it and followed her instructions to a shabby upstairs waiting room. Two other young women sat beside me on a worn understuffed couch, watching a video demonstrating how to do breast exams when you're in the shower. Neither of them looked too worried. They seemed confident and happy like they were just here to find out exactly how healthy they were. I, on the other hand, was starting to get a little sick. My muscles felt to be burning just under the skin. Sweat trickled from under my arms, down my sides.

When the breast video started itself over, I opened my folder. Inside was a handwritten note from Dotty, the nurse-practitioner who handled all my routine care: *6/3: Left message on answering machine, informing patient of "hormonal imbalance."* Now, on the fifth of June, my stomach cramped, wrung like a wet dish towel. The quotation marks around the words "hormonal imbalance" seemed exaggerated, as if Dotty had announced "quote, un-quote" before saying the words. It was like the things people say when they want to lie without committing perjury.

Before this, I'd liked Dotty. She was a tall, big-boned white woman who wore her stethoscope over a large flannel shirt and blue jeans. She liked to tell jokes with her hillbilly twang. She was the only health care profes-sional who had ever made me feel at ease while naked and spread in stirrups. When she asked me questions about my sexual past and present, I told her the truth. Why would I lie to Dotty? We were almost friends.

When I'd gone in for my pregnancy test on Monday, I showed her my ring as she pumped the blood pressure cuff on my right arm. My fingers tingled and I was ex-cited, talking way too loud. I giggled, explaining that my morning sickness had just lasted a week. The regular nurses, the ones who weren't dressed like lumberjacks, glanced up from their paperwork, clearly annoyed.

Dotty handed me a paper cup. "Sounds like you're a mama."

"I know."

I excused myself to the bathroom and returned hold-ing the cup aloft, as if proposing a toast.

She left and I sat on the table wearing my paper robe and waited, swinging my bare legs. Dwayne had offered to come, but I let him off the hook, telling him that meeting my family was enough excitement for one week. I waited for him to insist, but he'd just laughed and accepted the reprieve.

True to her word, Dotty returned after only a few minutes, but her face was deliberately blank, like she'd pulled down a shade.

"Aria, we want to take some blood, okay?"

"Okay," I said slowly. "But what about my pregnancy test?"

"It was inconclusive. We really need to draw blood before we can know anything for sure."

"Come on, Dotty," I said. "What do you think is wrong?"

"It's inconclusive. I can't really say."

"But, Dotty, you can tell me *some*thing. You're a doctor."

Dotty sat down at the computer and tapped the keys. She didn't look at me. "Aria, I'm just a nurse-prac. You're really going to need to see the M.D."

I recognized her tone. She was setting boundaries of the clear and firm variety. My pregnancy was not a personal matter between the two of us. She didn't owe me any sort of explanation. Dotty was here to do her job, which she had done. No matter how it may have felt before, we were not friends.

"Dotty," I said, making myself clear and firm too, "you cannot just send me away like this."

She pulled a green page from the printer. "Take this to the lab. There's really nothing to say until we get your blood work."

That was last week. Two days ago she'd spoken to my answering machine, as though leaving a message for a stranger.

Once again Dwayne had offered to come with me. This time he'd insisted when I said no. "If there is something wrong with our baby," he said, "I want to be there."

"What would you do if you were there?"

"Be there for you."

I shook my head. "I'll give you a full report when I get back."

Sitting alone in the waiting room, I regretted my decision to come alone. I surprised myself by not wishing for Dwayne. I wanted Hermione, bad and brassy, ready for anything. I could imagine her sitting beside me, smelling of orange hand cream. *This is not a problem, Aria.* I longed even for Keisha with her frank experience. *Don't worry, Miss Aria. People get pregnant every day.* And I knew that they would be right. But I still could not break free of a premonition of doom. A sick feeling that started in my stomach, traveled up to my chest, and burned there.

A nurse emerged three times, calling names. When she finally called for me, I said, "Not yet."

"Pardon?"

The robust woman beside me sighed and flipped through the pages of her pregnant-lady magazine.

The nurse weighed me, stuck something in my ear to read my temperature, took my blood pressure, and refused to answer any of my questions. "You'll have to wait and speak with the doctor," she said over and over. Finally she indicated that I should walk down the tiled hallway to room seven.

"Can I talk to Dotty?"

"Dotty is not here today. Your appointment is with the gynecologist." Then she shoved me into the small room.

Room seven was an ordinary examining room. In the center of the space was the examination table; tasseled golf club covers stretched over each stirrup. The walls were decorated with posters that reminded you in a nonthreatening way that unprotected sex is how you get VD. I sat on an uncomfortable chair to wait for the doctor.

From the other side of a door painted purple, a big voice said, "In here."

It had not come from a big man. Theodore Blackwelder was a little old white gentleman, dressed to the nines in a French-cuffed shirt and yellow and blue bow tie. His desk, an antique rolltop, belonged in a movie where the actresses wore dresses with bustles. Besides the desk, two chairs, and Dr. Blackwelder himself, the room was empty save several boxes of rubber gloves, syringes, and K–Y lubricant.

He walked across to greet me in his stocking feet; empty penny loafers peeked from under the beautiful desk. "Ariadne?" His amethyst cuff links shone under the fluorescent lights as he extended his hand.

"I go by Aria," I said. "Like in opera."

"Yes," he said, straightening his yellow and blue bow tie. "That's right. Do you like opera? I do, but my wife can't abide it. So we compromise by going to the symphony." He opened a folder and took out a couple of pages.

Dr. Blackwelder asked me a few questions about myself: what did I do for a living, where was I from, how did I manage to get rid of my accent, all of that. I knew he wasn't really interested, that he was just trying to make me comfortable. I kept my answers short and rubbed my sandals against the fraying carpet. After nodding a couple of times at my monosyllables he told me a little bit about himself: he was from Cincinnati, had been in Georgia ten years after he retired from private practice, had a granddaughter my age, etc. Taking a deep breath, he pulled his desk chair from behind the rolltop so that he and I were close enough to touch. He rubbed his shock of white hair. It was time to get down to business.

"You came in a couple of days ago, complaining of amenorrhea?"

"No," I said. "I came Monday for a pregnancy test."

"Yes, but you said you had been missing periods? That was one of your symptoms, yes?"

I nodded.

"That's what amenorrhea is," he explained. "So we did some blood work to see what the problem was." Now he handed me the pages he took from the folder. "These are your hormone levels."

The page was divided into three columns. The first was a list of unfamiliar words. Beside the words were numbers. The last column said "OK" or it said nothing. Almost everything was marked "OK," except two. I turned my eyes from the sheet and focused my attention on my shoes in an effort to relax myself enough to breathe normally. My lunch rose from my stomach to the back of my throat.

"Is something wrong with the baby? There's Down syndrome on my father's side."

"See the line that says 'FSH'?" He touched the page.

"Yes," I said without looking.

Dr. Blackwelder scooted back to his desk and flipped through an orderly stack of papers. "There was a diagram here, but I can't find it. Never mind. I can just explain it to you. The brain sends out FSH when it wants to tell your ovaries to release an egg. Your brain did just that. But the ovaries didn't do it. So your brain let out more. Your brain's yelling at the top of its lungs. It took out an ad in the *Times*. You've got *thrice* what's normal for your age. Understand?"

"No, sir."

He rubbed his chin. "So next we checked your estrogen. We need to see how much the ovaries are putting out. See it there."

I said, "Yes," again even though I wasn't looking.

"Well, your estrogen is so low that we can't even count it. Understand?"

"I understand what you just explained, but I don't think I understand what it *means*."

Dr. Blackwelder crossed his arms over his immaculate shirt and said, "In medical school we say this: when you hear the clatter of hooves outside of your window, it could be zebras, but it's probably horses. Understand?"

"No."

"That means that there are certain symptoms that almost always point to a certain diagnosis. When we see numbers like these, it generally indicates one thing."

The quaver in his voice is what scared me; it was just a little hitch, like a damaged record. My throat seized shut and I couldn't swallow the water that accumulated in my mouth. Female problems could kill you. Even if they didn't, it implied something nasty. It was the sort of problem that you spoke about only in embarrassed whispers. Whatever was wrong with me was the sort of thing that could make a doctor's voice crack.

"Premature ovarian failure."

I shook my head.

"In people your age we call it premature ovarian failure. But most people call it menopause."

I released the air that swelled my lungs. "That's it?"

Dr. Blackwelder shook his head. "You don't understand, do you? This means that you will be unable to bear children."

His language was so stilted, he seemed to be speaking from the Bible, or maybe from God himelf. It sounded more like prophecy than a medical assessment. Then Dr. Blackwelder startled me by lifting my hand from my lap. "I'm so sorry, Ariadne."

"No," I said. "That's impossible. I'm twenty-five. I had morning sickness."

Dr. Blackwelder still held my hand. "Morning sickness, or were you just sick in the morning?"

I shook my head.

"Coincidence, most likely. Something you ate. A bug?"

"No."

"Precocious menopause is very rare. . . ."

His use of my mother's word is what convinced me. I pulled my hand from his and used it to cover my face while the awful weight of truth pressed over me.

Leaving the doctor's office, I handed my parking ticket to the attendant, who opened the gate without charging me. I couldn't believe that I had been in the office less than an hour, that it took only around forty-five minutes for my life to be changed so completely. I took the city streets, feeling too unstable for the quick and cutthroat expressways. Stopping for traffic lights, I thought about myself and how stupid I'd been. A sensible person, Rochelle, for example, would have taken a home pregnancy test first. I hadn't because I was convinced that I knew my body. Now I couldn't even take the expression seriously. What did it mean, to know your body? This was a phrase that I'd picked up from women's magazines and television talk shows. I'd been living in this body twenty-five years and it was a stranger to me. I had gone through the Change and hadn't even seen the signs. Dr. Blackwelder said that it was easy enough to miss, that my body had been responding to the years of birth control pills I'd swallowed, taking its cues from the synthetic hormones. But still, a person who knew her body should have known that something was seriously wrong. I felt like an idiot, like the wives who are always the last to know.

Despite everything, I taught my late class that afternoon. I considered taking the rest of the day off; the thought crossed my mind as I waited at a light on MLK.

I could take a sick day, go home, and cry. But the idea of sitting alone in the house or sitting on the porch watching the crackheads made me even more unhappy, so I went on to LARC. At least there would be people there.

When I pulled into the driveway, I was relieved enough to weep. This was one of the benefits of teaching literacy, of do-gooding in general. It takes your mind off your own troubles. How could I worry that my eggs are all gone, that I have to tell my fiancé that we're not pregnant and never will be? How can I worry what my mother will say when I spend my days with young girls who could as easily go to jail as go shopping? How can I, a college-educated person with an above-average vocabulary, a person who eats every day and enjoys full health benefits including eye and dental, feel sorry for myself when talking to a teenager who can't even read? I work six-hour days, four days a week, and she works eight hours, six days, assembling submarine sandwiches. So how can I be sad? How *dare* I weep about my ruined ovaries?

The GED was in less than a month, so class attendance was fairly high and consistent. A couple of dropouts had quietly resurfaced. Early in the session we had spent our time reading poetry and talking about feelings, but during the final month I taught for the test and they learned for the test. It was boring, reading passages culled from instruction manuals for electronic devices; passages explaining the migratory patterns of certain South American butterflies. But this was the sort of thing that would be on the test, and this is what they were going to need if they were going to get their certificates.

I dimmed the light and clicked on the overhead projector. In the dark, with the door closed and the shades down, I was aware of the room's narrow dimensions. It was silly, really, to think that an old house could be converted into a school just because Lawrence decided to use it that way. Idealistic and silly. This room was not a classroom. Where was the chalkboard and the pull-down map of the world? This was a bedroom and a small one at that. We were eleven people crammed into metal desk chairs, which were then all crammed into a guest bedroom. What did we really think we were accomplishing here? To teach students this far behind you needed computers, current hip textbooks. Hell, you needed a real teacher. Not just me and Rochelle, people hired for our "energy."

I heard myself asking for a volunteer to read a passage beamed onto the white bedsheet used as a projection screen.

Keisha raised her hand and read carefully in her strong voice. She read slowly, considering each word, reading the way people read when they can't really read. "The" became *thee* and "a" was pronounced *ay. Thee butterflies nest in ay tree.* "Calling words" is how teachers described this. Not reading, just calling words. No inflection whatsoever.

The noise of her voice irritated me. I gritted my teeth with every syllable, her accent so slow it was almost bovine. I looked at the ceiling at each *thee* and *ay.* Keisha was somebody's mother. All of the girls in this classroom either had children or had the potential to do so. Some of them were pretty with shiny eyes and glossy hair. A few were ugly with their bad skin and discolored lips. No matter, though, no matter what they looked like, no matter what they had done, their bodies were young and fertile, teeming with eggs, soggy with estrogen.

I asked Keisha to stop her reading. Told the class to write the main ideas in their own words. "Please," I added.

Then I was bothered by the noise of their movements. All of them seemed to be wearing silver bracelets or multiple pairs of gold earrings. Their acrylic nails ticked together as they guided their pens across lined paper. The din was like every religious noise I have ever experienced or heard of. Like rosary beads clicking, the clanging of finger cymbals, the drone of church bells.

I turned away from them and wondered how a person knew if she was having a nervous breakdown.

Was I the only one in the world to ever notice that illiterate teenage girls under the supervision of the court smelled like candy? That they seemed to have a penchant for aromatic bubble gum? Did the smell of them make everyone nauseated, or was it just me?

I went to the window and jerked the green shade, sending it snapping onto its spool. I pushed up on the painted wood of the window frame, straining, using the heels of my hands, but the window stayed put.

"The windows are nailed shut, Miss Aria," Keisha said. Like on the first day of class, she spoke for the group.

"But that's a fire hazard," I said. "It's against the law."

The ten girls shrugged in what seemed to be a unified motion.

I willed myself to turn around and face them, to smile and do my job. I thought of my mother, back at the Institute just two days after the funeral. "The blind children need my help," she'd said. "Did you think they've all learned to see?"

I released the window, rubbing my sore hands together. With closed eyes I breathed in the fruit punch and sour-apple air, swallowing hard against the vomit rising in my throat.

"Let's turn on the light," I said. "Open the door and get some air."

With the lights on they scribbled in their workbooks. I usually walked among them, pointing out errors or offering little pats of encouragement. But today I sat in my metal chair with my arms crossed over my chest and my legs folded hard at the knee. I stared into the four-bulb fixture wondering if I was blinding myself, then wondering if it mattered.

There are certain concepts that you shouldn't think about when things go wrong. Fairness is one of them. You can't think about what you do and don't deserve. Hermione told me this years ago. "That's how you go crazy. Look at Mama. And anyway, who told you life was going to be fair?" I know that question is supposed to be rhetorical, but everyone tells you that the world is fair, or at least they let you know that it is supposed to be. All the work we did here at LARC and even my mother's work at the Institute. All that talk about leveling playing fields. That was about fairness. But what Hermione meant was that only a fool believes that she will get what's coming to her. That she will get only what she deserves.

And I wasn't naive. I never believed myself to have a charmed life. I wasn't like Rochelle, who assumed that people would like her, that landlords would be honest. She never counted her change, just stuffed it in her pocket, because in her universe things worked out. There are all manner of scams and cheats in my world. I have never been convinced that God is good. But there were some things I thought were unassailable. How many plastic dial packs of birth control pills had I added to Atlanta's landfills. Maybe landfills and pollution were no longer my responsibility, since I no longer had a direct stake in the next generation? Again I wondered how exactly a person could tell when she was having a nervous breakdown.

"I don't feel well," I said to the girls. "Let's adjourn early."

"Uh-uh," said Benita, the student with the worst attendance record. "You owe us another half an hour."

"Shut up," Keisha said. "Ain't like you paying for this."

"I pay taxes."

She was silenced by the other girls, who zipped their bags and slung them over their shoulders, eager to make it to appointments that I couldn't imagine.

After they had all filed out, Keisha approached me where I still sat in my chair.

"You okay?"

I nodded.

She leaned in and pressed her cheek to my forehead. I was overwhelmed by her smell, the combined scent of nail polish and banana taffy.

"You don't have a fever. It's your stomach?"

I hung my head and tried not to breathe too much of her.

"You went to the doctor today, didn't you?"

I nodded.

"You got your weeks?"

I shook my head. "I'm not pregnant."

Keisha covered her mouth. "You lost it?"

I nodded.

"You had to get scraped?"

The word was perfect, described how I felt, captured my very *condition*. Nodding again, I imagined the procedure, how it must feel to have the life abraded from inside you. "It was awful," I whispered, standing up.

Keisha hugged me, pressing the bulb of her stomach into my abdomen. I wanted to tell her to get away from me, not to touch me. But I didn't. I let my arms go limp and let Keisha press her swollen self into me and stroke the back of my neck. "I'm so sorry, Miss Aria. I'm so sorry."

I knew that I was the one who should be saying "sorry." I should ask her pardon for my thoughts because all I could think was how unfair it was. What had Keisha done to deserve a baby? And what had her baby done to deserve to have a mere teenager for a mother? Keisha was without a good man, a good job. She couldn't even read.

When Keisha let me go, I closed my eyes to black out the sight of her. Alone in the empty classroom, I sat thinking of Drew Alexander, the man from the Institute with the dirty magazine, furious and blind.

I made it home before Rochelle. Pushed through the doorway the cardboard boxes left for the bride. Took a handful of mail out of the box. Bills for me. A slip telling Rochelle to go to the post office for an insured package. Rochelle and all her abundance.

I sat at the kitchen table, waiting for her. I could not help remembering the evening when we became friends, when I'd given her the money I'd earned so that she could end a pregnancy. Had I dirtied my hands by helping her? But why hadn't Rochelle earned any punishment for herself? I'd been with her in the days after the procedure and even the years since. She didn't spend much time looking back; there were no screaming nightmares, no sobbing scenes of remorse. She'd had her abortion, taken a few days off from classes, and then resumed her life. Maybe I was her portrait, the image of her that felt all the pain, that bore the evidence of all the damage, while she lived and loved and thrived. Waiting for Rochelle, I watched a somber procession of ants make its way to the sugar bowl. I watched and I wondered.

Rochelle entered the house finally with a slap of the screen door and the tinkling of keys. My eyes watered with her patchouli scent, but I didn't turn to look at her.

"Hey, Penny," she said, making her way to the leaky refrigerator for a Diet Coke.

I didn't answer. She repeated her greeting. I opened

my mouth to respond, but my throat felt shut, like a drain clogged with dead hair.

Rochelle drank her Diet Coke in rapid, lusty swallows. She did this while I watched the ants. If I were to remove the top from the sugar bowl, there would be a hundred busy creatures swarming inside. Behind me I heard her open the cabinet for a bottle of wine. There was the hollow pop as she removed the cork. I wasn't crying. I did think about Genevieve, the wasted baby. She didn't cross my mind often. My little sister was dead before she could talk. I'd saved all my mourning for my father. But now I knew a baby's worth. My mind went to Keisha. I wondered what she knew. I put my finger on the trail of ants and they climbed over my flat nail.

Rochelle sat herself directly in my line of vision. In front of her was a glass of red wine, dirty with crumbled cork. "Penny," she said, "what's up?"

I didn't speak. The crush of disappointment paralyzed my vocal cords. I looked at my friend across the table. Sunlight from the kitchen window illuminated her so she glowed like a stained-glass saint. I wanted to ask her how it felt to have everything you wanted.

"I hope you're not still mad because I joked about your ring," she said.

I was still as stone and as silent.

"I've been thinking about it and I really am sorry. Dwayne is a good guy. He'll be a good father. I'm sort of horrified with myself that I even said anything." She stopped, her eyes falling on my finger and the ants crawling over it.

"Aria," she said slowly and softly, "say *something*. You're weirding me out."

I still didn't move; she took a small swallow of wine, set the glass down, and then moved my finger. Confused ants scattered in different directions.

"Aria," she said, "what is it?" Her voice climbed about an octave. I could tell she was getting scared. "Did something happen?"

I shook my head. Reaching over, I took the top off the sugar dish. The ants swarmed over the sugar cubes like mobile flecks of pepper.

Rochelle said, "Talk to me or I'm calling 911."

I didn't say anything.

"I'll call your mother."

I looked at Rochelle's face, lined with concern. I thought about Mr. Henry, the custodian from elementary school.

"I want to be you," I said.

Her face didn't quite relax, but she didn't move toward the phone. "What?"

"Your father is a veterinarian and your mother is a teacher. That's better than Cosby. You have Rod. Y'all are going to have kids and they won't be all fucked up because you aren't all fucked up."

Rochelle fastened the lid on the sugar dish. "Aria, my dad drinks too much. My mother is a martyr. Rod and I aren't even sure we want kids."

"But you have that choice," I shot back. My voice was too loud in my own ears. "You have all the choices. *Do you want to change your name? Is it sexist for your father to give you away?* All day you sit around deciding things.

When we were in college, you had an abortion. Don't forget about that."

The light in the room was different now. Rochelle's face was as gray as her hair.

"I don't really understand why you're bringing this up."

I didn't want to cry in front of her, but I couldn't help it. "I'm not pregnant."

She sucked in her breath.

"If you tell me it's a blessing in disguise, I'll never talk to you again. I'm serious, Rochelle. Don't say it."

And she didn't.

"I can't have kids at all," I said with a breaking voice. "The doctor almost cried telling me. Doctors have seen everything. This man has seen people dying of cancer and he almost cried when he told me. Everyone's going to ask me what happened and I don't know what I am going to say."

"Aria," Rochelle said.

"Dwayne wants kids," I said. "You don't know how much Dwayne wants kids."

"What do you want?"

"Kids."

"Then adopt," Rochelle said. "If you want kids, you can get kids."

I shook my head. "I don't want to *get* kids. I want to have my kids. I want them to come through me."

"Jesus," Rochelle said. "People kill me with all this nonsense about biology. Penny, remember who you are talking to. I'm adopted, remember? You can't tell me that my parents aren't my parents, that I am not their daughter."

"I want my own kids."

Rochelle closed her eyes. "Don't be so stupid. Don't be so closed-minded."

"You don't get it," I told her. "Sure, adoption is great for the person being adopted. You got to go live with a couple of really nice people. But don't you think about your mother? How do you think it felt when your hair went gray and nobody had any idea where it came from? I bet people in church were whispering, *Well, you know they adopted that girl.* I don't want people to feel sorry for me."

"So what if people feel sorry? You think my parents are wishing they didn't adopt me because of what people think? Who cares? I'd rather have people *feel* sorry for me than to actually *be* sorry myself."

Rochelle was losing patience. But she didn't know what it was like to be felt sorry for. When people are sorry for you, they look at your life and they go home and count their blessings. After the funeral for Genevieve and Daddy the neighborhood women came by with fast-food chicken presented on heavy crystal platters. Good cheddar shone atop their casseroles, but underneath there was only Velveeta, rubbery and bland. They came to our house, fed us box cakes, and touched our faces. They told us to pray about it. Reminded us that God was mysterious.

When they left, Mona Lisa smiles tickling their lips, they went home to their husbands who cheated on them and to their ugly, lazy children. They ignored past-due notices on their mortgages. Feeling sorry for us, they didn't worry about anything worrisome. When they went to bed that evening and many evenings to come, they slept easy, knowing that things could be much worse. They could have been *us*. Safe and secure that they were not, they counted their blessings on their fingers and toes.

"I don't understand why things keep happening to me," I said. But this was a lie. I knew why things happened the way that they did. Every misfortune could be traced to its obvious source. I needed comfort now, but there was no comfort for me. Fifteen years ago my father had wanted comfort as he sat trapped in the driver's seat, bleeding to death from the inside. He wanted me just to talk to him. Even at ten I knew what he wanted. But I'd plugged my ears and ignored him. He wanted so little and I gave even less. That's the kind of thing God can never quite forgive you for.

Chapter Eight

There was so much explaining to be done. The very idea of it burdened me, causing a tenderness in my joints, the achy way I feel when I am coming down with the flu. I went into the bathroom, my favorite space in the house. It was a common area like the kitchen or the living room, but it was intensely personal, a space that Rochelle and I shared. The bathroom is a place where you find yourself naked and wet from the shower, standing on the scale to see if you have gotten too fat. Every month I stood in the room examining my breasts, anxiously kneading the fatty tissue, feeling for hard knots that might mean that I was dying.

Standing before the sink, I turned my attention to the faucets, old-fashioned and shaped like daisies, the flowers that make you worry whether he loves you or loves you not. I twisted the left faucet, filling the sink with hot, cloudy water. Plunging my hands in up to the wrists, I concentrated on the throbbing in my fingers. Pain was good like that, cleared your mind.

I pulled open the mirrored front of the medicine cabinet. All Rochelle's supplements were there. Ginkgo biloba. She took this every day to preserve her memory. Sweet primrose oil was supposed to be good for her disposition. Dong quai to make her sexy. Then there were her birth control pills, fitted into a plastic compact like face powder. Hermione used to stash hers in the linen closet, between the folds of the fancy towels that we never used. My things were in the medicine cabinet too. Allergy tablets, bandages that didn't match my skin tone. Condoms. Tampax.

On the top shelf was the prescription bottle Rochelle's mother had left behind after shopping for wedding dresses. I followed the instructions on the child-proof cap, pressing and turning, and found fifteen blue pills in the vial. I eased the top off and borrowed only one. I liked the shape of it, perfectly round and scored in the middle. Alprazolam, the label read, but Rochelle called it Xanax. She saved them for special occasions. "These," she had said, "are for *high* drama."

Were fifteen tablets enough to kill yourself? Not that I was going to. I just wondered in the way that people wonder about things.

I chewed the tablet while running my bathwater. It was bitter, worse than Tylenol, but I liked the way it felt in my mouth, the taste brackish and utterly distracting. How would it make me feel? Xanax was a drug you heard about on talk shows. The new Valium. Something rich people take when they can't cope.

I stripped myself naked, mashing my dirty clothes into a ball. Balanced on the edge of the tub, I could see my body in the scarred mirror of the medicine cabinet. I held on to the towel bar scrutinizing my nude self like a used car on the lot. Things that I had taken for granted as just part of me were now symptoms, evidence of my malfunction. The skin on my legs was so dry that it was flaky, scored, and gray. Dry skin is a sign of estrogen deprivation. The pleats at the corners of my eyes. Weight gain. I slapped my thigh and watched the ripple travel down to nearly my knee. There were things happening, too, under the skin. My bones were likely hollowing out, especially at the hip. I had never wondered why old ladies broke their hips when they fell. Menopause. My body was aging, fast and sudden, like those little kids who start to wrinkle before they can walk, and fall over dead in third grade.

I always wanted to be special. When I was little, I'd fantasized about contracting illnesses. I wanted to be admitted into the hospital, be fed by the nurses, and receive plush toys as gifts. I would have loved to be stricken with something serious, so that a famous person would come to my bedside and my picture would be in *Jet*. My fondest wish had been to almost die, to come so close that everyone would regret being so mean, but would still have an opportunity to make it up to me, to show the love they'd hidden. This was a complicated fantasy involving handsome, quick-thinking doctors and beeping equipment. But I would have settled for a raging case of tonsillitis and a three-day diet of peppermint ice cream.

In real life I'd always been healthy. Horse healthy. I hadn't even needed to go to the hospital the day of the accident.

So now I finally had something. A sickness that would get me more attention than I could have ever wanted. It was embarrassing, really. The end of my menstrual cycle turned out to be as humiliating as the start of it. I remember how frightened I'd been that someone could somehow look at me and see that I had my period. I hid my supplies in the zippered compartment of my book bag, and even within that compartment I sealed them inside a makeup case. Now I worried that people would look at me and know that I was still different from other girls my age. That my body had stopped working in the way that a woman's body works. Female trouble. Has there ever been a phrase more shameful?

There was quite a lot of explaining to be done. Dwayne would have to be told. He had called three times, wanting to know what the doctor had said.

"We'll talk later. Tomorrow?"

"At least tell me if you're okay."

"I think I'm okay. I won't know for sure until tomorrow."

The lie had come easy, surprisingly so, like fast labor. I knew I would have to tell him. Some things can't be faked or pantomimed. It was only a matter of time before he realized that my stomach was still flat, that my breasts were still tight and small like sour apples. He'd soon know that although I looked the same as I always had, things would not be the same again.

The bathwater was not quite hot enough; it was only as warm as my body. It felt like slipping into a wet nothing. It would have to do. My mouth was still bitter from the pill, mashed bits of it jammed into the crevices of my teeth. I turned off the faucet, but the water still dribbled into the tub. I held my breath to feel the medicine working, to see if I felt like a rich lady who needed help to cope. I felt a little drowsy, but not different, transformed, or carefree. With wet feet I returned to the medicine cabinet and read the bottle. How many tablets did the doctor advise Rochelle's mother to take? Only one for problems like hers. So I took another one, bit it in half, and chewed.

"Are you depressed?" Rochelle had wanted to know after dinner. She was concerned in her genuine and sincere way. "Because if you are, there's nothing to be ashamed of."

Behind me the toilet ran like Niagara Falls. A place to get married, a place to drown in a barrel. Up to my chin in murky water, I'd forgotten to rinse the tub or add bubbles. A greasy brownish ring remained from the last time Rochelle had soaked. A film settled on my skin as I studied the mildew patterns in the grout.

I felt heavy and sleepy. Not relaxed. Was this coping? I felt pushed down and down, as if a man pressed his big hand on the crown of my head.

There were so many things that needed explaining. I was going to have to tell my mother. I wished I could hire a lawyer who could send everyone complicated letters via certified mail. Party of the first part, party of the second part, until everyone got the picture: no babies, nobody was liable. It was just the way things were.

This would be easier if Dwayne and I were already married. Then the matter of my ovarian failure would fall into the territory of "in sickness and in health." We could have gone together to visit a specialist, holding hands, explaining that we had been "trying really hard." Married, we'd be an "infertile couple." Now, without the benefit of a wedding and shared name, this was my problem. It was me.

Rochelle tried all morning to convince me that this crisis wasn't as serious as I figured it to be. She called it "an obstacle."

"Penny, Dwayne is not going to leave you," she promised.

I was sitting on the floor between her knees as she parted and twisted my hair. "You don't know that," I said. "He might."

"Dwayne'll be shaken," she said, "but he won't care. If he loves you, he won't care. Look at my parents. They've been together thirty years. It will work out."

I leaned into her promise, resting my head on the inside of her thigh as she separated the kinks of my hair. "But what if he does care? What if he wants his own biological children?"

She rubbed her finger, slick with hair cream, onto my scalp. "I know that Dwayne is sort of *literal*. But still. I think people are becoming more flexible about these things."

I closed my eyes and enjoyed the tug of her hands. I climbed into myself then, pretending to be a little girl, pretending that this was the afternoon that my mother combed my hair and everyone in my family was still alive. "But will he still want to *marry* me? That's the question."

"That shouldn't be the question. Love is the main thing." Rochelle's hands were fast in my hair, her ring casting rainbows on the wall.

Dwayne promised to come over after work; he left The Lock Shop over an hour ago, but I wasn't worried. It always took him a long time to reach his destinations, due to his choice of vehicle, a Crown Victoria, the same make and model of your average police car. Whenever he drove on the expressway, other drivers tapped their brakes, slowing to below the speed limit, frowning in their rearview mirrors as they tried to figure out if he was a state trooper or not. I would have thought that one benefit of this association would be that the car was off-limits to carjackers and other crooks. But to be on the safe side, Dwayne had the car decked out with all manner of antitheft devices—from a handheld remote that deactivated the engine to a metal club which he locked over the steering wheel. All this for a boxy white car for which he had been the only bidder at the police auction.

My handsome Dwayne arrived just after seven. He wore loose-fitting jeans and a stiff-ironed shirt with "The Lock Doctor" stitched on the pocket. Perched on his head was his favorite maroon baseball cap. It said the same thing. He looked comfortable and clean in his work clothes, like a local boy made good. Like the sort of man who would buy a big house for his mother were he to win the lottery.

Cynthia knelt in the driveway, furious with her searching, her face flecked with orange mud. She didn't even look up as Dwayne stood behind her, close enough to kick her hard in her hunched back. Shaking his head, he touched his pockets, feeling for his stereo faceplate, and bounded up my stairs, two at a time. I opened the door for him and he brought the heat of June into the cool living room.

"How can you live over here?"

"The same way you live anywhere, I guess."

Dwayne moved into the kitchen and helped himself to a beer, popping the top with his car key. He lifted his foot from the puddle of water in front of the fridge. "You and Rochelle are a trip. Most people work hard to get *out* of bad neighborhoods. I don't know why y'all like living with a bunch of crackheads, refrigerator leaking, and shit." He took a drink of beer and looked at the orange foil label. "What's this?"

I shrugged. "Something Rochelle and Rod like to drink."

Dwayne took a dainty sip. "Probably expensive. I'll drink it slow." He held the bottle out to me and then took it back just as I reached for it. "I forgot. No drinking for pregnant people."

"Let's go to the living room," I said. "I need to talk to you."

Dwayne set the half-empty bottle down with a concerned look. He took off his maroon cap and shaped the bill with a quick motion of his heavy hands, then put it back on. "That doesn't sound good."

"I'm not mad," I said. "It's nothing like that."

He relaxed a little and I knew I'd misled him.

Dwayne sat on the futon and ran his hands over the green and tan cover. "It trips me out to think that your mother made all of this." He waved his hand to include the matching drapes, throw pillows, and runners.

"She was on a sewing binge." These days she was on a crocheting kick. My throat tightened as I pictured her hooking an entire wardrobe of baby booties, sweaters, blankets, and tasseled caps.

Dwayne patted the space beside him. "Baby, what's the matter?"

I got up from Rochelle's leather recliner and sat where he wanted me to. We both faced forward like we were watching a movie together. The dirty window across from the futon was topped with a tan valance, stuffed with newspaper. From where we sat we had a panoramic view of the backyard, carpeted with crabgrass and ornamented with cinder blocks and litter. A stray calico sat, licking itself, on top of a dead television.

"Hey," Dwayne said. "Where's Rochelle's cat? What's his name?"

"Kitten. He's gone to the groomers for a clip-and-dip."

"Bourgie Negroes."

When there was nothing else to say, he took his hat off again, shaping the bill with careful squeezes of his palms. The cardboard core showed at the lip of the hat, where he had worn down the maroon fabric. When I spoke, I would talk to Dwayne's cap, timing my words to the slow, regular rhythm of his busy hands.

"Well?" Dwayne said over the scrape of cloth against his callused hands.

"Things didn't go well." I aimed my words at his fingers, his nails, his wrinkled, scarred knuckles.

Dwayne kept his hands on his hat. He cupped the bill, forcing it to mimic the shape of his palms. We were still sitting side by side on the futon, hips touching. He couldn't see my face and I couldn't see his.

"They ran all these tests and everything," I started again. "Blood tests. And they didn't come out right." There was a hitch in my voice. The pitch rising in my own ears. I breathed deep, tried to relax my throat enough to let the words out.

Dwayne rubbed his palms on the knees of his jeans, then he took the hat in his hands again. "Is the baby all right?"

The phone let off a shriek and we both snapped our heads in its direction. Dwayne and I were both old enough to remember when phones simply rang, they didn't sound alarms. When I was a kid, our kitchen phone actually had bells inside of it. I remember peeking into the plastic shell and catching a glimpse of dark metal. The memory hurt somehow; I touched my throat to feel the flutter of my pulse.

Rochelle's recorded voice spoke from the plastic answering machine. "Breathe and you will know peace."

Dwayne made a little circular motion at his temple. "What the hell does she mean by that?"

"You know how she is."

Rochelle's mother's voice sang out. She had seen a bouquet of burgundy calla lilies in a magazine. They were pricey but perfect. Could Rochelle call her back? The woman on the phone was Rochelle's mother, gray hair or no gray hair, biology or no biology, right?

"Do you want all that stuff?" Dwayne asked me. "Their wedding is going to set them back how much?"

"Forty-five grand and counting," I said.

He breathed through his teeth. "That's a down payment on a house. A good down payment."

I nodded, distracted.

"I can't give you all that," he said. "My sister, she just got married at our church. The reception was in the rec center. Wasn't no calla lilies involved."

"It's fine," I said. "I don't care about that."

"Rochelle and Rod, they probably going to have their picture in *Jet*, huh?"

"It doesn't matter."

"So what happened at the doctor's?" Dwayne said.

I put my left hand to my mouth and spoke through the screen of my fingers, and I knew why this conversation felt so sad and so familiar. I'd made my share of confessions in my life. I knew how words got caught in your throat, clotted and thick. I had more than a passing acquaintance with shame.

"It's got Down syndrome, epilepsy, or something?" Dwayne asked. He put his hands on my shoulders, twisting so that I had to look at him. He tightened the skin around his eyes, squinting, as though I were too small for him to see clearly. "Look at me, Aria. What happened?

Was it a miscarriage?" His hands on my shoulders gripped hard, hurt just a little bit.

This was the time to tell him. To just say, "It was a mistake. I can't have kids." That would give him everything he needed to know. I thought of Keisha saying that men don't care about the specifics, they just want the bottom line. But she was wrong; this news about my health, about my body, was what he would want to know, but it was the next-to-the-bottom line. The bottom line was that I loved him. That I wanted to make a family with him.

"I lost the baby," I said. "I had to get scraped."

After I said that, there was a new bottom line: I'd lied. From that moment on, this was all that would matter.

Dwayne moved his hands from my shoulders to the sides of my face. He pressed his lips to each of my closed eyes. "When?"

"Yesterday."

"Why didn't you tell me when I called?"

"I didn't want to disappoint you. I didn't know what to say."

"Are you okay? Are you in pain?"

"Yes," I said. "I feel terrible."

"You should be in bed," he said. "Trying to recover."

He helped me to my feet and we walked toward my bedroom. I leaned on him as though my ankle were sprained. Moving in tiny, careful steps, I concentrated on the scent of him and the squeak of his new sneakers on the wood floors. Dwayne was a good person and a good man. Generous and kind, all the things you would like in a person. Even Rochelle would agree with this. In all the things that really mattered, when you stripped people out of their bodies, out of the details of their lives, when you pared things down to the soul level, a person could do a lot worse than Dwayne. A person could, and I had.

"Can I get you something?" he asked me.

"Ice cream," I said. "Macadamia brittle."

"Okay," Dwayne said. "I'll be right back."

"Take my keys," I said. "So you can get back in."

"I don't need them," he said, picking up my key ring anyway.

While he was gone, I pulled on a yellow cotton gown, applied a bit of lip gloss, and climbed into bed. Cynthia's rhinestone barrette glinted under the glare of my bedside lamp; I fastened it around a handful of my twists. I lay there propped up in bed, trying not to think about what I had just done. I tried to think how lucky I was at that moment, in that instant. Dwayne was treating me the way you treat someone when you think you will love them for the rest of your life. I tried to gorge myself on this experience the way condemned men somehow manage to enjoy their final meal.

Dwayne wasn't gone long. When he returned, he rang the doorbell before opening my door with my keys.

"They didn't have macadamia nut," he said. "I don't know where you think you're at. You have to go to the suburbs to get Häagen-Dazs." He pulled a small tub of Sealtest chocolate out of a brown bag.

"That's fine," I said. "It's what I used to like when I was a kid."

I lifted the lid from the pint to find that the ice cream had melted and refrozen, a layer of gray frost covering the chocolate. I tilted the carton so Dwayne couldn't see and chipped at the mess with the plastic spoon. "Thank you."

"Are you going to be all right?" he said.

"Yes."

Dwayne knelt beside my bed, rubbing my arm, and I spooned freezer-burned ice cream into my mouth. "We have plenty of time for babies," he said. "Now we have time to do things right."

The ice cream tasted like dirt, but I forced it to the back of my tongue and down my throat.

"Not that I am glad about what happened. I'm not glad that you had to go through what you went through. The scraping and all. But I am saying that this might be a blessing in disguise."

"It is not a blessing," I said. "You don't know what has happened to me. If you had been there, you wouldn't say it is a blessing."

"Not a blessing, no, that's the wrong word. I'm just saying that we can make some plans. Okay, I'm screwing this whole thing up. I'm not good at talking." He reached into his jacket pocket and pulled out a blue velvet box. "Just take this."

The spring-loaded box fairly jumped open at my touch. There, wedged in blue satin, was an engagement ring. It was a simple affair, narrow gold setting, round cut, a little more than a third carat, less than a half. It was more than good enough.

"You want me to have it?"

"Naw," he said. "I just want you to look at it."

I handed it back.

"I was just kidding," he said. "Of course I want you to have it."

"I thought you just asked me to marry you because I was pregnant."

"It wasn't just that. Well, at first it was just that, because of the way everything went down. But I sort of got used to the idea of having you around." He smiled at me, showing his overlapping teeth, and I loved him so much that it made my head hurt.

I pulled the ring from its satin nest and gripped it tight, the metal prongs digging into my palm and me savoring the bite.

Chapter Nine

Each year my mother, Hermione, and I set aside my father's birthday as a day of remembrance. My mother shares with us her best memory of our father, the story of their courtship. She tells it the same way each time, as though reciting the language of a sacred text. As she speaks the words, I close my eyes to concentrate on the images produced in the factory of my imagination. Hermione shuts her eyes too, and though she would never admit it, I know that she does what I do: listen to the story and pretend that it had happened to me.

Daddy had gone to Morehouse, but he wasn't really "Morehouse material." He worked a couple of jobs to pay for his tuition and didn't have enough left for textbooks or cafeteria lunches. After classes he would climb the stairs of Graves Hall to sit in his teachers' offices, reading the lessons from their textbooks. He would eat a handful of peanuts for lunch before rushing off to sweep up hair at a barbershop. The barber, Old Man Phinazee, paid a dollar an hour.

When my father met my mother, she was eating a frosted cupcake, waiting at the front gate of Spelman for a ride. Daddy was hungry; he hadn't eaten since dinner the night before and it was now three in the afternoon. Mama wore a green dotted swiss skirt that stopped at her knee, and white shoes that fastened at the ankle. He said that he remembered the shoes because he was too shy to look in her face while she enjoyed the chocolate cake, because she might look in his eyes and see how hungry he was.

Mama asked him if he had a church key and he said, "No, ma'am." She laughed at him because they were the same age, both sophomores, nineteen. "I'm not your mother," she said, and popped the rest of the cake in her mouth.

Daddy pulled his handkerchief from his back pocket, checked that it was clean, and offered it to her, to wipe the chocolate from her lips. She did, and gave him the handkerchief back smeared with cake and frosted lipstick. I like to think that he rubbed it to his own lips after he was out of her sight, tasting sweet icing and grease.

Daddy saved his money for six months, cutting his budget by not buying pencils (he wrote with stubs he found on the ground). He ran extra errands for the barber, sharpening scissors, scrubbing toilets, after hours. Then he came down with the flu, missing a week of work, forcing him to dip into his savings to pay his rent.

But once he had the money, he asked her out to lunch and a movie. I've always wondered what he would have done with the money if she had said no.

Daddy met her at the front gate of Spelman and they walked a block to catch the bus on Fair Street. He was confident but shy in size twelve black penny loafers, borrowed from his best friend, Earl, the barber's son. Mama was a beautiful coquette wearing a navy-blue shirtwaist with yellow trim. When they walked to the rear of the city bus, she took his hand. Embarrassed, Daddy wished that he had been patient, saved longer, and had enough money for a colored taxi. But at least the bus was empty, except for the driver; they didn't have to walk past any white people as they made their way to the back.

The movie, *West Side Story,* lasted longer than they thought it would. Neither of them enjoyed it much, but they were happy to sit close together in the dark, fingers touching in the bag of oily popcorn. When they came down from the balcony—Mama always called it the balcony, never nigger heaven, which is what everyone else called it—it was twenty minutes until my mother's six o'clock curfew. When I was a student at Spelman, our curfew was two a.m. on weekends. If we violated this rule, the punishment was "social probation," which was more an inconvenience than anything else. But in 1962 the students wore white gloves on Sundays and the penalty for missed curfew was expulsion.

She would have to go home in a taxi. In his pockets Daddy had money for their bus fare and twenty cents that he had planned to use to treat her to an ice cream cone. Daddy gave her all he had in his pockets, and then he bent down and took two dimes from his borrowed loafers. Wondering where he would get the dimes to replace the ones he'd stolen from Earl's shoes, he put her in the taxi. I can remember Daddy's laugh when he told this story, saying that the wind smacked him all about the head and shoulders as he walked the six miles from downtown to the rooming house where he lived. His coat was thin and a little small for him. Earl's shoes rubbed blisters the size of quarters. But Daddy said that even when it started to rain, he was warm because my mama had kissed his cheek before she climbed in that taxi.

This is my most vivid memory of my father, although it happened years before I was born. My father has been dead most of my life. I don't have many real memories of him, no stories that haven't been retouched from multiple tellings. This story, the one of how he loved my mother the moment he met her, is my best memory of him, even though it happened before I existed. It's my favorite memory of Mama too. I like to imagine her through his eyes, pretty and swiss-dotted, chocolate-eating and laughing. My memories of my mother's smile are as distant and blurred as those of my father's face.

When I die, I want to be cremated. I don't have plans for the ashes, but I want them to be discarded, dumped somewhere with no marker.

On my father's birthday we go to the cemetery to lay flowers on his grave. We bring blossoms for Genevieve too, but we don't make a special trip for her birthday. I suppose it would be more democratic to commemorate the April day that we lost them both, a day equally significant to a thirty-eight-year-old man and a girl less than one. But this would be dishonest somehow. Genevieve's death was just insult. Daddy's was the injury.

Lincoln and Genevieve Jackson are buried in Westview Cemetery, five gorgeous acres of grief. They lie side by side, like man and wife, under matching brass plates.

When I was a little girl, we used to cut through the cemetery to avoid the traffic on Gordon Road. As we wound through the green hills, I'd mash my face to the car window admiring the plaster angels, heavy-winged and weeping. In the center of the graveyard is a four-story tower with a notched top, the sort of structure where fairy-tale princesses are held hostage by ogres. Before I was ten, I never thought of the dead people under the elaborate markers. When I saw fresh dirt heaped under a green funeral tent, I only noticed the flowers.

Daddy and Genevieve are at the back of the cemetery, nearly a quarter mile from the nearest marble monument. In this section of Westview the graves are marked with flat metal plates, so that the groundskeeper can just roll over them with a riding mower. I wondered about the other families who buried their loved ones out here. Were they the sort of people who asked that mourners make donations to charity in lieu of flowers? Maybe they were wealthy misers who'd rather buy stocks instead of paying high rent for the dead. Or maybe they were like us, feeling guilty and poor as we passed some other "beloved father's" monument. This back pasture plot was all that we could afford at Westview.

Although the cemetery itself is opulent, the neighborhood around it is decayed and rotting. I would never be willing to live over here. People like Dwayne think that all depressed areas are the same, but anybody who lives in a less-than-desirable zip code can tell you different. This stretch of MLK, just before it branches off to Abernathy, near the Marta station—this mile or two really has nothing to offer anyone. The real estate agents are not buzzing about its possibility. Even if you were to raze the buildings—the crumbling apartment buildings with No Trespassing signs, these condemned homes in which people live anyway, people with children—even if these structures were leveled, it wouldn't be right to build on this land. The sadness permeates the soil like nuclear waste.

Mama sighed as we waited at a red light on MLK. When our family ran into the magnolia, this was called Gordon Road. Now the road bears the name of Martin Luther King and at the fork honors Dr. King's number two man, Ralph David Abernathy. A neon sign advertised "Best Buy Caskets" to get the attention of the people of the neighborhood who would need both discounts and coffins. Beside it was a liquor store. My mother sighed again and I knew she was thinking that this was not what Dr. King died for.

"When I was a girl, it was nice over here, a real high-class area." Mama shook her head. "But now that all of *us* have moved in here, just look around." She snorted. "I bet the white folks wish they could have taken the cemetery with them when they all moved to Buckhead."

"It's kind of sad," Hermione said.

"Don't tell me about sad," Mama said. "I know all about sad."

I knew all about sad too. Dwayne gave me my engagement ring nine days ago. I was happy to have it, pleased to reach for items with my left hand. But I knew that this was a temporary happiness. I'd accepted the ring under false pretenses. I'd be found out eventually because there are some things that you just can't hide. I lay awake many nights, fondling my engagement ring, tapping my nail against the stone, rubbing the narrow gold band like a magic lamp. I woke in the mornings exhausted from wishing and missing Dwayne in advance.

Hermione stopped the car and got out. The chirp of the car alarm startled a pair of squirrels sunning themselves on Genevieve's marker. It was noon on the tenth of June. The heat and humidity swaddled us like a filthy blanket.

I wish that I could think of some other way to pay my respects to Daddy, to honor the memories that I think are mine. When I go to the cemetery with my mother and sister, I can't tell which stories of him live in my head, what information was reported by my eyes, ears, and hands. Much about what feels like memory to me happened before I was born or in the hours after I was sent to bed. I know that he liked to drink seven-and-seven, that he loved his mother, that he was overly competitive at dominoes and bid whist. But these memories are not mine. The thought pictures that belong to me are the silly incidents recorded by a ten-year-old, a kid who didn't know that these memories would be all that I would have to carry me into my womanhood.

So what I remember are things like this: Daddy chewed gum two sticks at a time, different flavors. He would force me to clean my room, and when I finished, he would come in, compliment me on the clean floor, and say, "This is a good start. Call me again when you're finished." Daddy never gave in to fake tears, but would melt if my sobbing was genuine. I remember things like this. Things that are not enough when I try to remember him as a father, let alone when I try to remember him as a man.

The graveside ritual never lasted for more than a half hour. There really wasn't much to do. I put most of the flowers in the depression in the plaque with Daddy's name and dates; we gave the rest to Genevieve. The three of us stood there quiet, as though we were waiting for something to happen.

"Lincoln would have liked Dwayne," Mama said. "They are cut from the same cloth."

I lifted my bowed head and looked at Hermione, who nodded.

Dropping my eyes to my navy-blue shoes, I wondered if my mother was right. I wondered what my father would have done if my mother had told him that she couldn't have children. If she had whispered that truth while he fished through his pockets for a metal church key.

"Oh, Ariadne," Mama said, touching my stomach. "Who's going to give you away?"

The only time you could really see my mother's age was when she cried. Tears snagged in the grooves under her eyes. On her neck the loose skin trembled with her quiet coughs.

Hermione took a few steps toward our mother, nudging me aside. My sister was taller than Mama, rounder and bigger as well. She pulled Mama to her chest and rocked her in a moment of role reversal that made me jealous, dizzy, and lonely. I stood there, beside them, quiet and respectful. My heels sank into the grassy yard and I twisted them in further, trying to ruin my good shoes, trying to sacrifice something, since I couldn't make myself cry.

Two rows east, a funeral had just ended. The box, slim and baby pink, was poised over a grave, red and open as a mouth. A blanket of Astroturf hid most of the displaced earth. The casket, pastel and cozy, was perfect for a ten-year-old girl. Hermione rocked Mama, the two of them turning their memories over in their heads like dough.

With eyes so dry they burned, I looked over my shoulder at the men burying the girl. An orange bull-dozer was parked nearby, but the workmen completed this job by hand, quietly piling shovelfuls of bloody earth, pausing to blot their sweaty faces with their dirty shirttails.

I remembered myself when I was ten, the age of the girl in the box. The year Daddy died. I had gone to the beauty parlor for the first time, on my birthday, for Shirley Temple curls, held off my face with a wide purple ribbon. I remembered how disappointed I had been not to look sweet like Cindy on *The Brady Bunch*. Instead, I looked like me, too tall and too developed to be just ten, a woman's face under a mop of oily ringlets.

Where was Daddy at that time? Did he like my new hair? Did he try to cheer me up and tell me that I was pretty as Lena Horne? Did he worry about me? Did he know that I wasn't safe at ten years old wearing a B-cup? Did he and Mama talk late at night about me, finally deciding that they would ignore it? Treat me like nothing was happening so that maybe nothing would happen?

Two rows over, the dirt fell on the pink coffin in a fine flurry like wedding rice. I shut my eyes respectfully and tried to remember my father. When had he decided that I was too much of a woman to sit on his lap? I was nine when I tried to climb up and he shoved me onto the floor. Was that when I decided that I wanted curls for my birthday?

I sucked in clean air to clear these memories. This is not what I wanted to recollect. I wanted to remember times that he took me for ice cream or maybe a time that he and I snuck out and went to the circus without Mama and Hermione. I am sure that we went on some special outings, just the two of us. After all, I had been Daddy's girl, by all accounts. When he was alive, I was somebody's favorite.

Why couldn't I remember it?

Mama prayed a moaning prayer into Hermione's breast.

The workers kept shoveling red clay with small spades. Listening to their grunts, rhythmic like the men on a chain gang, I remembered my father's voice. "Have you taken Ariadne to the doctor?"

I had just gotten home from school, fourth grade.

Mama said, "I made an appointment. It isn't exactly an emergency."

Daddy said, "I saw her today, walking up the driveway. Just out of the corner of my eye. She looked like a grown-ass woman."

I'd gone into my room and looked at myself in the tall, narrow mirror tacked to the back side of my bedroom door. I had been wearing a navy-blue pullover with my green jumper, even though the weather was warm, so boys couldn't see my bra strap. My B-cup breasts pushed against the green and white embroidered flowers on my girl-sized sweater. I may have looked like a grown woman, but at the same time, I looked like me. I'd kicked the door with my orange and white sneakers, hoping to ruin the mirror in an angry smashing of glass. But it had stayed whole, reminding me how much I'd grown in the last year.

When we left the cemetery, the girl was only half buried.

Mama noticed her as we walked back to the car, three unhappy women. "It's so hard to lose a child."

The phone was ringing when I got home from Westview. I undid the locks in a hurry, hoping that it was Dwayne. He often called when I was just walking in the house, like he knew somehow that I was available. I scurried into the kitchen, racing for the wall phone. I needed to hear his voice to remind me that he was still mine.

Rochelle was home, sitting at the oak table with her fiancé, Rod. They were drinking organic beer from purple bottles. I've never quite gotten used to their fantastic otherworldly appearance as a couple. There was Rochelle with her dark skin and silver hair; Rod was nearly her perfect inverse. He was about as white as you could get and still be black. His inky locks fell just below his shoulders. I wondered what sort of children they would produce.

Rochelle shook her head as I reached for the phone.

"It's your mother," Rod whispered as though she could hear us through the phone.

"She called four times already," Rochelle added, just as my mother's voice spoke out from the answering machine.

"Rochelle, this is Mrs. Eloise Jackson. I am trying to reach my daughter."

Rod pulled two beers from a cardboard carton and handed one to me. "She was crying when she called a few seconds ago."

I took the beer, feeling slightly embarrassed. How much had Rochelle told him about me?

Rochelle said, "How'd it go?"

I said, "Everyone's still dead."

Rod winced.

Rochelle massaged my shoulder with one hand and held tight to her bottle with the other. I tilted my face and kissed her fingers before taking a swallow of beer, which tasted faintly of raspberries. They talked honeymoon destinations and made fun of their travel agent. I tried very hard to care, or at least appear to care.

When my mother called again, I talked loud over her

voice streaming from the answering machine. I tried very hard not to care, or at least to appear not to care.

The phone rang a third time as Rod was making the case for honeymooning in a developing nation.

Rochelle said to me, "Do you want to take that in the living room?"

I could imagine my mother sitting at the smoky-glass kitchen table, still wearing her beige suit with gold brocade. She'd have removed her contact lenses, experiencing the world by touch through her blurry gaze. I didn't know why she wanted to talk to me, but my mother is a woman who doesn't strive to be understood. I didn't want to have this conversation, but I had to. I took the call with a two-beer buzz, lying on the hardwood floor, staring at the water-stained ceiling.

"I'm worried about you," she said.

"There's nothing to worry about," I said. "I just got a little emotional out there, that's all."

My mother sighed. "My girls just lie and lie. Hermione's so good at it. She should figure out a way to make her living from bending the truth. Do you think I would have let her marry Earl Phinazee if she had been honest about it?"

"No, ma'am."

"But you are not much of a liar. You try, but it's just not you. I am your mother. I know you. I was the first person to ever see your face."

"I know."

"So tell me," she said. "What's going on?"

It felt like a question that wasn't really a question, as

though Mama knew already and just wanted to see if I was capable of honesty, if I would fess up, tell the truth.

"Dwayne is going to leave me," I said at last.

Kitten padded into the room and settled himself on my chest. I rubbed his furry back and waited for my mother to speak.

"What did you do?" she said.

"Nothing." I stroked the cat and he closed his slit-eyes. "I just think he's going to leave me, that's all."

"Oh, baby," she said. "What happened?" Her tone was soft and sugary. This was the way mothers were supposed to be. Warm and omniscient at the same time. Her words were like kind hands, soft and scented. I wasn't used to this sort of affection from her. Tears pricked the corners of my eyes.

"I don't know."

"He wouldn't leave you with a child to raise on your own. He has his shortcomings; I won't lie and say he isn't a little rough around the edges, but he wouldn't abandon you."

"There are so many things about me he doesn't know." I was crying for real now. I'm sure Mama was surprised; she hadn't seen me cry since Hermione left us. "So many things about me that you don't know."

"I'm your mother. I've known you since you were born."

"If Dwayne leaves me, I'll have a breakdown. I know I will."

"He's not going to leave you," Mama said. "And if he did, you wouldn't break down. You're a strong girl. Always have been, always will be."

I was reminded of a story that my mother likes to tell to show the world how "strong" I am. When I was four, I mentioned that there was a sore on my little arm. Mama was late for work; Daddy was out of town. She promised to look at it later and dropped me off at kindergarten. The "sore" was some sort of oozing, ulcerous wound that had to be lanced, drained, and stitched. The upshot of this story is that I didn't cry. Not even while the doctor sewed the wound together with hard tugs. Of all my childhood stories, this is one of my least favorites; it seems to me that someone should have noticed my condition earlier. Do you have to cry for your own mother to notice that your arm is festering?

And then there's another story that nobody likes to tell but that everybody remembers: I was only ten when Daddy died, but I didn't cry then either. I wore my nappy gray coat in the overwarm sanctuary to hide how my lace dress strained across my chest. Beside me, my mother and Hermione both cried quiet, ladylike tears. From the corners of my eyes, I watched each of them dab her eyes with the hand that was not holding the other's. I faced forward with my eyes on the box, so gray it was nearly silver, and tore at my cuticles with my nails. When that didn't hurt enough, I used my teeth. Blood scribbled down the first joints of my fingers and settled in the creases of my knuckles, where it dried. When I flexed my fingers, it flaked like old paint.

"I miss Daddy," I said into the telephone.

"Don't tell me about missing Lincoln. I know all about missing Lincoln."

When I first got my period, I didn't tell Mama for four months. Daddy hadn't been dead a month. I had known it was too soon for me to hit puberty and she would cry, so I used my sister's supplies for the first two times. Then I got caught trying to figure out how to use a tampon and Mama shook me hard by the shoulders and said that keeping secrets was the same as lying.

With a queasy sense of déjà vu I said, "I went to the doctor the other day. I'm sick."

"Oh my God," she said. "Is it HIV?"

The phone was slick in my wet, hot hands. I wiped them on the carpet and said, "They don't know how it happened. Maybe I was exposed to radiation, or maybe it's just because I got my period so early in the first place. It's not lupus, they checked for that."

"Cancer?"

"Mama, I'm menopaused. Already."

"You're twenty-five," she said.

"I know."

She was silent, even after I called her name three times. On the fourth time, I spoke loud enough to bring Rochelle trotting in from the kitchen. When my mother answered with a quiet "yes," I shooed Rochelle away.

"Mama?" I said. "You still there? Don't worry about what I just said. It's not that important. We can talk about it later. You're not crying, are you?"

She didn't say anything, but she was still on the line. I heard the clicks as she tapped her tongue against her teeth. "Mama?"

"He *is* going to leave you." She made this pronouncement almost casually, as if she were predicting rain. I could picture her busy, tidying up the kitchen as she spoke to me. "Oh, Ariadne, why didn't you meet somebody in college?"

"Mama, who was I supposed to marry in college? Nobody asked me."

She said, "It's the way you carried yourself."

"Mama, I'm sick. Are you listening to me?"

"It's the way you carried yourself," she said. "You and your sister both. I've been telling you about that ever since you were in high school. You stayed out all night when you were just sixteen. How did you think things were going to turn out?" Her voice splintered with tears. "You always thought it was cute to run around with this boy and that one. That's why nobody is on their knees for you—because you're always on your knees for them."

"It's not my fault," I said.

"Nothing is ever your fault," she said.

"I wanted to meet somebody," I whispered. "I tried." And this was true. What I had wanted from college, more than anything, was to star in a love story just like my parents'.

I hung up the phone and crawled to the corner of the empty living room, held Kitten close. I tried to be grateful. What my mother had said to me was bad, but it could have been worse. Kitten pressed my thigh with his paws as if he were kneading bread. Rochelle once said he does this because he was taken away from his mother when he was too small.

When the phone rang, Rochelle and I picked up at the same time, giving a simultaneous hello. My mother on the other end sounded confused, disoriented. Her voice quaked a bit, giving me a fleeting sense of what she would be like when she was old. Rochelle hung up, leaving me alone on the wires with my mother.

"Ma'am?" I said to her.

"Ariadne, we've been foolish. There are doctors, you know. Don't worry about money. Don't worry about anything. I am going to get you all fixed up."

Having delivered her message, she hung up, leaving me cradling the quiet handset in my trembling hands.

Chapter Ten

Keisha failed the GED examination. She hadn't missed it by much, but this was a pass-fail situation. Like so many things in life, almost didn't count for anything. She came to my office on the Wednesday afternoon that she had gotten the results. I hadn't seen Keisha in nearly a month. Her session was over and I had a new class of students. These were traditional GED students, adults who wanted nothing from me but assistance in learning to read.

Rochelle and I shared our office, which had been a bedroom in LARC's earlier incarnation. It was a good-sized room and we shared it like feuding sisters. While there was no clear line of demarcation separating her side from mine, it was obvious that the space was shared by two very different women. I was something of a minimalist at work. I brought the things I needed to help me do my job and that was it. My desk was nearly free of all clutter save a large calendar/blotter and a brandy snifter filled with potpourri. On the wall was my framed college degree and a plaque of the Serenity Prayer. Rochelle's desk was littered with photos in eclectic frames, snapshots mostly of herself, documenting each of the phases of her life. My favorite was a faded and cracked picture of her at the age of about four. She was in a petting zoo, all dressed in yellow and green. The photographer caught her fighting a baby goat over a cone of cotton candy.

Whenever people came into the office, even my students, they went right to Rochelle's side, drawn by the pull of something invisible but irresistible. I was marking papers when Keisha tapped on the door.

"Come in," I said, smiling when I realized that it was her.

Keisha walked in and snatched a photo from Rochelle's desk before plopping herself into a chair. The frame seemed to be carved from a coconut shell.

"Which one you got there?" I asked her.

She turned the shell toward me so that I could see a three-by-five of Rochelle and Rod dressed in ski gear. Rochelle's hair was as white and sparkly as the snow.

"You ever been skiing, Miss Aria?"

"Nope," I said, snapping the top onto my red pen and putting it in my desk drawer. "Where I'm from, black folks don't ski."

"Me either," she said. "I haven't ever really seen snow. I mean real deep snow."

"Me either." I smiled at her. "Look at you." It's amazing how much a pregnant woman can change in just five weeks. The last time I'd seen Keisha, she was obviously pregnant, but the evidence was only in her middle. From the breasts on up and the hips on down, she had looked like the other seventeen-year-old girls in the neighborhood—slim-faced with thin arms and shapely legs. But today she looked pregnant all over. Her cheeks were round and her forehead shiny. Her ankles protruding from under her sleeveless dress were thick and bloated. She wore her sandals unfastened.

"I don't know what I am going to do, Miss Aria."

"What's wrong?"

"I failed my GED." She handed me the pink computer-generated report. Looking at the little column of numbers, I wasn't terribly surprised. Only about fifteen percent of our students make a passing mark the first time around. Keisha had been my favorite student in terms of personality, but there had been others who worked harder.

"You'll take it again in the fall."

She shook her head. "It's not fair. Other people have their high school diplomas and they can't read and write and do math any better than me. I know all kinds of people who got their diploma and they don't even know what an adjective is." She reached her hand into her hair and scratched, shifting her blond braids up and down. "I'm fixing to have a baby and I don't have anything at all. I'm living with my mama, my job is tired, and now I failed my GED."

Her eyes were shiny with tears and I opened my desk drawer, offered her a tissue, and then returned the box to its place. She dabbed her eyes carefully so as not to disturb her fluorescent eyeliner.

"You can take it again. Brush up on vocabulary and take it again."

"I don't want to take it again. I want to have my GED right now."

Lawrence tapped on the door. He stuck his head in and I smiled at the way he had arranged his curly hair to camouflage the thinning patch in the middle.

"Come on in," I said.

He entered the room, bringing his citrusy cologne. He wore his usual uniform of khakis and rumpled oxford shirt. "I don't mean to interrupt," he said. "I just need to get some paperwork from Rochelle's desk." He went to the desk and surveyed the heaps of manila folders. His hand hovered over the piles. "Do you think there is some sort of system here, or will I have to look at all of them until I find the one I want?"

"Well," I said, "I think the stuff closest to the center is what she was working on last."

"Aha," Lawrence said, reaching across the desk to pluck a green file folder from the middle. "NEH," he read aloud from the tab. "Just what I am looking for." To Keisha he said, "How are you, young lady?" He smiled and gave a nod of his head that seemed almost courtly.

"Terrible," she said.

"What's wrong?"

"GED results came back this week," I said, looking at him over her head as though we were her parents.

"Bad news?" Lawrence said.

"She almost passed," I said. "I am trying to cheer her up."

Lawrence knelt before her with crackling knees and said, "Lots of people don't pass the first time."

Keisha shifted in her chair. "Don't try and be nice to me."

Lawrence eased up with more knee-popping and took a step back. "What do you mean?"

"You're not getting my baby," she said. "Just because you have money and a nice job. I know what you're thinking. You think that now that I failed my GED, I really don't need to be raising a child."

"That wasn't what I was thinking at all," Lawrence said.

"It was," Keisha said. "It is exactly what you're thinking."

Lawrence looked to me, but there was nothing that I could do to help him. He looked at his watch as though he had just remembered some pressing appointment. "I'll have to bid you ladies adieu," he said.

"I can't stand faggots," she said when he was gone. "If God had meant for them to have babies, he would have gave them the right equipment to make them."

"Keisha," I said, "you know hate speech is not allowed at LARC."

"I'm sorry, Miss Aria," she said. "But people make me mad how they always think that they are better than you."

"Lawrence is a really nice person," I told her. "His partner, Eric, is nice too."

She rolled her eyes. "They are not getting my baby."

"Okay," I said. "No one is trying to force you to do anything. But you could do worse."

Lawrence and Eric did want to add a baby to their family. Lawrence more so than Eric, I thought. They tried to go through an adoption agency, but they couldn't get approved. As Eric put it, "There is no way in hell that the state of Georgia is going to give a newborn to two faggots like us." Lawrence tended to say things like, "Times are changing, but I don't know if things are going to change in time for Eric and me." The bottom line was they wanted a baby and they didn't have a way to get one. A couple of years ago they were negotiating with a pair of Senegalese lesbians. The women wanted green cards and Lawrence and Eric wanted a baby. I am not sure what became of that situation. All I know is that the ladies stopped coming around and Lawrence was depressed for three months.

"You can't tell me what to do," said Keisha.

So we sat in my office thinking our separate thoughts. Keisha fiddled with her hair. I used my teeth to peel dead skin from my lips. She put the coconut back on Rochelle's desk and picked up a red glass frame.

"I don't know why I am so depressed," Keisha said, looking at Rochelle, twelve years old, wearing a pale green pageant gown. "It's not like I was going to get my GED and my whole life was going to change. I would still be working at Subway. It's not like somebody promised me a raise. I just wanted to have it before the baby got here."

I nodded.

"And Omar, he has his diploma and I know he's not

smarter than me. He's the one gave me money to take the test, and now I have to tell him that I failed it. I get tired of disappointing everybody." She leaned forward and planted her elbows on the edge of the desk and rested her face in her hands.

"What are you doing now?" I asked her.

"I'm sitting here." She rubbed her stomach.

"I mean this evening."

"I have to work at ten," she said. "But until then, nothing really."

"Dwayne is coming to pick me up in a few and we are going to get something to eat. Do you want to go with us?"

"I'm on a budget," she sighed.

"Dwayne will pay."

"I don't eat pork."

"That's okay."

I sent her to the front porch to look out for Dwayne. As she walked toward the front door with her sandals flapping against her heels, I tiptoed to Lawrence's office and tapped on the door.

"Yes?" he said.

"I just wanted to tell you that I am leaving."

"That's fine," he said, flipping through the green folder that he had taken from Rochelle's desk.

"I'm sorry about that scene in there."

He looked up from the folder and raised his eyebrows and tried to appear arch. "Nobody said working non-profit was easy."

"She didn't mean it the way it came out," I said.

"Yes, she did, Aria. Your gifted student and the state

of Georgia are of one mind." He turned his face back to the folder. "Lock the front door when you leave. I'm going to be here until late."

I wanted to tell him that I knew how he felt, though I probably did not. How can you know what another person is going through when your own life is so different from his? People had done this to me often enough, telling me that they knew how I felt because they had suffered this or that loss, felt some sort of pain. The words were in my mouth to tell Lawrence that I knew what it was not to be able to make the family you want to have, not because you are a bad person or because you haven't tried hard enough, but because you just can't. I could predict his response, his words, polite enough, thanking me for my empathy, my generosity of spirit. And I could imagine his thoughts, that no, I couldn't possibly empathize. Our situations were not the same at all.

I told Lawrence to have a good night. I asked him to say hello to Eric for me, easing myself out of the room and closing the door gently so as not to disturb him more.

Keisha waited on the wooden swing on the front porch. She moved herself back and forth by bending her legs. "Dwayne's not going to mind that I'm coming with you?"

Assuring her that it would be all right, I sat on the wooden swing beside her and we watched bees force their way inside the buttercups growing in the yard. Keisha picked at a bump over her brow. I moved her hand from her face. She smiled over at me and I realized how much I'd missed her over the last five weeks.

When Dwayne pulled up in front of the house, I waved at him. He let down the window and smiled. Keisha got in the back and I slid into the front passenger seat. Dwayne leaned over and kissed me quick on the lips. He did this every time that I got into the car, but it seemed more special when we had an audience. I introduced him to Keisha and she gave him a demure hello.

"Where do you want to go and eat?" He looked into the rearview mirror when he spoke.

"I don't care. Something American," she said.

Dwayne nodded his head. "That's what I'm talking about. I'm going to start bringing you with us every time we go to dinner. I need another vote for regular food. Aria, she always wants to try something different—Thai, Vietnamese, Ethiopian. Keisha and me are in the mood for plain old American."

"Let's get pizza," Keisha said.

"There's Felini's on Ponce," I said.

"Let's find some regular pizza," Dwayne said. "I don't want no pineapple or artichokes on mine."

"Gross," Keisha said.

"Where's a Pizza Hut?" Dwayne looked to me.

"Nearby?" I said, thinking. "There's one all the way on Fairburn Road. We used to go there when I was little. Make a U-turn and go the other way down MLK."

He put on his blinker and I breathed deep to still my twitching stomach. Why did I insist on doing this to myself? I could have sent him down I-20 or we could have taken Cascade Road and crossed over. The way we were headed, we would pass the curve, the bend in the road where my father had veered from the pavement into the bark of a one-hundred-year-old magnolia.

Keisha asked Dwayne to turn the radio up and she sang along in a reedy soprano. I closed my eyes and concentrated on my breath. Breathe, Rochelle said on the answering machine, and you will know peace. I pulled the air inside of me and let it out. I pulled it in again and again. My head floated with so much air. I touched my forehead to the glass and looked the other way while Dwayne rounded the curve easily, driving with only one hand, and didn't hit anything at all.

We passed Westview Cemetery a few moments later. "That's where my father and sister are buried."

Keisha stopped singing and Dwayne gripped the steering wheel with both hands. "Sorry," Dwayne said. "Sorry," echoed Keisha. We rode the rest of the way in silence. I'd ruined the mood. "Sorry," I said.

Pizza Hut was closed. Not closed for the day, but closed for good. The burgundy building with its triangular panels had been converted to a beauty salon. A sign staked into the dirt said "Walk-ins Welcome." We could see the four barber chairs and shampoo bowls, but a Pizza Hut still looked like a Pizza Hut no matter what you did with it.

"When was the last time you were here?" Dwayne asked me.

"I don't know. A few years?"

"So now what?" Keisha said. "I'm hungry."

I was disappointed that the restaurant was gone. Pizza had been Hermione's and my favorite treat. In the seventies food was different than it was now. Then pizza delivery was an innovation that existed only on television shows, along with Chinese food that you ate right out of paper cartons. If we wanted pizza, we had to go to Pizza Hut on Fairburn Road. It was an expensive meal, so we went only on special occasions like birthdays, but the Pizza Hut Man, tall and lean, always remembered us. Mother had taken us there only once after the accident; the Pizza Hut Man must have seen the article, recognizing us from our family Christmas photo, printed on the crease of the morning paper. He didn't ask after Daddy or Genevieve, nor did he charge us for our meal. Mother thanked him; I realize now that we never went back.

"It's a Church's across the street." Keisha pointed.

"That'll work," Dwayne said.

We left the car in the Pizza Hut parking lot and stood on the curb, waiting to cross the street. Dwayne put his hand on Keisha's shoulder as cars zipped by.

"Okay," he said, and we advanced to the median. The breeze from the passing vehicles lifted the hem of Keisha's dress. "All right," he said, and we followed him to the opposite side of the street.

Keisha, flushed and excited, trotted ahead to the door of the restaurant. "Y'all are too slow," she called over her shoulder.

"That chicken ain't going nowhere," Dwayne said.

He went to the counter and ordered ten pieces of chicken, coleslaw, corn on the cob, and sweet tea. Keisha and I put ourselves to work gathering plastic cutlery, condiments, napkins, and straws. She and I chose a booth and sat on opposite sides, waiting for Dwayne.

Keisha said, "You remember when they used to say that Church's Chicken was owned by the KKK?"

I laughed. "That was an urban legend."

"What's that?"

"A lie."

Keisha laughed. "It was probably KFC that started it."

Dwayne walked over with a heaping brown tray. "Here it is." He set the food on the table and slid into the booth beside Keisha. I had scooted close to the wall to make room for him, but now I eased myself toward the middle.

My mother used to say that when you have a daughter, you lose your husband. This was, of course, before she lost her husband for real. She'd say this after church, laughing, when people would comment that Hermione and I were such daddy's girls. We'd each hold one of his hands and Mama would walk behind, reminding us girls to stand up straight or warning us not to ruin our stockings.

Keisha pulled a glistening ear of corn out of its greasy plastic sheath and plopped it on her paper plate. She sighed, picked up the corn, held it to her mouth without biting it. She put it down and sighed again.

"What's up?" Dwayne asked her.

"I just have a lot on my mind," Keisha said. "I lost my appetite."

"Things on your mind like what?" Dwayne winked at me.

"I failed my GED," she said.

"Will they let you take it again?"

She nodded with a little-girl pout. Her braids, festooned with glass orbs, covered the left side of her face like a beaded curtain.

"Aria will tutor you and you'll pass it. Right, baby?"

"I told her she would pass it the next time."

"See," Dwayne said, and tapped her shoulder with his.

Keisha flicked the braids over her shoulder and smiled like she believed him.

"Eat," he said. "Chicken is brain food."

She smiled without showing teeth and pulled the fried skin from a chicken thigh. Under the table I felt Dwayne's hand on my knee.

He bit into his own drumstick. "The KKK know they make some good chicken."

"That's an urban legend," Keisha told him.

"Straight?" Dwayne said. "That's good. Now I don't have to feel guilty."

"You so crazy," she said to him. "Move over so I can get out. I need to go to the ladies' room."

While she was gone, Dwayne leaned across the table. "How old is that kid?"

"Seventeen."

"She looks fifteen. I hate to see young girls pregnant like that. It's depressing."

"There are worse things that could happen," I said.

"And she doesn't even have her GED?"

"She'll get it next time."

"But you know what I mean. What chance does she have?"

Keisha came back to the table wearing a fresh coat of lipstick. Dwayne told her that she looked very pretty.

"Do you have kids?" she asked Dwayne.

He took two bites of slaw before he spoke. "Yeah," he said. "A little boy."

I wished he hadn't told her. It cheapened Dwayne somehow, his having a little boy living in another state.

"How old were you when he was born?"

"Eighteen," Dwayne said without looking at her. He held an ear of corn by its wooden stick and gnawed at it.

"Are you a part of his life?"

"I try to be," Dwayne said.

"That's good," Keisha said. "That's good." She rooted around in the box of chicken and found a wing. Pulling it apart, she said, "A lot of people have kids young. It's not like I'm the only person this ever happened to."

We dropped Keisha at home after eight o'clock. She was flushed, happy, and tired, like kids after a day at Six Flags.

"I wish I didn't have to go to work," she said. "If you ever get hungry late at night, come to Subway. The one on Abernathy. I'll hook you up with a twelve-inch."

"Cool," Dwayne said. "I like the roast beef."

We sat in the car and waited for her to make her way into the apartment. She blinked the lights on and off to let us know that she was in safe.

"Seems like you should have to get some sort of license before you have a child," Dwayne said. "She's a nice kid and all of that. But can you imagine if she was your *mother*?"

"She might do okay," I said, suddenly protective of Keisha. Dwayne had no idea what it was like to be a teenage girl, to be evaluated constantly by strangers and people you loved. When you are a young woman of a certain age, people older than you and some of your peers are always looking at you sideways, deciding if you are fast, if you are easy, if you were the kind of girl who was born to break her mother's heart.

"Look at you," I said. "You had a kid young too."

"It's different for a man."

"It shouldn't be."

"But it is. A seventeen-year-old girl that's a mother is in a lot worse shape than a seventeen-year-old guy that's a father."

"What about Trey's mother."

"What about her?"

"I mean, what's her story? What is her life like?"

"Charla? I don't really want to talk about her. That's all over and done with."

"All right," I said, thinking that I probably knew more about her than was good for me anyway. She was his first girlfriend; he'd taken her to the prom. The boutonniere she'd given him was dried and dead in the box with his aunt Iola's ring. Charla and Dwayne weren't related, but they had cousins in common. That's how things are in little towns. Charla was the kind of woman that Dwayne didn't have to explain things to. They sang from the same hymnbook in church. When her daddy passed, Dwayne's own father was one of the pallbearers.

I only asked because I wondered where she was right now. I wondered if her ambitions included Dwayne.

He shrugged. "Trey is happy where he's at. I send money every month. Charla has never, not once, taken me to court. I take care of my boy; I see him when I can."

"When we get married," I said, "you could send for him if you wanted to."

He leaned over and kissed me. "Why would I want to do that? Mix his life all up? Trey's happy where he's at."

"But are you happy, Dwayne?"

"Grown men don't get to be happy."

After we had picked up a video from Blockbuster, we drove over to my house. Rod's Honda was parked on the curb. "It's Cosby time," Dwayne said.

I swatted him on the arm. "Don't make fun of them. I like Rod; he's cool."

"He looks gay with that ponytail."

I shushed him as I slid my key in the lock. Opening the front door, we found that Rochelle and Rod had beat us to the TV in the living room.

"Hey, Penny," Rochelle said, rising from the Huey Newton Seat that she had dragged in for the night. She took my face and kissed it. She tiptoed, hugging Dwayne, pressing her cheek to his. Dwayne jerked his head upward in a gesture to Rod, who replied with a weak wave.

"Want to watch a movie with us? We just started looking at it. We can rewind."

I stole a glance at the television screen. The movie was black-and-white and the characters looked European and depressed. "Thanks, but we are going to watch something in my room."

"We're going to watch *Rocky III*," Dwayne said, shaking the plastic video case at them. "I like to see some action."

"Have fun," Rochelle said, waving us away.

Dwayne was still chuckling when we closed the door to my bedroom. "I just like messing with them. Did you see Rod's face when I said what we was going to watch? That brother is too uptight for me."

I slid the video into the mouth of the VCR and sat on the bed beside Dwayne. I didn't care much what we watched; I just enjoyed sitting in the dark with him. He wrapped his arm around my shoulders and I rested my head on his chest, listening to his bass-drum heart.

"Your mother called me today," he said.

"What did she say?" I tried to make my voice casual, but the muscles in my shoulders kinked tight.

"Nothing. She just wanted to say hello."

I didn't like the idea of my mother talking to Dwayne without my supervision. What if she said something to him about what a good man he was not to leave me despite my problems? I could see her telling him this, since she made a point to tell it to me at least once a week. "Don't talk to my mother when she calls you. Just let the machine pick up."

"How come? Don't you think I need to be friendly with my mother-in-law?"

"I just don't like the idea of her being in our relationship, okay? Just trust me on this one. I know her better than you."

"You make your mother out to be such a big bad wolf, but she seems like a nice lady to me."

"She's not. You've got to take my word for it."

After the first twenty or so minutes of the movie Dwayne said, "You know what I said in the car about not wanting to talk about Charla?"

"Yeah."

"I was just thinking about the way that might have sounded. I don't want to talk about her, but it's not like I still have feelings for her. She was my girl back in high school, but that was a long time ago."

"I understand."

He rubbed his hair with the flat parts of his hands. "Charla. That girl. She called me about six months ago to tell me that she was getting married to some dude in the service. I tell her I'm happy for her. What the hell else am I supposed to say? So I'm saying congratulations over and over."

I moved my head from his chest, propping myself up on my elbow so I could look at him. Behind me on the television screen a boxer spit out a bloody mouthpiece.

"She says that she is going to send me some paperwork that she wanted me to sign so that her new husband can adopt Trey. The dude is going to give Trey his name and everything.

"I didn't know what to say to her. She called me up asking it all casual, telling me this is just so that Trey can get health benefits and things like that. But I'm not crazy. I know that when you sign a paper saying someone else can adopt your kid, it means that you are giving up your whole parental-rights situation." He shut his eyes and shook his head.

"So what did you say?"

"Hell, no."

"And what did she say?"

"She told me that I was being selfish."

His chest heaved as he scraped his lower lip with his teeth. "I don't want to lay all this on you."

"Don't worry about it," I said. "We're getting married. We don't have separate problems anymore."

"There is no way I can say this without it coming out wrong."

"Just say it."

"When we first got engaged, before you lost the baby . . ."

My heart splashed in my chest. My pulse beat in my ears. This was not a conversation I wanted to have. This was not information I wanted to know.

"When me and you were having our baby, I went ahead and signed the papers."

"Why did you do that?"

"Because it seemed like she was right. I *was* being selfish. Here I was, getting mad because some other dude wanted Trey to have his name. Trey didn't even have *my* name. Well, he's Dwayne the third, but he has Charla's last name. And when I thought that I was about to have another baby, and I was getting to go ahead with my life, I decided to stop tripping and just get out of Charla's way."

I covered my mouth with my hands. "Dwayne, I wish you hadn't done that."

He shrugged and pulled me back down so that my head rested on his warm chest again. "It's okay." He stroked my hair. "We'll have our kids anyway. We'll do it right."

"Can't you call her and tell her you changed your mind?"

"I didn't change my mind," he said, lifting my chin so that he could kiss me. Dwayne shifted our weight so that I lay flat on my back. Without ending the kiss, he unfastened my blouse.

This was his way of talking without talking, saying that things were going to be all right, that he wasn't angry with me. But I knew things that he didn't know.

"Wait a second," I said, moving his hand, speaking through his kisses. "But what about Trey? You can't just give him up, swap him out for a baby we haven't even had yet."

Dwayne moved away from me and lay back on the pillows. "He's my son, but at the same time he's not mine all the way. I grew up with my mother, father, sister, all in the same house. I'm not Trey's father the way my old man is my daddy. I don't know if I can really be a father with me and Charla not being together. With me living out here and him being back in Anniston. So this other dude wants to be Trey's dad. He wants to be Charla's husband. I feel like I'm just getting in the way."

I moved to touch him then. It was my turn to talk without talking. If telling him my secret would have given Trey back to Dwayne, I would have stared down my fear of losing and told him everything that the doctor had told me, but there was nothing I could do to reconnect the two of them, Dwayne II and Dwayne III.

Sooner or later he would have to know about the failings of my body. But on that particular moment on that particular night, I would offer him everything that I knew to give. I knew what it was like to look at your kin and not feel what you know you should. More than anyone, I understood why a person would want to make a new family, to create a new ring of relations, new possibilities for love and acceptance. If I couldn't give Dwayne exactly what he wanted, I could offer him empathy, the thing that connected us from the beginning.

Following my lead, Dwayne undressed us both in a determined and melancholy silence. He reached for my nightstand where I kept the condoms, but he didn't open the tiny drawer. Instead, he picked up the remote control and made the television louder to camouflage our noise for the benefit of Rochelle and Rod, watching their foreign film in the living room. Dwayne turned back to me and looked into my face. He raised his eyebrows, asking for permission. I closed my eyes against his question.

"Why does it seem so sad?" he said.

"It's hard to lose someone."

He stroked my face, kissing my shut eyes, then my forehead, then my mouth. I was touched by his tenderness and his earnest caresses. Making love is different when you are trying to make a baby. Dwayne was open to me in a way that he had never been before. He looked in my face as we moved together. He whispered that he loved me. I stared at the water-stained ceiling, listening to the noise of us, the noise of the television, and the noise of the night.

Chapter Eleven

Phinazee's, the barbershop, is in a good location that has stayed pretty good for the last forty years. It's on Lee Street, just a couple of blocks from the express-way—near where the east-west freeway crosses the north-south one. It's convenient for anyone who wants a haircut bad enough. Mr. Phinazee likes to brag that in almost fifty years of business—when his father ran the business to when Earl himself took over—there has never been a robbery. "It's because we are part of this community," he said. "I let my little girl work in here by herself," he said.

The little girl he is talking about is his thirty-four-year-old daughter, Colette, who more than *works* in the family business, she *runs* the place, although her daddy keeps all the paperwork in his own name. Before Little Link was born, Coco was heir apparent for the shop, which had grown to accommodate four chairs. It only made sense. Nobody said it out loud, but she could cut heads better than her daddy ever did. On top of that, she was gifted on the business end of things. She changed Phinazee's to keep up with what the college students wanted without alienating the neighborhood types. A sign above the pricing sheet said "Locktician Available Upon Request." She let her daddy come in on Wednesdays to take care of the old heads who wanted scissor cuts and hot-lather shaves.

When Little Link was born, Mr. Phinazee called his lawyer to change his will. When he dies, Phinazee's will be handed down from father to son as it was in the previous generation. Even Hermione, who has no love for Coco and vice versa, protested that this wasn't right. Mr. Phinazee listened to my sister and added a codicil indicating that Coco would always have the right to work there and if Little Link dies first and childless, Coco would be next in line.

"What if Link doesn't want to be a barber?" Hermione asked.

Mr. Phinazee said, "Every man wants to be his own boss."

"What if you die tomorrow?" Coco asked. "Who will sign the checks?"

"Baby," Mr. Phinazee said, "I'm healthy. And I thought of that already. You'll hold power of attorney until he's old enough. And don't be down in the mouth, Colette. I love you. I've taken good care of you, too, in my will."

❧

Coco didn't greet me when I came into the shop. She lifted her head at the jangle of the brass bells, but she didn't smile or say hello. Her silence is understandable, I guess. In addition to her anger about the lost inheritance, she was in her early twenties when Hermione married her father, and it must have been difficult to accept as a stepmother a kid she used to babysit. Even still, Coco knows enough about our family to know that we lived under extenuating circumstances. She was there the day of the accident. She was the one who answered the police's call. She should know as well as anyone that none of us can be held completely responsible for the things that we have done.

Despite Coco's territorial behavior and the general negative vibe, Phinazee's was a historic landmark for my family as well. Daddy once worked here sweeping up clots of hair, washing toilets, and polishing the plate-glass window. Whenever I am in the shop, I picture him there wearing worn but clean clothes. This is an image concocted entirely from my imagination, I know, but it is as real to me as anything else.

Walking in the shop on a Saturday morning, I was glad to see that business was good. All three barbers were busy and five men waited for their turn in the chairs. I looked around to see what had been added since the last time I had come by, almost a year ago. Coco was always building, improving things. I made note of the credit card logo in the window. A glass case displayed shampoos and oils.

I was also pleased to see Coco, although the feeling was far from mutual. She had no use for any of the women in my family—not even my mother, who had been against Hermione's marriage as much as Coco herself, and not me, who had no say in the matter. I never understood how she could throw us away so easily. She had been the one to rescue me from the car on the day of the accident. She had spoken my name in my ear and worked it into my heart.

"Is Hermione here yet?" I asked over the buzz of clippers.

Coco looked up from the fade she was working on, not smiling, not acknowledging me as anyone more special than one of the guys that came into the shop selling counterfeit watches and colognes. "You're looking at everyone that's here."

I took a seat in a row of men variously aged and variously unkempt, each waiting for a seat in one of the barber chairs. A few years ago, right after I stopped relaxing my hair, I wore my hair in a short fade that required weekly visits to a barber. When I would walk in the door, the men would hush whatever conversations had raged before I arrived. I sat in the barber's chair, feeling faintly guilty, an uninvited guest who had no other place to go. Phinazee's wasn't like that; Coco's feminine presence shaped the character of the place. She didn't do anything obvious like plant flowers out front or require the barbers to iron their shirts, but she managed to civilize it a little bit. It was like being in the home of a favorite aunt, the kind of woman who would let you drink but wouldn't let you curse.

I looked at the clock over the wall of mirrors. A quarter past ten. Hermione was fifteen minutes late.

I picked up a year-old *Jet* that fell open to the Beauty of the Week. The Beauty was a big girl, one dessert away from a weight problem. Posing in such a way to emphasize her cleavage while deemphasizing her stomach, she reminded me of Hermione. Colette, on the other hand, was nothing like my sister. Short but lean, she wore a loose-fitting sundress covered by a white barber's jacket. Her hair was Caesar shorn and neat. Her only ornamentation was a pair of heavy gold hoops.

"Your sister said for you to meet her *here*?" Coco said.

"That's what she said."

"I don't understand people," Colette said, swabbing her customer down with bay rum.

When the chair was empty, a young man stood, wearing the red and black uniform of the Shrine of the Black Madonna. Light-skinned and chunky, he reminded me of Head Cheese. And this, of course, reminded me of Dwayne.

"Coco," I said, "did you know that I was getting married?"

"Colette," she corrected me. "I think my father said something about that."

"Colette. Do you think you would like to be in the wedding party, maybe?"

"You have a date already?" She folded the customer's ear and buzzed the clippers behind it.

"Not this November, but the next one."

"In my book," Coco said, "it doesn't count if it is more than a year away."

"Okay. Maybe I'll ask you later."

She nodded to the guy from the Shrine. "Now, Jamal," Coco said, "that don't make no sense. Waiting this long to do something about your head."

Jamal smiled. "My money been funny."

"You need to sell some more bean pies, then."

"The Shrine don't sell bean pies."

"All I know," Colette said, snapping a black cape around his neck, "all I know is that it's going to take me half the morning to turn you back into a human being."

She chuckled and I remembered how kind she'd been before Hermione married her daddy. I suppose she had a right to her anger; Coco has known her share of loss too. Her mother died only three years before we lost our father. Lupus had taken Mrs. Phinazee. I was only seven or so, and the word was frightening and myste-rious.

"I hope that you would be able to be a hostess, at least," I said. "I think Little Link will be the ring bearer."

"Uh-huh," she said over the buzz of clippers.

I sat and looked out the plate-glass window, deciding not to say anything else to Coco. I was sincere in my de-sire to include her in my wedding, but I didn't want to seem to be bragging. On more than one occasion I have run into some vague acquaintance in the mall or at the bank. The hellos would be barely over before the girl was shoving her ring in my face, gloating at the sight of my naked knuckle. Or at least that is how it always seemed to me. Colette wasn't married, and as far as I knew, she wasn't even dating anyone, had never dated anyone. But she didn't wear her solitariness the way a lot of single women did. For her it seemed like a choice. For everyone else it seemed like a sentence.

I fidgeted in my seat, waiting to spot Hermione's minivan. Some people look like their dogs, but my sister looked like her car: large, round, but strangely aerodynamic.

The road just outside Phinazee's was busy like a Third World market. Vendors sold incense, bootleg CDs, body oils, T-shirts, and baked goods. Cars of all types, from SUVs with rhinestoned vanity plates to rusted Toyotas without air-conditioning, inched down Lee Street. Across the four-lane road, at Popeye's Chicken, a couple of pedestrians used the drive-through. There were also a few college students, the ones who didn't go home for the summer, seeming both at home and out of place in this environment. I could spot them easily, not just because the girls wore knit shorts with the name of their school stitched across their behinds, but because of their way of moving place to place, gesturing with their pretty hands, noticing only one another.

Among the throngs of people, I noticed a pregnant girl buying incense from a skinny Rastafarian. I got up from the chair and pushed open the front door. The brass bells jangled behind me. "I'll be right back," I called to Colette.

I trotted out of the shop, but slowed down and stopped myself several paces behind Keisha, who held three sticks of Egyptian Love incense to her nose.

"Buy five," the Rasta said, "I'll give you one free."

"You not trying to cheat me, are you?" Keisha said. "You see I'm pregnant and everything."

"No, sister," said the Rasta. "I wouldn't cheat my queen. Buy three, I'll give you two."

She seemed different somehow than she did sitting in my office. Her blond braids and airbrushed nails were not so garish. Her pregnancy was more graceful; her motions as she traveled were evidence of the perfection of nature, like the clumsy bumblebees who manage to fly anyway. I raised my hand to call out to her, but I closed my mouth, not wanting to interrupt whatever magic was working for her this afternoon.

Keisha turned toward me as though she had heard my unvoiced greeting; I pretended to look at a selection of T-shirts offered by a nearby vendor, hiding my face among silk-screened cartoon women with Scarlett O'Hara waists and Hottentot behinds. Souvenirs from the last Freak-Nic. Half off if you bought two. The shirts buckled in the dirty breeze, waving their arms like they were struck with the Holy Ghost. Smiling, Keisha turned her attention back to the Rasta and went away with six sticks of incense without having to pay for any of them.

"Hey," I called finally. "Keisha!"

She turned on the ball of her foot, bobbing a little as she scanned the faces around her. I waved again, but somehow Keisha managed not to see me. I let her go, feeling oddly shy amid the throng.

When I returned to Phinazee's, Hermione's van was parked in the handicapped spot at an almost forty-five-degree angle. She was waiting in the shop, sitting in front of the shampoo bowl, arms crossed hard over her big chest.

The easy laughter and camaraderie that had enveloped the shop just fifteen minutes before were gone. The men were still there and the television was still turned to SportsCenter, but the only people in the room that mattered were Hermione and Colette.

"I was here at ten o'clock," I said as soon as I saw her expression.

"She was," Coco said, still working on the same guy's head.

"Let's go," Hermione said. "Let's just go." On her way out she grabbed two bottles of shampoo from a glassed-in display case. "Get whatever you want."

I looked over at Colette.

"That shampoo is six ninety-five," she called.

Hermione took another bottle. "Tell my husband to give you the money."

Hermione left. I was embarrassed to follow her, but I didn't know what else to do.

Hermione's minivan smelled of old french fries and vanilla air freshener. My seat was covered with a purple bath towel.

"Little Link spilled juice there," she explained.

At the stoplight, just before the freeway, a filthy man approached the window.

"Can you help me out?" he said.

Hermione thrust a bottle of shampoo into his pleading hands. He was still examining it when we drove off.

"I'm sorry," she said, "for being in such a bad mood. Colette is such a bitch."

"Why did you meet me over there in the first place? You know she has issues with us."

"Earl wanted me to hand-deliver her invitation to Link's birthday. Like that would help. That bitch makes me crazy."

"She used to be nice."

"I used to be nice too." Hermione changed the subject. "Are you ready to go see the wizard?"

This was the whole point of the escapade. Mama had made an appointment for me to see a reproductive endocrinologist at Emory University Hospital. My insurance wouldn't cover it, but Mother was prepared to pay out of pocket. According to Hermione, Mama was going to use the money from the college funds we never got to use.

"What's Dwayne saying about all of this?" she asked me.

"He doesn't know."

"About the appointment?"

"About any of it."

My sister put on her blinker and pulled into the parking lot of John A. White Park. We were technically out of the West End. The area was still sort of blue-collar, but it was what Rochelle would probably call blue-collar middle-class. A neighborhood very much like the one where I grew up. The parents here had money to pay for Little League but probably suffered from preemptive ulcers whenever they thought about the cost of college educations. But no one was worrying about that today; kids suited up in baseball uniforms milled about, laughing and knocking each other's caps off. Parents set up lawn chairs and wore ridiculous hats with umbrellas on top. Hermione put the van in park and turned toward me.

"He doesn't know that you're sterile?"

"Hermione," I said, "can we use a different word? 'Infertile' is what people say now."

"You know what I mean."

I did know what she meant, but there are some words that I just don't care for. If it were up to me, people would not be allowed to use the word "sterile" at all, not just when talking to me. The two syllables just hung in the air, like a mist of cheap perfume.

"But he doesn't *know*?" my sister persisted. "You're getting *married* and he doesn't *know*?"

I shrugged and looked at the debris on the floor of the minivan. Saltines ground to powder, stray napkins, ketchup packets. "If this doctor is everything she is supposed to be, there may be nothing to tell him."

"Aria," she said, "have you ever heard of honesty?"

"Why are you even asking?" I mumbled. "It's not like we are close."

"Would you believe me if I told you I feel terrible about that?"

"No," I said, softening my voice. "Not really."

I turned my face toward the tinted glass and watched a little boy swipe a granola bar out of the lunch cooler while his mother laughed with another lady. It was a beautiful Saturday morning and it made me want to cry. More than cry, weep. What would it be like to roll in the grass, beat my fists against earth, and just cry, scream, howl even? I'd been crying dainty tears for nearly three months now, but I didn't feel any better. It was like my emotions were constipated, caught in my gut and making me ill.

"Living at home was just too much," Hermione said. "You and Mama act like you were the only ones in the car that day. I was there too. Fifteen years old. Not as young as you. I respect that it must have been tough being in the car with Daddy all that time. But I was a child too. I was there when they took Genevieve. I was the oldest, but I was a kid too."

"You never talked to me after you got married. Never took me anywhere."

"I just wanted to escape," she said. "I love Earl and I am so happy with my life and with Little Link. But when I was eighteen and he said he would marry me, all I was thinking about was getting out. Getting away."

"Getting away from Mama? She was never mean to you. Not like she was with me."

"Please," Hermione said. "What do you know? You were just thirteen." She took a pack of cigarettes out of the glove compartment.

"You smoke?"

"There's so much that you don't know about me."

She opened the car door. "Let's walk. Earl doesn't like me to smoke in the van."

I got out and followed her to the far side of the park, where the bleachers stood empty. I plunked down beside her on the third row. She shook a dainty Capri cigarette out of the box and offered it to me. I took one, though I didn't smoke.

She lit hers and inhaled, then she took mine and held it to the red tip of her own until it caught. I took it from her, held it between my fingers, and took a foul-tasting breath.

"When I started seeing Earl, I was almost seventeen. Remember how he used to take us out right after Daddy died? I think he was trying to impress Mama, show her how good he was with the kids." She sucked hard on her cigarette, contracting her jaws. She blew rings. "See?" she said. "Bet you didn't know I could do that."

I shook my head and tried to remember the days she spoke about. Mr. Phinazee used to pick Hermione and me up and take us to the movies. He'd ask Mama to go, but she'd say, "I don't care for films." He had been old even then.

"Then he started taking me out by myself. Remember? You must have been thirteen? Colette was the first one to figure it out. I was hanging out in the barbershop more and more. One day she pulled me aside and said, 'You need to stay away from my motherfucking daddy.' Just like that. I'm *sixteen* and she's cussing me like that. This was right after she finished college.

"Anyway, I told her I didn't know what she was talking about and she started crying, talking about how her mama was spinning in her grave. I told her that I can't live my life worrying about offending the dead."

I was shocked. "You said that to her?"

"You goddamn right." Hermione pulled on her cigarette.

"What'd Coco do?"

"Slapped the shit out of me."

"What'd you do?"

"Nothing. Just stood there, hating her. I think she

was the one who told Mama. Remember when Mama started going through our stuff, making us take our baths with the door unlocked? Don't you remember all of this?"

I nodded. I did remember our room in disarray when we came home from school. That was when Mama kept asking us, *Why is it that you girls are determined to be sluts? I tried so hard to raise you right. I had to do it by myself but I tried so hard. Look at you. A slut and a slut's apprentice.*

"She really went apeshit."

"And even before that. Remember when you got caught messing around with your gym teacher?" Hermione said.

"It wasn't really like that. I didn't sleep with him."

"That's because you got caught."

"That wasn't my fault. I was just in the ninth grade."

She blew out a mouthful of smoke and waved it away. "I'm not trying to say anything about that. I'm trying to tell you what happened. Remember that dinner Mama fixed for us that night? The bloody chicken and the burnt potatoes?"

Of course I remembered this. We had been sitting at the glass table and Mama put out a platter of chicken and the bowl of potatoes. I could see that the potatoes were crusted dark brown and the carbon smell filled the dining room.

"Eat," my mother commanded us. "I cooked for you. I've been in the kitchen all evening. Eat."

I had cut my eyes at Hermione. She had grown into her plumpness by now and looked like a ripe peach.

She'd tightened her face on one side, a "hell no" expression.

Mama looked at me and said, "Are you hungry, Ariadne?"

"Yes, ma'am," I had said, and spooned the potatoes on my plate and took a chicken thigh.

"And you ate it," Hermione said. "I watched you. You ate it. You bit that chicken and the blood ran out. The meat was sort of see-through and slimy. I watched you chew it, swallow it, and when it started to come back up, you swallowed it again."

"But I had to," I said. "She was so mad about what had happened with Coach Roberts. And I felt guilty."

"I knew right then that I had to get out. Get away from Mama, get away from you. All this craziness. I called Earl that night and told him he was going to have to marry me right away because I was pregnant."

I tapped the ash of the slender cigarette into an empty Coke can. "You were pregnant?"

"No," she said. "But I had to tell him *something*. I got the idea from soap operas."

"So you lied too."

"That was different," she said, exhaling smoke.

"Different how?"

"Aria, Earl was our *play uncle*. It was sort of a bad situation from the jump. But where you're at is different. You and Dwayne can be like regular people. Don't screw it up playing these games. This is your chance to be *normal*. Don't you just want to be normal, finally?"

Looking into the pink tip of the smoldering cigarette, I said, "I'll never be normal."

My sister took it from my hand and took a deep drag. "Look, Aria. I'm sorry. I *am*. I had to get away from Mama. Crazy is contagious. How could I live my life if I had to stay in that house, stuck like flypaper?"

"So you just left me there with her?"

"I had to save myself," she said.

"You just left me."

"I had to."

"I hate you," I whispered.

"No, you don't."

Hermione was right in calling my bluff. I didn't hate her. Could I blame her, really? Would I have done the same thing if I had been her, offered a get-out-of-jail-free card from a most unlikely source?

"You still didn't tell me what you are going to do about Dwayne."

"I don't know," I said. "I am sort of hoping that things will work themselves out."

"Well," Hermione said, "you better hope this doctor is as good as everyone says she is."

We rode to Willow Street making easy, meaningless conversation about the personal lives of celebrities. I didn't share Hermione's breadth of knowledge on the subject, but I did my best to keep up with her. Mostly I smiled, pretending to be emotionally invested in the lives of the stars.

When we pulled up into the driveway, she looked at me and said, "Ready, Freddy?"

I smiled. This was what she'd say when we were kids after school. She'd say, "Ready, Freddy?" just before we'd open the front door and see what Mama had in store for us.

"Ready," I said.

"Okay." Hermione honked the horn twice. I climbed into the backseat, sitting on a blanket of crushed Goldfish crackers.

Mama bounded out of the house in an excellent mood, lipsticked and smiling. She was well dressed as always, in a smart linen pantsuit. Lilac.

"It seems like Dwayne should be here with us," Mama said over her shoulder as Hermione merged onto I-85. "If he's going to be your husband, he should be involved with this."

I was in the backseat, beside Little Link's empty car seat. My mouth tasted burned from the cigarette in the park. I sifted through the debris for gum or a mint.

"Well, this is just a consultation," Hermione said. "There's plenty of time for him to get involved."

"I told you that the doctor is a black lady, right?" Mama said, talking loud over the air rushing in the windows. "She's supposed to be the best."

"That's good," said Hermione.

"Well, she's got to be better than that old man you went to at first."

I didn't appreciate her potshot at Dr. Blackwelder. He was a nice enough man and I appreciated his empathy. But Mama was probably right. Dr. Blackwelder was seventy if he was a day. Although he'd had decades of experience, I questioned his mastery of the latest technology.

Still, it had seemed disloyal to ask him for my records.

"Getting a second opinion, are you?"

"My mother's making me."

"Where you going?"

"Emory," I mumbled.

He brightened. "Emory? Oh, yes. That's a fine idea. They really know what they're doing out there. Pricey, though." He looked at me through his oval spectacles.

"Dr. Blackwelder, why is this happening to me?"

He crossed his arms over his chest; his yellow-dotted bow tie bobbed as he spoke. "The human body is so delicate. When anything goes wrong, hormones, enzymes, just the slightest thing, everything starts to malfunction. Ariadne, the miracle is that people are able to live at all."

As I was leaving, he had taken my hand and spoken quietly. I worried that he would cry. "Come back after they've had a look at you. Come back here and tell me some good news."

"Yes, sir," I said.

"Good," he said before releasing me. "Chin up, young lady. Don't count yourself out just yet."

Regular people's lives are different than rich people's lives. This is something that everyone knows, either from watching TV or just from plain common sense. People who have things have things, and people who don't, don't. But short visits to the other side really let a person see what this means in a daily sort of way.

Reproductive endocrinology must pay pretty well; the doctor's office was well appointed, to say the least. It wasn't so extravagant that the nurses offered you cappuccino or anything like that, but it was nice. Paintings hung on the wall, the real thing, not just framed prints. The whole place smelled sweet like a high-end gift shop.

Mama, Hermoine, and I sank into comfortable chairs in the waiting room, where a white couple sat, heads bent over a shiny brochure. The woman was about Hermione's size, but she didn't carry it as well. Where Hermione favored close-fitting V-necks, the woman in the waiting room wore a beige cotton tunic, expensive but shapeless, and a faded pair of leggings. Red acne dotted her forehead. Her husband, thin and rangy, seemed to be taking better care of himself. His chinos and polo shirt looked pert and fresh from the dry cleaners.

A framed poster on the wall asked "What is infertility?"

"This is nice," Mama said.

"Nicer than my house," I said.

The couple looked over at us and the woman gave an uneasy smile, a look people give you when they think they are better than you are, but are too nice to show it. My mother gave Hermione a stern look, warning her to keep quiet. Had the rich couple not been within earshot, Mama would have said, *Hermione. Don't act like you have never been anywhere before. This is not what Dr. King died for.*

Hermione caught the glance and then picked up a magazine, *Fit Pregnancy.* A pregnant supermodel on the cover was credited with saying, "I love my new curves." Hermione rolled her eyes and put the magazine down. "When I was pregnant, I looked pregnant."

The couple looked over at us now, with interest and maybe even a touch of envy. I am sure that they thought that my sister was the patient, the one who had been given some sort of miracle cure. Hermione jiggled her key chain with the photo of Link frowning in a small plastic frame.

I picked up a copy of *Managing Menopause* and Mama gently slid it out of my hands, handing me *Modern Motherhood*.

As it turned out, Dr. Ruby Morrison gave us no reason to doubt her knowledge of all the latest technologies, but she didn't give us much reason to like her either. Tallish and blade thin, she was about the same age as my mother but smaller. Mama prides herself on wearing the same size eight she wore as a bride, but Dr. Morrison was a six. Her black pantsuit pinched in at the waist.

When she walked into the examination room, she seemed a little taken aback to see so many of us wedged onto the love seat.

"Oh!" she said before acknowledging us with a nod each. "Which of you is Ariadne?"

I raised my hand.

Dr. Morrison nodded. "And these are your . . . friends?"

"I'm her mother, Mrs. Eloise Jackson."

"They're here for moral support," I said.

"That's fine," said the doctor, easing her slim self past us to a small desk. She pressed a few keys on her computer and frowned. Mama stared at the doctor, taking in her hair—cornrows that fed an austere French twist down the back of her head. Even her braids were thin. I saw Mama scrutinize the doctor's jewelry, a chunky amber pendant and matching earrings. No wedding ring on the fingers moving rapidly over the keyboard.

It was difficult to pinpoint exactly what was so offensive about Dr. Morrison. It wasn't simply the matter of her physique. We'd seen narrow women before. There was something in her manner that seemed a little superior. When she took my hand, it was as though she wore rubber gloves.

"Where are you from?" Mama asked with suspicious eyes.

"Johns Hopkins," Dr. Morrison said without looking up.

"No, where are you *from*?"

"Detroit, Michigan."

"Oh Jesus," my mother said.

I saw the remark register with Dr. Morrison, but she ignored it, opening a drawer and producing a paper robe. She handed it to me and left the room.

"It's hot in here," Hermione said.

"I don't care for that woman," my mother said. "Did you hear how she talked to me?"

"I didn't notice anything," Hermione said.

But I knew what my mother was talking about. Dr. Morrison spoke with the same quiet condescension as bill collectors, the way they call you ma'am but don't mean it.

I looked at the paper robe in my hand and stood up. I've never liked undressing in front of anyone. Maybe I was still traumatized by my "precocious puberty." Even with Dwayne I was shy. He'd step out of the shower in his full glory, walk across the bedroom, go to the kitchen

for a beer. He'd stand in the yellow light of the refrigerator, naked and dripping wet. When I showered, I
emerged wearing a robe, maybe something sexy and re-
vealing, but I preferred to have fabric covering me if the
lights were on.

I stood before the examining table and unhooked my
belt, and pulled it from around my waist.

"It's cold in here," I said.

"I haven't been cold in years," said Mama.

"Do you want us to give you some privacy?"
Hermione asked.

I gave my sister a grateful smile.

Mama pulled her fingers through her short hair.
"We're all ladies here. She doesn't have anything we
haven't seen before."

"I guess," Hermione said.

I unfastened my skirt and slid it over my hips and
took off my blouse. I tried to move quickly, pulling my
panties over my thighs in a blur, unhooking the bra in an
embarrassed flurry of motion. Hermione looked away,
but I felt my mother's appraising eyes. Mama, I knew,
thought I was a little too heavy. My stomach sagged at
the navel. On my back there was a little fold of fat where
my bra fastened. I wiggled into the stiff paper gown and
sat goosefleshed and shivering at the edge of the table.

Dr. Morrison returned with some sort of computer
and a rolling cart. Mama and Hermione pressed their legs
aside as Dr. Morrison shoved the cart to the table where
I waited.

"It's a portable ultrasound," she explained with that
quiet condescension of hers. "We'll insert the wand into

the vagina and get a better look at your reproductive organs."

She held the wand and turned it a couple of times like she was trying to sell it to us.

She stood aside as I scooted to the edge of the table and spread my legs until my feet touched the stirrups. Thankfully Mama and Hermione could only see my profile.

"Scoot up a little more," the doctor said. "Put your bottom at the very edge of the table."

I moved forward, hoping that I wouldn't fall off.

"Good," she said. "Right there." She slathered the wand with clear jelly. "I'm going to insert now. There'll be some pressure."

I closed my eyes and battled the urge to cry out. The procedure didn't hurt exactly, but the wand inside me was hard and cold. Dr. Morrison maneuvered it like a joystick, grunting at the images on the computer monitor.

"Doesn't look good," she said, pulling the wand sharply to the right.

I wasn't sure if she was talking to me, Mama, or Hermione. She spoke in a voice as bland as egg white, like her words would be of no particular interest to anyone present.

I rose up on my elbows, hoping to see the monitor, but a sharp pain forced me back onto the paper-draped table to recover.

Mama said, "What doesn't look good?"

"See," Dr. Morrison said, wiggling the wand to the left. "The ovaries are very shrunken. Atrophied." The wand banged against my cervix, but I didn't flinch. *Breathe and you will know peace.* I took my air in small mouthfuls, drying out my tongue and lips.

"I don't see anything," Mama snapped.

Over my knees I studied my left foot. The knuckles of my toes were gray and dry, but my nails were pretty, sparkling with bronze polish. I noticed what looked to be the beginnings of a bunion.

Hermione said, "Maybe if you could just explain things to us."

Dr. Morrison touched the monitor. "Her ovary is here, but we can barely see it. Afollicular."

"Speak English," Mama said.

I could tell from Mama's tone that she had turned a corner. She spoke quietly now, with a little pause between each word, as if she were struggling to restrain herself.

"Mama," Hermione said, "we're here to help Aria. Please behave."

Mama said, "Her name is Ariadne."

I was glad that Mama didn't listen to Hermione. I wanted her to misbehave. I'd seen Mama unleash her fury on strangers before. She'd been evicted from Rich's at Cumberland after slapping the rouge off a saleswoman who demanded ID before taking her credit card. I had been seventeen and ashamed—thrown out with her, although I hadn't struck anyone. My sympathy had been with the racist salesclerk. When we left, my mother's handprint stained the clerk's powdered cheek like a birthmark. But this time I wanted Mama to act up, to overreact, to be violent and a little crazy. I'd seen her erupt dozens of times, but never had she rained fire on my behalf.

The doctor remained calm, even when Mama rose from the leather couch and studied the computer screen from over her shoulder.

"Her ovaries have stopped functioning," Dr. Morrison said.

"We knew that when we came here. I didn't drive across town for you to tell me something I already knew. We came here to ask you what we can do about it. I've got money," she added. "So tell me what is possible, not just what you think I can afford."

"Can you take the wand out?" I asked.

"And maybe turn on the light," echoed Hermione.

"Of course," Dr. Morrison said, and did both. I took my feet off the stirrups. Sitting up, I let my bare feet hang from the side of the table and pressed my knees together as the sticky lubricant wet my thighs.

Mama looked fierce and dangerous with the polished nail of her index finger inches from Dr. Morrison's nose. "I know your kind. I grew up with girls like you."

"Mama," Hermione said in a voice clear and firm. "Calm down; you're going to get us thrown out of here. Sit down." She patted the space beside her on the couch.

Dr. Morrison was scared. You couldn't see the fear in her face, which remained fixed in her careful half-smile, but her fingers fluttered in her nervousness. I wasn't sure what would happen if Mama were to hit the doctor, but I was excited by the idea.

"Mama, sit down," Hermione said again. "Dr. King

didn't die for you to come in here and fight with the doctor. Come on now."

Hermione patted the couch and Mama sat down. I marveled at Hermione, who wouldn't look my way. Closing my eyes, I wished my sister had been there all those years when I needed someone to put oil on the water, to extinguish my mother's wrath.

Mama breathed a couple of heaving breaths and unzipped her jacket before Dr. Morrison retreated to her dainty oak desk. She crossed her legs in her smart pantsuit and then, as her shoe swung away from her slender heel, said, "Aria is infertile. She has no genetic material."

Hermione said, "Well, aren't there options? Can't she freeze the eggs she has left?"

Mama said, "What about that?"

Dr. Morrison shook her head. "It doesn't quite work like that. We can't freeze ova. We can only freeze embryos."

Mama said, "I know I have heard of women having their eggs harvested. Career types."

"That's purely science fiction."

"You know what," Mama said. "I don't like your attitude."

"I'm engaged," I said. Everyone turned and looked at me as if a pet turtle had suddenly spoken. "Could my fiancé and I make some embryos and freeze them?"

Dr. Morrison spoke to all of us in a voice like a gavel. "Ariadne, you are afollicular. There are no ova to fertilize."

This pronouncement was so grave and so absolute.

Everyone stopped talking and I put my fingers in my mouth. "Why is this happening to me?"

Dr. Morrison shook a chiding finger at me. "Now, don't start feeling sorry for yourself. Your heart is fine. You have two perfect lungs."

"Is that enough for *you*?" Mama was on her feet again in the crowded examining room. "Dr. Morrison, I asked you a question."

"What exactly do you want to know?" The doctor spoke evenly, but her eyes were skittish, darting to the shut door and back again.

"I want to know if you get up every morning content because you have two lungs. Two *perfect* lungs. Why should Ariadne have to be grateful for things everyone else gets to take for granted?"

"I'm not sure I understand," said Dr. Morrison.

"When I lost my husband and my youngest daughter, people kept telling me what I needed to be grateful for. How I needed to be satisfied with what I had left. Who are you to tell us what we should be grateful for, what should make us content?"

Dr. Morrison waited until Mama sat back down. "I apologize if I have offended you." She paused. Her boundaries were clear and firm. This was not personal. This was just her job. "What I really want to help Ariadne with is hormone replacement. When the ovaries stop producing estrogen, there are two major results: bone loss and thickening of the arteries, heart disease."

"I know all about hormone replacement," my mother snapped. "I'm fifty-three years old."

Now Dr. Morrison turned to me. "You've lost a lot

of bone. You have osteopenia. It's not as bad as osteo-porosis, but it's still serious."

"We didn't come to talk just about that. My daugh-ter is just twenty-five. She is engaged to be married. We want to talk about fertility." She read from Dr. Morrison's card. "You are a reproductive endocrinologist, right?"

Dr. Morrison looked at me and said, "Is this what you want to talk about?"

"Yes," I said.

I looked at Hermione, to see if she was planning an-other intervention, but she studied her leather sandals.

"This is something that I usually prefer to discuss with a woman and her partner. Maybe the two of you would like to make an appointment?"

"You can just tell me now," I said. "I'll tell Dwayne whatever I find out."

"There's always the slim possibility that you could conceive naturally—sometimes the ovaries release one last egg—but the odds against it are even greater than the odds of early menopause. I have a colleague whose FSH was higher than yours and she managed to have a child. But as I said, it is rare. There are fertility treatments, but they are expensive and virtually ineffective for someone in your condition."

"Are there other options?" I said.

"Egg donation. Your womb is in wonderful shape." She went to her desk and pulled what looked like an X-ray from a cardboard sheath. Holding it carefully by its edges, she showed me the film, but all I saw were vague shapes in deepening shades of gray. "Look at it, look at

258

Tayari JonesTayari Jones

the curve. It's a beautiful uterus. You could carry a child to term with no problem."

"But why? What would be the point of going through the whole pregnancy ordeal just to give birth to another woman's baby?"

"We have a great egg donation program here. You use a donor egg and your partner's sperm. We screen the donors for all sorts of genetic defects—diabetes, breast cancer, et cetera. It would be your baby in almost all ways—your womb, your placenta, your blood, everything. There's only one problem."

"Besides the fact that it wouldn't be my child?"

"Yes," Dr. Morrison said. "None of our donors are African American."

"That doesn't really matter," Hermione said. "If you have a black daddy, you end up a black baby no matter what."

"But she would sort of stand out," Mama said. "We don't have any really light-skinned people in our family, and Dwayne is rather dark."

Dr. Morrison waited until they finished jabbering and said, "And there's the other option. You can use the egg of someone you know."

My mother was quiet only a second before speaking up. "My eggs are probably too old. But Hermione could help, if she wanted to?"

"I would," Hermione said. "I know that I owe you, Aria."

"This could work," Mama said slowly. "This way Dwayne can still be a father, and you can have a child that is still part of our family. But things are never as easy as they sound."

"Is it expensive?" I asked.

"Not really," Dr. Morrison said. "Not compared to the other options."

"How much? Like in numbers."

Mama said, "Don't worry about money. A decision like this shouldn't come down to money."

I bit the nail away from my finger until I felt pain, kept pushing until I tasted blood. I understood why it would be best to have a family egg, but I didn't want to give birth to Hermione's child. I wanted Dwayne and me to make our own family, an immediate family, not some space-age extension of the family I already had.

And how would Hermione feel? No matter what papers she signed, there would be a part of her that would consider my child to be hers. Like Dwayne, who still considered Trey to be his son, even though he had signed away his parental rights. Charla could draw up another set of paperwork for her new husband to sign, changing Trey's last name, but he would still be Dwayne's boy.

And where would it leave me, to be the mother of a child and not its mother too? What about Little Link having a brother or sister that was also a cousin? There was something sordid in all of the overlapping of relationships, like in the movie *Chinatown* when the woman sobs, "She is my sister, she is my daughter." In a healthy family the lines are clear, unassailable.

Breathe and you will know peace. I breathed deeply, filling out my stomach and then upward to my chest. I did it again and again, inflating, deflating, until my head felt light and the room shifted in gentle waves. I lay back on the cold table, drunk with so much air.

Mama and Hermione were still talking, but I couldn't quite make out what they were saying. It was as though they spoke in some exotic foreign accent, still speaking English but not in a way that I could understand.

Dr. Morrison said, "Mrs. Jackson, would you and your daughter mind going out in the hallway? I need to talk to my patient alone."

I lay on the table looking at the ceiling as they left, biting my cuticles, chewing into the soft skin.

After they had gone, Dr. Morrison turned to me and said, "How are you?"

"Pretty bad," I whispered, tucking my throbbing hand under my thigh.

"Your family situation is difficult. Don't you agree?"

"Don't talk about my mother, Dr. Morrison. You don't know anything about us."

She handed me a box of tissues, although I wasn't crying. "Do you want to talk to someone?"

"Like a therapist?"

"Yes, we can refer you."

"My health insurance won't cover therapy," I told her.

"I see," she said delicately. "Let's talk about hormone replacement. It's very important. We don't want you to break your hip when you are thirty."

I nodded.

"Do you want to talk about this without your mother?"

"You might as well bring her in, or else I'll have to tell her everything in the car."

"What about your fiancé?" Dr. Morrison said. "You shouldn't have to go through this alone. Infertility is a couple's challenge. It's not your problem by yourself just because you are the one with the endocrinological obstacle."

"He doesn't know," I whispered. "I was hoping you could fix me so he wouldn't have to know."

Dr. Morrison shook her head. "I'm so sorry."

I pulled a tissue from the flowered box. "Sorry seems to be an epidemic these days."

Mama and Hermione returned to the examining room simmering with the possibilities. Sitting there on the small sofa hip-to-hip, they seemed determined and relieved. I was still on the examining table, naked under my paper robe, freezing.

Dr. Morrison wrote me a prescription for birth control pills. Ortho-Novum, twenty-eight-day cycle, the same prescription Dr. Blackwelder had recommended, the same prescription Hermione had taken me to Planned Parenthood for, just before she left home for good.

"I don't understand," Hermione said. "She can't have kids anyway, so why does she need birth control?"

Dr. Morrison explained that for younger women she preferred to prescribe regular birth control pills. The medicine was almost the same as the hormone therapy. "But this way Ariadne will get to have periods each month. No one will look at her strangely at the pharmacy. In other words, it will make her seem more normal." She turned the corners of her mouth down for a moment, considering, and then she scribbled out another prescription. "Something to help you sleep tonight."

Mama and Hermione nodded, satisfied.

I sat bare and goose-pimpled on the edge of the table, trying to be like the blank-eyed blind children, the ones who never complained.

Chapter Twelve

Rochelle hired Keisha to address all five hundred wedding invitations in burgundy calligraphy. She would pay a dollar and a quarter for each invitation. This included the outer envelope, inner envelope, and reply card.

"Do you know that is more than six hundred dollars?" Keisha said to Rochelle once she had made the offer.

Rochelle nodded. "I'm giving you the going rate."

When Rochelle left the office, Keisha bounced in her seat. "That's rent plus enough to get a good stroller for the baby. The kind that lays out like a crib on wheels. When you and Dwayne get married, I could do your invitations too."

"Don't get your hopes up," I said to Keisha. "Me and Dwayne won't be having *that* kind of wedding."

"But other people with money, do they need people to do calligraphy? Because I am good at it. You know, you learn all this crazy stuff in vocational training, but you never think that somebody might really pay you to do it. Six hundred dollars."

"Just make sure you do a good job. I vouched for you."

"I know, Miss Aria. What am I supposed to wear?"

"Something comfortable. Nobody cares what pregnant ladies wear."

She pouted her bottom lip. "That wasn't a nice thing to say."

"I'm sorry, Keisha. I'm just in a mood. Ignore me."

This was a mood that had lasted the better part of a month. It had started as a sort of depression that intensified each time I saw Dwayne, each time he touched me with the force of his intentions. But my sadness had sharpened into a sort of irritability, the way that dogs get mean when they are scared.

Babies are all that Dwayne thinks about. The making of them.

"Do you think you can tell right away if you conceive? My mother says that she can tell me the exact date that her and Daddy made me. She said she dreamed that her mother kicked her out of the house and she knew that she must be pregnant." Last night Dwayne sat up in bed, sheet tucked tight around him, looking pleased with himself.

I wanted to tell him then, let him know what I had

learned from Dr. Morrison. At least now I could give him some options. Tell him about Hermione's egg.

"What if something went wrong?" I said to him. "Like if I just keep having miscarriages over and over. What if we had to do something sort of high-tech?"

"Test-tube baby?" Dwayne reached for the remote control and turned on the TV to watch sports highlights. "You never hear about black people doing stuff like that."

"Really," I said. "I'm worried."

"Don't be worried. We haven't even been trying but a few weeks. And look at last time: one little mistake and boom, you got pregnant. It was the same way with Charla." He turned his eyes to the television and watched a few seconds of baseball. "And what did you tell me about your mother? That your little sister got born even after your mama had her tubes tied? Seems like we got some serious genes on our side."

"But what if something went wrong?" I said again. "I mean, what if we had to do something drastic? Like a surrogate mother."

"That's too weird for me," Dwayne said. "That's the kind of thing they have on talk shows. Anyway, I'm trying to have a baby with *you*."

Then I cried, a soggy explosion of sadness and frustration and guilt. I twisted away from him, embarrassed by my own instability. This was not the sort of woman I wanted to be.

He smiled. "You are acting like a pregnant lady already." He pulled off his T-shirt and twisted me so that I had to face him. With the crumpled cotton shirt he dabbed my face delicately, the way my father used to comfort Hermione and me with his dime-store handkerchiefs.

This didn't soothe me the way I would have imagined. Dwayne's gesture toward me, his kindness, all of it made me feel helpless and ridiculous, like a kitten stranded on the upper branches of a magnolia tree. I accepted his ministrations, allowed Dwayne to kiss me and fondle me after he'd scrubbed the tears from my face. I lay there through it all, wanting to go home, return to my own quiet bed. I missed the occasions when Dwayne would reach for me because he couldn't help himself, when something about me—a flash of my thigh or the sway of my walk or even the way that I laughed—when something about *me* would motivate him to kiss me. Now sex was like work, some uphill battle, a pitiful aiming for a long shot.

I slept a little, skimming only the surface of dreams, like a water bug, or maybe Jesus treading over the water's transparent skin. In the morning, at first light, Dwayne would begin his new morning ritual, stroking me awake. I would comply, without opening my eyes. If I looked in his tranced face, I might tell him everything. Stop him in the middle of his passion and exertion, shout out the whole truth.

And what would happen if I did? Would it be like Rochelle predicted, that Dwayne would be like her own kind father and reassure me that this was about love, not about babies? Maybe Hermione was right: that he would be disappointed but would go on with our plans. He's the kind of guy, my sister said, who would be willing to make a sacrifice.

Keisha ignored me, arrived at our front door dressed as though she were expecting a job interview. She wore a black gabardine skirt fastened over the broadest part of her stomach and an off-white satin shell. She walked up the driveway taking the mincing steps that high-heeled sandals required. She looked at the strip of paper in her hand three times before committing to the trip up our front stairs. I opened the door.

"It's the right house," I said.

She crinkled her nose. "I knew you stayed over here, but I thought you lived in one of the ones that was all fixed up."

I found myself constantly defending the house, the way you might take up for a lover who refuses to get a job. "It's not such a bad place."

"It's better than where I live at," she said. "Don't get me wrong. But you kind of expect somebody who got six hundred dollars to spend just on envelopes, somebody like that is supposed to live someplace plush."

"Come on in," I said, moving from the doorway to make space for her.

Keisha rubbed her arms with her hands. "Y'all got the A/C cranked up like white people. I don't know why rich people like to keep their houses so cold."

"I'll warm it up a little bit," I said. "Sit down on the futon. Rochelle will be right back."

"I'll sit out on the porch," she said. "You let me know when it's warm in there."

I turned the thermostat up to seventy and joined Keisha on the porch. She had settled herself into the Huey Newton Seat and taken off the patent-leather sandals.

"Where is Miss Rochelle anyway?"

"She and Rod are gone to taste wedding cakes."

Keisha smiled. "For real?"

"For real."

She smiled and then giggled. I laughed with her. It was nice for a while, having a laugh at Rochelle's expense, Rochelle who could certainly afford it. Then Keisha stopped laughing. She pressed her hand to the center of her face.

"What's wrong?" I asked her.

"It's not funny. Every time I see Miss Rochelle it makes me feel like shit. Just talking about her makes me feel bad."

"Don't think like that," I said.

"But really," she said. "She's eating cakes and what am I doing? I'm so broke, I'm sitting around the house eating grits with no butter."

I got off the wicker love seat and squatted on the porch at Keisha's knee. Her belly rested on her lap like a sack of groceries. "You have your health," I said to her. "You have this baby coming." I ventured to touch her extended stomach, its hard tightness spurring thrills down my arm.

"Miss Aria, having a baby is not that much of a accomplishment. Even crackheads have babies."

I took in a sharp, wounded breath, imagining Cynthia skittering down the street with her electric hum.

Yes, she probably could have a baby too. Most everyone could.

"Still," I said to Keisha, "there are women who all they want is to have a baby. And they just can't."

Keisha said, "I get the point, Miss Aria. But I just wish I wasn't having a baby *right now*. I want to get married, and Omar wants to get married or whatever. But since this is not his baby, the first thing he is going to want to do is have a baby, so me and him can have a kid together. To make it official. If you count Dante, I already got two kids with different daddies. This time next year it's going to be three. And that is just so ghetto. And if things don't work out with me and Omar, and I can meet somebody else, then they are going to want to have a baby too. Miss Aria, things are not looking good for me."

"But at least you can *have* kids," I said to her. "If you meet somebody and he wants to have a baby, you can do that if you want to."

"That's what I hate about men," Keisha said. "They so baby crazy. But I am grateful, in a way."

I fingered the sleeve of her blouse.

"You said Dwayne is giving me a ride home?"

"He'll come by after work," I said.

"Here is something anyone can be grateful for," Keisha said, nodding toward the street. "Just be glad that you are not a crackhead."

I turned to see Cynthia making her way up the street. She walked close to the curb, not looking up at Keisha and me on the porch.

"I'm not bothering you," Cynthia said to no one in

particular. She stopped at the foot of the driveway and shoved the gravel with quick thrusts of her white sneaker.

"What is that all about?" Keisha wanted to know.

I pretended not to understand.

"She lost a rock out there. I bet that's what it is."

"You don't know that," I said. "It could be something else. Maybe she dropped her earring."

It was hot outside, the air thick and damp from last night's rain. Cynthia squatted in the dirt, looking away from us, searching with the tips of her fingers.

"Crackheads don't care about earrings. At least not like that," Keisha said. "Let's go on in the house before she ask us for some money."

I followed Keisha into the house, without saying hello to my neighbor or even looking back.

Rochelle came home a few minutes later, smelling of sugar. She smiled at us, flashing the results of years of orthodontia. "Sorry," she breezed. "That took longer than we expected. Have you been here long? I brought samples."

We followed her into the kitchen and sat at the table. Rochelle lifted four or five Styrofoam cartons from a brown shopping bag with handles. She grabbed two forks and a spoon from the dish drainer. "Eat," she said to Keisha and me.

She stood before us, still smiling, hands on her hips. "Eat."

I pressed a little tab on the carton nearest me, causing the cover to flop backward. In the center, resting on a paper doily, was a hefty square of single-layer cake. Both the inch-thick icing and the cake itself were chlorine-bleach white. I held my fork over a frosting flower, but I couldn't bring myself to destroy it. "It's too pretty to eat."

Keisha had opened a different carton. Her cake was the yellow of pollen, the icing buttercream beige. She sat frozen before it, one hand on the hump of her stomach. "I don't want any," Keisha said. "I just want to do the invitations for you."

Rochelle stood in front of us, amused, it seemed, and a little annoyed. "Can't you at least just taste it? I need an opinion."

The sweet stink of butter and sugar was thick in the kitchen. I touched the tines of my fork to the white icing, leaving a row of punctures. "I'm not hungry," I said.

"Fine," Rochelle said, fastening the containers and stacking them on the counter. "We'll wait until after dinner."

To Keisha she said, "Are you ready to get started?"

Keisha nodded, saying something about a square brush. Rochelle mentioned Levenger ink. For my part I couldn't pull my mind away from the squares of cake. I wondered if I would have eaten if Keisha hadn't been here. Would the opulent perfection of the icing have seemed to be inedible had it just been me here, with my good friend Rochelle? I thought of the hand soaps in the bathroom. They came out of the box, gardenia-scented and -shaped, triple-milled, soft almost. We washed our hands with these soaps every day, wearing them down with our dirty palms until they were just sweet-smelling slivers. My mother kept such soaps on a china saucer in her bathroom. For decoration, she said. For our hands we used clunky rectangles of Ivory.

Keisha said that being around Rochelle made her feel bad. Well, being around the two of them at the same time made me feel worse. I felt rich and poor at the same time. Deprived and wasteful, all at once.

Keisha did have a gift for calligraphy. Rochelle and I watched as she wrote out the first ten or so RSVP cards, the square brush barely scraping the soft yellow envelopes, leaving rich burgundy letters in its wake. Her lips didn't move when she did this sort of writing. Her face was firm, unmoving—determined, almost. Rochelle, satisfied, went to her room. I went outside to sit on the porch.

Cynthia was still there, not sifting through the gravel, but sitting on a chunk of broken curbstone, watching a cluster of children draw on the street with chalk. She was still for once, not tapping her foot or worrying her neck with her busy fingers. Even though I could see only her back, I could tell she was tired.

"Come onto the porch," I called to her. "You can sit in the Huey Newton Seat."

"That's all right," she said. "I can just stay right here."

"Whatever makes you happy," I said.

We watched the children for a moment until Cynthia called over her shoulder, "I hate them Bebe kids. No respect. They got no respect at all." She shook her head and stood up, straightening her clothes. She was dressed up in a men's dress shirt, still creased from the package, and a pair of dark blue jeans; white plastic earrings hung nearly to her chin. She joined me on the porch, skipping the stair where the brick had come loose.

"You look nice today," I said.

She smoothed her hands over her narrow hips. "My mama came around to see about me today. I haven't been feeling so good. She brought me these clothes. Some food she had fixed."

"Your mama lives around here?"

"Sort of," Cynthia said. "Over by the Beautiful Restaurant. You know where that is?"

"For real?" I said. "That's where I grew up."

"Where you go to high school?" Cynthia asked me.

"All over," I said. "My mama pulled me out of school every time I had a boyfriend."

"I went to Brown High," Cynthia said.

"I went there for a minute."

"We could have knew each other," Cynthia said, brushing off the Huey Newton Seat before sitting down.

I dragged the love seat so I could sit beside her. Cynthia smelled clean, like dish detergent and new clothes. "Do you get along with your mother?"

Cynthia picked at a gray scab on her forearm. "She's okay. She's my mother and everything like that."

"My mother doesn't understand me," I said.

"That's just how it is."

We watched the kids in the street. These were grade-schoolers writing letters in chalk because they had just learned how. They wrote mostly three-letter words, in big letters—a foot high at least. They laughed, pleased with themselves.

"What's it like for you?" I asked as she pried a small scab on her wrist. A bubble of blood rose to the surface. "What's it like when you do what you do?"

"Miss, you don't want to know about me." She stood up and walked back to the driveway, tripping a bit on the rotten step. Through the new shirt I could see a hump forming at the top of her spine. She returned to the driveway, kicking the gravel with her new tennis shoes.

"I do want to know about you." I followed her. "Do you have children?"

"I'm telling you," she said. "You don't want to know about me."

She squatted, causing her jeans to ride up, exposing ankles shiny with Vaseline. She picked up a handful of rocks.

I put my hand on her arm and tried to tug her to a standing position. "Not with all the kids out here."

"Not like I'm doing something that's X-rated," she said. "These kids seen worse than what I'm doing. And anyway, they stole that chalk, you know."

I looked to the children in the road, who had switched from writing to drawing a hopscotch board. Three girls drew careful blocks.

"You never seen a rock before, have you?" Cynthia said, smiling as she caressed the gravel in her hands.

"Not in real life."

"Well," she said, "it looks like a rock. That's why they call it that."

"I don't think there's anything out here, Cynthia. Don't you think you would have found it by now?"

She said, "Keep hope alive."

I looked at the pebbles in her palm. Most of the rocks in this part of the country were chunks of gray granite, pieces of Stone Mountain, the South's answer to Mount Rushmore. Granite was an igneous rock. This was the sort of thing I learned in grade school, the sort of information that was utterly useless, but I couldn't seem to forget.

A gray roly-poly bug crawled out onto the tips of Cynthia's fingers. She turned her hand over, sending the rocks to the ground and dirt floating up into our faces.

"So tell me," I said. "Do you have children?"

She was still squatting, her head about level with my hip. She looked up. "I told you. You don't want to know about me."

"Tell me," I said. "I just want to know. Do you have any kids? Do you want children?"

She shrugged. "What do you think?"

Bugs congregated around my head, trying to drink my sweat. "I don't know."

"You know," she said.

I didn't answer her. The children in the road hopped around the grid they had made. I wondered if they had stolen the chalk and I wondered what difference this made.

Cynthia looked at me with an expression that was hard for me to translate. Her mouth was stretched, turned up at the corners like a smile, but her face wasn't amused or warm.

"You know." She stared hard at me with that same not-smile.

"I'm going in the house," I said, scared suddenly and backing away. "I got company."

"Just stay with me a little while longer," she said. "You see I didn't say nothing about that money you owe me."

"I gave you that dollar a long time ago."

"No, you didn't," Cynthia said. "But I'm not tripping about it. I'm just asking you to help me with this, that's all. Help me a little bit and we can talk about what all you want to know about. Come on." She patted the driveway beside her and gave me what looked to be a real smile. "We're friends, right?"

I lowered myself beside Cynthia and picked up a handful of dirt, although I had only the vaguest idea what I was looking for.

"You have kids, don't you?" I said.

"You want to know how many I had, or how many I got?"

"Whichever."

"I had three. Don't have none with me."

"Where are they?"

She shrugged. "Don't make me get to lying. I lost track of them. I move around too much."

"I really have to go back in the house. They are probably wondering what happened to me."

"I'm just asking for a little company," Cynthia said. "I gave you my good hair clip and didn't ask you for nothing. All I'm asking you to do now is just sit out here with me for a little while. I just want somebody to talk to." She grabbed my wrist. The move was sudden and the force of it almost tipped me forward.

"It's cool. I'm not going anywhere." I tried to make my voice relaxed so she would let me go. Her hand was ropy with veins, the nails beige and thick. As I looked up, Cynthia met my eyes. Her pupils were pinprick tiny, the whites the color of candlelight.

"Why you act so biggity? You don't have nothing, besides that diamond on your hand. Y'all don't even have a couch, just some fold-up bullshit. Liquor in the freezer, like you don't want nobody to find it. Clothes strewn all over the bathroom floor. Panties right there in front of the bathtub." At this she squeezed my wrist, my left hand went limp, my ring heavy and bright.

"Cynthia," I said, "you were the one who broke in our place?"

"I didn't take nothing," she said. "I just wanted to see. And I saw everything." She laughed a wet laugh, still holding tight to my wrist.

"Let me go," I whispered. "What do you want?"

"I want what everybody wants." Cynthia leaned in close enough to kiss me. Her breath smelled of mint over rot. "Stay out here with me," she said. "You said you was going to keep me company."

I pulled myself into a standing position, and Cynthia, still attached to my left wrist, rose with me.

Cynthia was wire thin in the way that only drug addicts can be. I was a big girl, healthy looking. She wasn't a physical threat, exactly. I didn't doubt that I could overpower her. But the idea of grappling with her, having her touch me, maybe wrestling me to the ground and covering my body with hers, was terrifying in the way that a nest of daddy longlegs is terrifying even though you know the spiders are blind and can't hurt you.

"A whole drawer," she said, "with nothing but snot rags."

With my free right hand I slapped her, hard across her chapped mouth. I swung hard like I was trying to hit the back of her head from the front. Cynthia's skin was softer than I would have expected. She took a step back and I took one forward. I balled my hands into fists and struck her mouth again. Her teeth nicked my knuckles before she grabbed me, two handfuls of my hair, close to my scalp. She pulled my face toward her.

"Don't you ever touch me again," she said.

"Fuck you," I said, reaching for her hair, but it was too short and oily to catch. I looped my fingers through her plastic hoop earrings. "Fuck you," I said. "I'll pull them out."

"Do it," she said with her lips scraping my cheeks. "Do it and I'll kill you, motherfucker." Her hands tightened in my hair.

"Those handkerchiefs were my father's," I hissed into her ear. "He's dead."

She didn't respond as I waited for my words to sink in, for her to fully understand the extent to which she had invaded my privacy, how she had desecrated my father's memory by merely looking at his handkerchiefs with her yellow eyes.

Finally she spoke. "Cemetery is full of people's daddies."

She let go of my hair then and I retracted my fingers from her cheap earrings. We stood there for a moment, looking at each other across the humidity of the afternoon. I took steps toward my house, walking backward, facing her. She eased away in the same fashion, understanding that she should never turn her back on me again.

Chapter Thirteen

For Little Link's birthday Dwayne bought a shiny
metal cap pistol, leather holster, and a dozen or so
rolls of red and black caps. Dwayne had volunteered to
shop for the birthday present and I'd let him. For one
thing, I didn't want to drive all the way to Buckhead to
find a decent gift. Although the West End was crawling
with children, there were no toy stores in at least a ten-
mile radius. The only potential gifts for sale at the West
End Mall were miniatures of expensive basketball shoes
or tiny versions of teenagers' baggy pants and athletic jer-
seys. The other reason I let Dwayne take control of the
gift buying was that I liked the idea of him asking to be
the representative of our relationship. Whatever he
bought would be presented to Link, to Hermione and
Mr. Phinazee, and to my mother as a gift from Dwayne
and me. A gift from our branch of the family to theirs.

The fact that the gift was of Dwayne's choosing made it clear to everyone involved that he was as committed to the institution of our tiny family as I was. This was just further proof that he and I would *stick*.

Dwayne brought his package into the house in a paper shopping bag. It banged against his legs as he bounded up the porch steps, almost tripping when his shoe snagged on the gap where the brick had fallen out.

"I got something good," he said, kissing me lightly on the lips.

"Come on in the kitchen," I said, tugging his hand.

Rochelle had insisted on buying a gift for my nephew, even though she and Rod were not invited to the party. Now she and Rod sat at the kitchen table staring at a wooden xylophone with painted metal keys. At Rochelle's elbow was a single sheet of gift-wrapping paper, blue with yellow sailboats and a coordinating bow. Rod looked to the glittery sheet of paper and back to the xylophone. "I don't know," he said to Rochelle.

"That's what y'all got him?" Dwayne said, pretending to cover his laughing mouth. "Don't no little boy want an accordion."

"It's a xylophone," Rochelle said. "Kids like things that make noise."

Rod said, "I had one of these when I was little. It was one of my favorite toys."

"Admit it." Rochelle hit his shoulder. "You still play with it."

As everyone laughed, Rod used two of his locks to tie the rest into a ponytail. "How to wrap this thing is an entirely different matter."

"I kept telling you to just buy a gift bag," Rochelle said. "The gift bag is the best thing to happen to American consumerism since the invention of the credit card."

"But little kids like unwrapping toys. They rip open the paper, throw the ribbon around."

I am sure that Rochelle and Rod had problems, like all other couples. More than once, she had told me that relationships take *work*. In my experience people only say this when their significant others are getting on their last nerves, so I was fairly certain that all was not perfect with my roommate and her fiancé. Even so, they seemed to get along easily with their implied consensus on everything from pizza toppings to the suitability of this gift for my nephew.

"So," Dwayne said, "you think I should wrap this?" With a sharp crackle of the paper shopping bag he pulled the cap pistol from under the table. He pointed it at Rod's forehead, twirled it around, then blew a puff of air over the barrel. It was a good-looking toy. Realistic, as far as I could tell. The barrel was real metal, not molded plastic; the handle shimmered with mother-of-pearl.

Rod was the first to speak. "Um, do you really think that is appropriate?"

"It's better than a xylophone."

Rochelle said, "Maybe something a little less violent?"

Dwayne aimed the gun again at Rod's forehead, pulling the trigger. "It's a *toy*. Why do you have to take everything so serious?"

Rod flinched at the hollow crack of the metal hammer. "Not to be judgmental. But with so many black men in prison for violent crime, don't you think we should try to be a little bit more positive with our gifts?"

"What do you know about kids anyway?" Dwayne said to Rod. "I got a little boy back at home. And I gave him this exact same gun when he was three. Trey is ten now and he's not turning out to be some sort of freak. He's a good kid. He ain't no punk, but he's a good kid."

Rod said, "You can't deny that there are certain correlations . . ."

"You going to tell me you never played cowboys and Indians when you were little?"

"Actually," Rod said with a glance toward Rochelle, "my parents had a political position against that sort of thing."

"Whatever," Dwayne said, crunching the bag under his arm. He stalked out of the kitchen, moving toward my room. I looked over my shoulder at Rochelle as I trotted out behind my boyfriend.

"Ouch," she whispered.

Dwayne yanked open the door to my bedroom, flopping himself onto the bed. "What was that all about?"

"Rochelle and Rod just don't think that kids should have toy guns. A lot of people think like that."

Dwayne tossed the brown shopping bag onto a chair and lay down on my half-made bed, covering his eyes with his large hand. Seeing him stretched over on my flowered sheets, I was aware of how much of a man he was, how much space he occupied. He was dressed for the birthday barbecue in long denim shorts that reached his knees and a purple and gold basketball jersey. Tufts of wiry hair protruded from under his arms. "I don't know how you live over here. It's the worst of both worlds. You live in the ghetto with a bunch of bourgie Negroes. Did you look at Rod's face when he saw what I had bought Link? You would have thought I was fixing to give the little boy a box of pornos or something. *Do I think that is appropriate?* Just the way he was talking. Your girl was trying to be nice, but you could tell that they are of one mind."

I sat on the edge of the bed beside him. I knew how he felt. It was hard to move in a world where you don't know the language, can't quite figure out the rules. I pressed my face to his chest and stroked his muscular arms. I'd missed him over the last week. "Don't worry about them," I said.

"I'm not worried about them," he said. "Like I said, I have a son myself. It's not like I never thought about what kind of things are good to give kids." He rubbed his hand over his short hair. "Trey is still my boy. I might have signed the papers, but you can't sign away blood. He got my hair, my mama's big feet, my sister's dimples."

"You're right," I said. "He's still yours."

"So Rod don't have no right to talk to me like he's the first person in the world to have ever thought about something. It's like that all the time when I come over here. They will be sitting there eating something crazy like tofu and Triscuits and I'll bring in a pizza and they will just look at me like I'm crazy because it's got pepperoni on it."

"Dwayne," I said, "don't read too much into this."

Dwayne struggled to sit up, forcing me to move my

head. "It's not about reading into things. Disrespect is disrespect."

The ringing of the phone startled me. I jumped, biting through the soft meat of my jaw.

"It's for you," Rochelle called.

At first I didn't catch Keisha's voice. She spoke quietly and carefully, as though she were reading her words
from a cue card.

"Miss Aria," she said, "are you busy?"

"In a way," I said. "I'm on my way to my mother's for
my nephew's birthday party."

"Who's with you?"

"Everybody. Rod, Rochelle, Dwayne."

"That's good," she said. "Could you come over here?
Could you come over here and bring Dwayne with you?
It's important."

My impulse was to tell her that we couldn't make it.
Little Link's party was in less than an hour. My mother
didn't believe in the notion that late could ever be fash-
ionable. I didn't want to make her angry and possibly
ruin the party with one of her creative tantrums.

"Please, Miss Aria?" Keisha said. This time she was
begging. Not in the pouty teenage girl way that she em-
ployed to convince me to take her to Taco Bell after
school, or to keep me from being mad when she didn't
turn in her homework. In her voice was the pleading
that occurs on a soul level. How could I refuse?

We took Dwayne's car to Keisha's apartment. He
didn't talk much on the drive over. I could tell from his

flexing jaw muscles that he was still angry about the scene in the kitchen. I knew that his mind was racing, zipping with things that he could have said if he had only thought of them in time. I empathized. I knew exactly what it was like to think of the right thing to say years too late.

I guided him through the twisting parking lot to reach Keisha's place. He pulled halfway into a parking space and then backed out, seeing green bottle glass scattered on the pavement. He chose another space and backed in.

"This is worse than your neighborhood," he remarked, chirping his car alarm. "At least where you live, people are spread out. Here, they are all on top of each other. Look at all this trash."

I shrugged. I'd been here so many times before, the jagged asphalt and soiled mattress jutting from the Dumpster barely registered with me. My mind was on Keisha. The more I thought about her phone call, the less I liked it. It was her, certainly—I recognized her voice— but she didn't sound like herself. Even the first time I'd come here, when she'd missed so many days of school, she'd seemed like herself. She had been tired, defeated, but she was still the girl I knew.

At the foil-covered door of the apartment I grabbed Dwayne's hand before knocking.

"What's wrong?" he whispered.

"Something," I said just as the door opened.

I was startled not to find Keisha standing in the doorway. Instead, we were invited in by a small woman who looked to be a little older than Hermione.

"Come in," she said. "LaKeisha will be right out."

Dwayne and I stepped over the threshold into the living room. Inviting us to sit on the couch, the small woman snapped a dying leaf from a creeping philodendron plant. Dwayne ducked to keep from knocking his head on a hanging flowerpot.

"Oh, I'm sorry," the small woman said. "We don't get too many tall folks in here."

"It's all right," Dwayne said. "I'm Dwayne."

"Yes," said the woman. "That's what I figured. And this is the famous Miss Aria."

I gave a little nod and sat on the couch, close to Dwayne. He took my hand, stroking my knuckles with his palm.

"I didn't catch your name," Dwayne said.

"I'm Mary Montgomery. LaKeisha's my daughter."

I looked closely at Mary and I could, in fact, see the resemblance. I don't know why I didn't assume that she was Keisha's mother as soon as she opened the door. I knew that Keisha lived with her mother, that her mother was the one responsible for all of the foliage. But since I'd never seen her, the woman was only an abstraction for me, like the ever-absent mother in *Grimm's Fairy Tales*.

Keisha emerged from the back room at last, wearing the same skirt and blouse set that she had worn to ink Rochelle's invitations a week ago. Her hair was held back from her face with a blue grosgrain ribbon. Dwayne and I were dressed for a barbecue. I shifted, feeling half naked in my tank top and shorts.

"I don't know why you got all dressed up," Mary said.

"I'm not dressed up," Keisha said. She gave me a shy smile and sat in the covered chair at her mother's end of the sofa. I will admit that I felt a little hurt that she didn't choose the chair that was closer to me. It was awkward being in the apartment with Mary. I felt like the Other Woman. Mary was Keisha's mother, her blood, so of course Keisha would sit beside her. I shifted a little so that I would be closer to Dwayne. He was my family, in a way.

"I went to the doctor today," Keisha began.

Dwayne's hand tightened around my fingers.

"Can we turn on some lights?" Mary wanted to know. "It's so dark in here. It's like a haunted house."

Keisha got up and went to the doorway and turned a plastic knob. The room filled with a gentle yellow light.

"See," Mary said. "That's better. Go on, baby."

"Like I was saying, I went to the doctor today." She patted her belly and didn't say anything more.

"Is everything okay?" I flexed my legs to rise from the sofa, but I stopped myself, wondering if it was appropriate to comfort someone else's daughter.

"Everything is fine," Mary said. "The doctor said that Keisha is having a healthy baby. A big healthy boy. You brought the ultrasound pictures to show them?"

Keisha looked stricken. "I didn't bring them, Mama. I should have brought them."

"It's okay," Dwayne said. "We can see them another time."

Mary spoke. "I know you had wanted a little girl. Keisha told me. But a little boy is good to have as your first baby. Sometimes I wish that Keisha had a older brother to look out for her."

"Any child at all is a blessing," I said.

"I knew you'd feel that way," Mary said. "From everything Keisha told me about you. She talks about you all the time. Miss Aria says this, Miss Aria says that. Miss Aria got a diamond ring. Miss Aria's fiancé is so nice. You know, like that. The way young girls can be." There was a bit of an edge to her voice. Dwayne heard it too; I felt his body stiffen into something hard and even more solid.

"Miss Aria," Keisha said, "I know I failed my GED and everything. But I have a good mind. You even said that yourself. It's nothing wrong with my mind. My little boy, I think he's going to be smart. And he's going to be really big and healthy. The doctor told me that."

"That's good," Dwayne said. "And we don't mean to be rude. But we have to get over to Aria's mother's house in a few."

I, too, was wondering about the occasion for this gathering, but I was embarrassed that Dwayne would be so direct. Keisha looked away from us, studying her mother's profile.

"Mama," she said softly, so quiet that Dwayne didn't hear, but I heard it and so did Mary. She didn't nod or nudge Keisha, she just turned herself to look into her daughter's face. Keisha pushed herself up from the flowered chair and stood in front of Dwayne and me. She carefully lowered her pregnant bulk until she was kneeling in front of us.

"Stand up," Dwayne said. "I don't want to see you down on the floor like that."

I looked to Mary, who didn't glance toward me. Her eyes were fixed on her daughter. Dwayne moved his jaw around invisible gum. Anticipating something I couldn't see coming.

"It's going to be a real good baby," Keisha said again. "We don't have nothing in our family. Cancer, sugar, nothing like that."

"I don't understand," I said.

"She's just a little girl," Mary said. "She's not but seventeen. She's not ready for a baby. She's a good kid herself, but she's not ready."

Still on her knees like a suitor, Keisha looked up at me, shy but hopeful. "I know you wanted a baby."

I closed my eyes as the magnitude of this offer rolled over me. It was the sort of thing that made me believe that maybe God did have a plan for me. That my whole life was leading to this moment. Dwayne and I would take this baby, make it our own. We could make our family around this little boy. This big healthy boy that was growing now inside of Keisha, right here at our feet.

"And we would leave town, Mama and me," Keisha said, looking at Dwayne. "Just listen. Okay, Dwayne? Let me tell you my whole idea. We would leave town so you and Miss Aria could just be a regular family. I know you wouldn't want me hanging around, confusing things. And I would respect that. I wouldn't call y'all on the phone, or want to see pictures, or anything. I would be gone, like I never was here." Her voice caught on the last sentence and she sucked in her cheeks and held her head back, trying to let the water run into her hair instead of down her cheeks. "Okay?"

I slid off the couch and knelt beside her, on my bare knees on the worn carpet. "Don't cry." I hugged her, burying my face into her neck, breathing the coconut oil in her hair.

"Aria," Dwayne said, "can I talk to you outside for a minute?"

I lifted my face to look up at him. "Okay."

Outside, in front of the foil door, the day was hot. I leaned against a rusted metal railing.

"What's going on?" he wanted to know.

"You were right in there," I said. "Keisha wants us to adopt her baby."

"Aria." Dwayne covered his eyes and shook his head. "Aria, I'm not a bad person. It's not like I don't understand. But this is real life, Aria. This is not a after-school special."

"What do you mean?"

"Aria, first off, adoption is supposed to be anonymous. You are out of your mind if you don't think her or her mother is going to show up after a couple of years saying they want their baby back. People don't just walk away from their kids. Blood always is going to call you back. I don't care what kind of papers she signs.

"Number two: we are not ready to be parents next month. And besides, we have been trying to have babies of our own."

"But, Dwayne, did you see her face? We have to help her."

Dwayne leaned against the metal railing of the porch.

"It's a bad situation," he said. "But it's not up to us to fix it."

For the second time in two weeks I found myself with the urge to hit someone in the face. With my hands in tight fists by my side I turned away from Dwayne, taking deep breaths through my nose. I took a few steps down the walkway, to the stairs, and then back to Dwayne.

"Can you at least say that you will think about it? Do you have to feel like you know everything and can come up with an answer right here, right on the spot? It took a lot for Keisha and her mother to make this decision. The least we can do is to think about it. Take it seriously."

Dwayne said, "All right. Go in there and tell them that we're thinking about it. But thinking is just thinking. Don't get their hopes up."

I left Dwayne outside while I went in to speak with Keisha and her mother. The two of them sat on the couch, their faces brown and blank against the background of ivy. I told them that Dwayne and I were thinking it over. I told Keisha that I loved her.

Chapter Fourteen

Dwayne and I parked the car in front of my mother's house but didn't get out. We'd made the drive in near silence, each busy with our own thoughts. Sweet Keisha. When I met her on that spring day last year, I thought that my job was to save her. Who would have thought that she would end up saving me? So maybe this was how life felt for other people, people like Rochelle. She had been dealt a bad hand of cards at birth, been abandoned, but the universe corrected its error and sent Mr. and Mrs. Satterwhite to adopt her.

Dwayne finally let up the windows and turned the car off. "All that pain in that girl's face. When I close my eyes, that's all I see."

"We can help her," I said. "Maybe it was meant to be."

Dwayne and I opened the side door to go into my mother's house just as Hermione pressed the red button on the Polaroid camera she'd bought at a garage sale.

"You're late," she said, pulling the picture from the camera.

It was such a shame that instant cameras had gone out of fashion. I loved how you took the photo and knew in just a few minutes what your memory was going to look like. Mama didn't care for them much, said the pictures always came out too small and fuzzy. The prints were never suitable for framing. "Patience," she'd say, popping out the film cartridge from her camera, a slim 110 model. "If you're willing to wait, you'll get a better picture." And we did wait, and wait. Sometimes we wouldn't see the photos until the significance of the event had worn off. Snapshots from a wedding or party six months after the fact just didn't mean as much. Memories are best when they're fresh.

In a quiet voice Hermione explained that she hadn't planned to use the camera until later in the afternoon; she had bought only three packages of the expensive film and wanted to save them for the cake and candles phase of the gathering. She brought it out early in an effort to amuse her husband. Mr. Phinazee was depressed because Coco didn't accept Hermione's hand-delivered invitation to the birthday party. Hermione had begged her husband not to get his hopes up. If Coco hadn't made it to Link's christening or to the hospital when he got his hernia fixed, it was unlikely that she would show up today. But Mr. Phinazee thought that Coco would have mellowed by now. It was one thing for her to disapprove of her father's marriage, but rejecting Little Link was another matter altogether. How could she hold a grudge against a baby? Hermione whispered all of this as we waited on the milky squares to develop into pictures. "He acts like Little Link is Gandhi, Jesse Jackson, or somebody. If he can get Coco to act right, they will have to give him the Nobel Prize."

I looked over to my sister's husband. His plastic chair was situated near the chain-link fence that separated our yard from the neighbors'. He angled his neck to see between the houses, to the street. Mr. Phinazee rubbed his jaw from time to time and yawned.

"It's pitiful," Hermione griped. "Doing her daddy like that. I even went to the shop again to ask her to come. I was *begging* her. Well, maybe I didn't beg all the way, but I was *nice*. Finally I had to just tell her: 'Your daddy's not for always.' And I should know."

Hermione moved as she talked, sometimes picking up one of the pictures and shaking it like a thermometer, making the image show itself sooner, but I liked to let the faces take their own sweet time. I squinted at the blue-white surface, waiting for the colors.

Since Link was the birthday boy, there were many pictures of him, sitting somber and quiet in his cone-shaped cardboard hat. He fiddled with the elastic band under his chin, looking like a worried, depressed head of state. I wondered if he would have been happier if other children had been invited. My mother had gone overboard, baking and frosting nearly one hundred pink-topped cupcakes for the gathering of only six people. In one photo she is frowning at the tiny cakes, each smeared in buttercream and accented with sugar flowers.

The photo of Dwayne and me was the last to develop. In the eight and a half months we'd been together we hadn't taken many pictures as a couple. Hermione had caught us unawares as we stepped into the house. Dwayne is about two paces ahead of me, not smiling, his eyes focused somewhere ahead of him. I'm trying to hold his hand. My eyes span the space between us; my reaching hand is a blur.

Hermione sat down beside me on the picnic table. "That's it for the Polaroid. We're out of film. Three rolls and I couldn't even get Earl to look at them."

"But I wanted me and you to take a picture together."

"Mama has her camera."

"But we'll have to wait a million years to see the prints."

My sister looked pretty for Link's birthday. She'd styled her hair in a curly upsweep with loose ringlets hanging from her temples in lazy spirals. She wore a silk tunic, the pale green of seedless grapes, and matching Capri pants. For a fleeting moment I envied Little Link, wishing that Hermione had been my mother, so round and pretty, obviously sane.

She looked over her shoulder to the porch. "Your boyfriend is spiking the punch."

"Make him stop," I said. "Mama is going to shit a brick."

"We just won't tell her," Hermione said. "People deserve to have some fun. Maybe Earl will cheer the hell up. It's ninety-something degrees out here."

I scanned the yard for Dwayne. He sat on the grass beside the baby pool, speaking to Link, who sat in the waist-high water, staring at his own tiny hands. I waved at them, but neither seemed to notice.

"I wish you had made more of an effort to get here on time," Hermione said. "Mama thought you were blowing her off."

"Something important happened."

Hermione gave a quick shrug. "It wasn't pretty here for the first half hour or so. Earl was mooning over Coco, and Mama was fretting over you and Dwayne. It's a good thing that you finally showed up. Mama was raring herself up for a big one when I saw you and Dwayne sitting in the car out front. Since then, it's been all smiles. But who knows how long it will last?"

"I didn't plan to be late."

"All I am saying is that you should try to think about Mama's feelings. She's been through a lot."

"What about us?" I blurted. "We've been through more than Mama."

Hermione stretched her lips into one of those smiles that don't show teeth. "Mama thinks she's cornered the market on misery."

"But what do *you* think, Hermione? Don't you think it was worse for us? I mean, she had her whole life before everything happened. We were *kids*."

"Aria, what's the point of even thinking about things like that?"

"Come on, Hermione, please tell me what you think."

My sister took a potato chip from a plastic bowl, broke it into pieces, and spoke to the crumbs. "Before I had Link, I would agree with you. But now that I have a child, I think that Mama was hurt more. Because of Genevieve."

"But Link is the only child you have. Mama still had us."

Hermione licked the tip of her finger and touched her finger to the crumbled chips. Tapping the pieces onto her wet tongue, she said, "Don't get so upset, Aria. I don't know why you even spend your time thinking about these things. It's not really the point."

"What is the point, then?"

"The point is your life right now. I think about you all the time, Aria. I've been thinking about Dwayne too. You are just going to have to tell him."

"I'm going to tell him tonight," I told her.

"I'm serious about the egg," Hermione said. "You say the word and we can harvest the next day."

"That costs money," I said.

"Earl will pay. He'd do anything for you, Aria."

I wasn't comfortable having this conversation outside like this where our words could carry on the wind. Dwayne was over at the barbecue now, painting sauce onto the chicken. Mr. Phinazee laughed. I'd forgotten how men were together. After the accident we hardly ever had men at our house, and never more than one at a time. I'd forgotten how they play together like young horses, drink, and laugh. How they seem to make each other happy.

"I want a big wedding," I said to Hermione. "I want to invite three hundred people. An outdoor reception."

"Oh God," Hermione said. "Earl and I stood up before the judge and that was that."

"Three hundred guests isn't that many people. Rochelle is having twice that."

"You don't even know three hundred people. Who would Mama invite? A bunch of blind people? You'd be a fool to spend a thousand bucks on a dress to wear in front of a bunch of blind people." She laughed a little. When she choked on her potato chip, I refused to clap her on the back.

Link toddled over to us with his arms outstretched. "Hey, birthday boy," Hermione said. "What's wrong, sweetie?"

Link didn't speak, he just waddled closer with his arms open. Hermione picked him up and plopped the wet baby across her thick thighs. "Have you been swimming?"

He nodded the way some children do, bobbing his entire upper body.

Suddenly shy, Link hid his face in the front of Hermione's tunic, making a dark wet spot.

"Let's dry you off," Hermione said.

She moved toward the sliding glass door with Link riding her hip. I marveled at how easily she carried him, how snugly he fit there, clamped to her side with his wiry legs.

I followed Hermione into the bedroom that my sister and I had shared in the years before her famous elopement. Mama kept the space just as I left it when I moved eight miles away to a dormitory at Spelman. She's not the kind of mother to preserve our artifacts as a shrine to our childhoods. It was more like she had no use for this room once we were gone, no reason to alter or visit it. The posters I had loved as a teenager—Michael Jackson dressed in a yellow cashmere sweater and Prince wearing an impossible purple blazer surrounded by a haze of smoke—still hung on the wall, secured by push-pins shaped like daisies. Our narrow twin beds still pressed against opposite walls and were covered with the same green plaid spreads worn thin in places. While Hermione dried Link with a heavy towel, I lifted an ancient lipstick from what had been my side of the dresser. The pink plastic case caused me to smile a little, remembering how expensive and elegant Fashion Fair makeup had seemed to me then. How sophisticated I had been to buy makeup from a department store counter, rather than stealing from the drugstore. I twisted the tube and found it empty. I must have used a brush to dig out every expensive purple bit. The bottom of the case bore a round sticker, "chocolate raspberry." I held it to my nose and remembered the strong perfume of Fashion Fair, a scent so overpowering that it flavored your food and your kisses.

"It's weird to be in here," I said. The air in the room was cooler than the rest of the house.

Hermione laid Link on the bed that had been hers and pulled off his wet trunks. The baby looked horrified and covered his private parts with his small hands. "Are

you shy?" Hermione said. "Nobody is looking at you."
She leaned down and kissed his hernia scar with a smack.

"The scene of the crime," Hermione said, rummaging in the diaper bag, which also matched her clothes.
"This whole house is a crime scene, really."

Hermione slipped a pair of pull-ups onto Link, snapping the elastic around his waist. "Now you don't have to
be so shy."

"I think I want to adopt a baby," I said to my sister.

Hermione continued to dress Link, smoothing lotion
on his skinny legs, tickling his potbelly. There was only
the rustle of clothing and Hermione's coos and clucks.

"Then I won't even need the egg."

"You can have the egg, Aria."

"You don't understand," I said. And I told her about
Keisha. "It's going to be a real good baby," I assured her.

"What did Dwayne say?"

"He wasn't all that enthusiastic. But he might change
his mind once I tell him about my medical problems.
See, right now he's looking at it out of context. When I
tell him, he'll see how it all fits together, how it is more
fate than anything."

"He's not going to go for it," my sister said. "This
baby is due in a month? It's too soon."

"But it's a special situation," I said.

"Doesn't matter," Hermoine said. "If there's one
thing I know, it's men. I know how they are." She swung
Link back to his place on her hip and moved toward the
door. He crossed his arms around her neck, holding on
like he was drowning.

For a moment I wanted to rise from my bed and

snatch Little Link, to untangle him from her and hold him on my own lap. My sister could be terribly smug, secure in what she had. She was the kind of person who could make a way out of no way. She had found a way out of this house, out of this room, by latching on to Mr. Phinazee, our father's best friend. An old man even when we were little, five years older than our father. Hermione thought herself to be very smart, and I supposed she was. Who could have known that old Mr. Phinazee had the ruby slippers all along?

But maybe it was my turn to be at the right place at the right time.

"Do you have any idea," I said to my sister, "what a big deal it is for someone to offer you a baby? It means that she trusts us, that she thinks we will be good parents."

"Goodness, Aria," Hermione said. "You said this kid's seventeen and doesn't even have a GED? Of course she's going to think that you and Dwayne would be a better option for the kid. I mean, think about it."

I didn't have a response to this remark. Of course Hermione was right, on some level. Everything she said about Keisha was true, but this bare outline didn't capture the heart of the matter. I was still trying to think of something to say, some way to explain, as Hermione and Link moved toward the door. My nephew gave me a backward wave, with his palm facing his own face.

"When you tell Dwayne," Hermione said, "tell him about the egg. At least that way he can have his own child. Trust me."

I stayed in my bedroom a long time, watching Dwayne through the window. No one seemed to notice that he kept his distance from me this afternoon, cavorting with my mother and even horsing around with Mr. Phinazee, but saying nothing to me. I suppose it was because Keisha's offer was between us. Until we talked about that, there was really nothing else to say. Through the metal burglar bars I saw Dwayne swing Link around by his arms, my nephew's bony shoulder blades like undeveloped wings.

Chapter Fifteen

At four o'clock, after Little Link had blown out the candles on three cupcakes, Mama lowered herself onto the blanket where I had spread myself out, enjoying the warmth of the day on my eyelids, reliving the moment in Keisha's house when I sank to my knees and hugged the girl. Dwayne hadn't been a part of that moment. If he had been there and felt what passed from Keisha's skin to mine, from my body to hers, he would understand that this was what was meant to be. From where he had sat on the couch he could only feel the sadness, but I had been near enough to feel the love.

Beside me, Mama lay on her stomach. She looked good for a woman her age, for one that has seen what she has seen. There were shallow pleats at the corners of her eyes, but that was all.

"Ariadne, do you think your sister is happy?"

"As happy as anybody," I said.

I rolled on my stomach to watch Hermione bouncing Little Link on her lap and covering his face with lip-sticked kisses. He looked like a cartoon sweetheart, his face wallpapered with prints the shape of his mother's mouth. He didn't bend his face, but his eyes seemed happy enough.

"Mama, did I laugh when I was a baby? Little Link never smiles at anything."

"He didn't get that from our family. You laughed all the time when you were a baby. You laughed so much that I took you to the doctor. Sometimes you can think a baby is laughing and it is really having a seizure."

"Mama, that is a really morbid thought." But I liked the idea of myself as an unnaturally happy infant, smiling without obvious provocation.

She touched the tip of her nose. "Honeysuckle. Do you smell it?"

I suppose the fragrance was there all along, but it seemed like she released the perfume in the air with her words. As I breathed fantastic sweetness, she pointed toward the back fence and I saw the vines, twined through the chain-link. They, too, must have been there all along, but it seemed like my mother conjured them with the tips of her fingers.

"Genevieve would have been fifteen this year. Can you picture that?"

I remembered myself at fifteen, overgrown and under-cherished. "It's hard to picture what we would be like if the accident didn't happen."

"Your sister thinks I should move on with my life. She thinks I should date. Can you picture that?"

I turned myself to face her strong profile. "You're not too old."

"You girls were just children, and children have no choice but to grow. But for me to move on? Move on to what?"

We lay there on the blanket, on our tummies, our chins cushioned by our folded hands. Dwayne and Mr. Phinazee sat facing each other in plastic lawn chairs, their knees almost touching. Lying beside my mother, watching everyone, I thought about my mother and wondered when was the last time anyone had touched her. Maybe this was why she liked working with the blind: there was much unintentional brushing of skin. Occasionally someone might actually touch her face. Angling my face toward my mother, I moved to kiss her forehead, like Hermione kissed Link, but timidity seized me, some strange notion of protocol. Mothers kissed daughters, not the other way around. Instead, I studied her neck, softly speckled with freckles. I placed my hands there, where her neck disappeared into her cotton blouse, just where her pulse throbbed lightly against her skin.

Mama's hand jerked upward, but she didn't move my fingers. "Genevieve would have been fifteen this year, did I say that already?"

"Yes, ma'am," I said. "You did."

My mother rolled onto her side, so close to me that she spoke these words almost into my mouth. It felt like CPR, the way someone forces your lungs to accept air.

"It could have been avoided. There were no car seats

back then. Everybody held their babies on their laps. So when Lincoln swerved off the road, I held her hard to my chest. It was reflex, I didn't think about it. There was no plan. Children are delicate, you know."

I remembered my mother running from the car with Genevieve and the impossible angle of her little head.

"That's not what happened," I said. "She probably hit the windshield or the dashboard."

"No," Mama said. "I would never let my baby hit a windshield. I held her to my heart."

I reached toward my mother again, resting my fingers in her soft hair. "I always wanted you to hold *me* to your heart."

"You aren't hearing me." She rolled herself over, leaving me to stare at her slender back.

"Yes, I am. Keep talking. Mama, please turn back around."

She did keep talking, but without turning to face me. "I didn't mean to hurt her."

"Mama," I said, "I know you didn't. Please turn around."

I reached for her shoulder and she let me move her. Mama lay on her back now, staring into the bright sky without shading her eyes. "You're not hearing me."

"I do hear you."

"Then why don't you say something?"

"There's nothing really to say, Mama."

She seemed to lose control of her hands then. They clenched and unclenched at her sides, with a clatter of bracelets, then flew to her head and tugged at her delicate graying hair. Her eyebrows buckled with her effort.

I looked around the yard for Hermione but saw only Dwayne and Mr. Phinazee, huddled deep in conversation. I covered my mother's hands with mine, prying open her fists, freeing her hair. She struggled still, but my hands were larger, stronger, and younger.

"Is that what it was, Mama? All these years, that's what it was?"

"You say it like it was nothing."

"It's not nothing. But you could have told us." Her hands still resisted my strength, but I held them still. "You should have told us a long time ago."

Her hands went slack, as though suddenly disconnected from whatever source powered them. I released them, slowly, carefully, ready to stop her, but she let them lie unmoving on the blanket.

"Hermione knows," Mama said. "I know that she knows."

I smoothed her hair where she had ripped at it. "She doesn't know."

"Yes, she does. She was there with me. You stayed in the car with Lincoln. But your sister was with me." Her fingers gave little jumps.

"No, Mama," I whispered until her hands lay quiet again.

"Ariadne," Mama said, "if she doesn't know, then why did she leave us?"

When I didn't answer, Mama stood up, nearly herself again. She straightened her clothing and walked toward the picnic table. While she stacked plastic cups and paper plates, I rolled myself onto the warm space she had left. With the hands that had touched my mother's hair I felt

my own dancing pulse, parting my lips as I slept, tasting
the honeysuckle air.

I opened my eyes to find myself alone on the blanket, the rubber tip of Dwayne's sneaker just inches from
my nose.

"I need to talk to you," I said, wishing that there were
better words to start a conversation as important as this
one. Somewhere between dream and memory was the
image of my mother and her guilty, dangerous hands. I
saw her neck, the veins straining under her loose skin.
See, she seemed to be telling me with the bunched muscles of her face. Her hands tearing at her hair in desperate sign language. *This is what my secret has done to me.*

"I need to talk to you," I said again to Dwayne,
stretching out my hand. "Pull me up."

Steady on my feet, I rubbed my arms, swollen and
blotchy with insect bites. It was after sunset; lightning
bugs dotted the air like incandescent snowflakes. The air
was still rich with honeysuckle.

"We need some privacy," Dwayne said.

"What's wrong?"

"Where can we talk?"

I said, "Let's talk when we get home."

"I want to talk now." Dwayne walked toward the
house in long, hard strides.

"No," I said. "Not here." I wanted to do this in my
own space, in my own house with all its promise and
possibility.

Dwayne pushed open the sliding glass door, and the
rolling noise seemed too loud. I planted my feet on the

soft grass outside, but he tugged me over the threshold. In the living room the television was still on, but no one was watching.

"Where is everybody?"

Dwayne sat on the couch and rubbed his palms against his ashy knees. "Earl's daughter called, said she had a gift for Link. So Earl took Link over to her house to get it. They'll be back after a while to get Hermione."

"Where's my mother?"

"In the kitchen with your sister. Aria, I need to talk to you right now."

The urge to run was as strong and undeniable as the impulse to duck when there's a softball spinning toward your head. I went into the kitchen, where my mother and sister stood at the double sink washing and rinsing serving dishes.

"Hermione?" I said, not knowing quite what I wanted to ask her.

They both turned toward me with stricken faces. I had never noticed the strong resemblance between them, but there they were, mother and daughter. As alike as Keisha and Mary.

"What's wrong?"

Hermione caught her lip with her teeth.

"No one died," Mama said. "No one is hurt."

I nodded, glad to process that information, waiting for the rest. Dwayne's feet trod on the carpeted hallway behind me with a hissing like water scattered on a griddle. I left the kitchen and took quick steps to my former bedroom and shut myself in, pressing the little button in the handle to lock the door.

Sitting on the low twin bed where I slept for most of my childhood, I crossed my arms over myself, looking for a way to escape. But were there a hidden hatch, a trap-door, an unbarred window, I think I would have discovered it years ago. There on the bed I closed my eyes hard, covered my ears to shut out his knocking. "I can't hear you."

The door opened, of course it did. I opened my eyes a crack, half hoping to see Coco, hoping that she would sing to me. But Dwayne filled the threshold.

"Calm down. I just want to talk to you." He closed the door and pressed the privacy tab. "I talked to Earl this afternoon."

He sat on Hermione's old bed, facing me. He spoke and I could easily picture the scene. Mr. Phinazee, well-meaning Earl, old enough to think that he knew what was best for everyone else. Mr. Phinazee had sat Dwayne down in a man-to-man way. Probably he had intended to pour vodka but discovered that Hermione and I had drunk everything in the liquor cabinet years ago, filling the bottles with tap water. So he and Dwayne had sat down with cups of spiked punch between them, and Earl had told him not to worry about money.

Dwayne said, "Aria, I thought he was talking about the wedding. That he would pay since your pops had passed and everything. So I am nodding my head, saying, 'Yes, sir. I really appreciate it,' and everything like that."

I could see Earl, old and interfering, assuming every-one knew everything, explaining that he and Hermione would stay out of our business when it came to the mat-ter of the child. To think of the egg as a gift. It was only the egg that Hermione would be contributing; the child, the baby itself, would be ours.

"Then he goes on about how lucky we are to be living in this day and age. When there is technology. He's going on and on, talking about his wife that died and the daughter that don't half speak to him. He's talking about your sister and about Link and even about your dad, but I can't get over what he just told me."

Dwayne was on his feet now, pacing across the small room. His sneakers were dirty, leaving faint tracks on the already stained beige carpet. From the top of the chest of drawers, he picked up the glass ring-holder, shaped like a finger. He jiggled his hand as though weighing it, like he was considering throwing it, but he replaced it on the dresser top.

"I was going to tell you. I was going to tell you as soon as we got home."

"So what's going on, Aria?"

"It's like Mr. Phinazee told you."

Dwayne stood in front of the mirrored closet door and met my eyes in reflection. "No," he said. "It can't be like he said, because you *were* pregnant at first. I gave you my aunt's ring because you were having a baby. You were sick in the morning. I heard you in the bathroom being sick."

"The doctor said it was just a coincidence."

He took two steps toward the door, three steps the other way, then again. His feet were too heavy for this room. The ceramic figures on the tops of the dresser and chest rattled with his walking. "You are telling me that you came down with the *flu* and decided that you were *pregnant*? Didn't you take a *test*? Didn't you at least *pee in a cup* before you started telling people?"

In the mirror I stared into his face, which wasn't quite angry. His mouth hung open in something like disbelief, but his eyes were narrowed like he couldn't bear to watch what would come next. I also looked at myself, sitting on my childhood bed, my face and hair appearing girlish and vulnerable.

Dwayne sighed, still pacing. "I gave up my boy behind this." His voice was quiet, but I knew Hermione and Mama could hear him. This house had never been able to conceal private conversations. "I signed the papers, had them notarized." Dwayne closed his eyes and let air out of his mouth. He uncurled his fist like a flower past its prime, unfurling until the petals fall to the ground. "So what am I supposed to do?"

I moved my lips to speak, but there was no air.

"I feel so stupid," he said, sitting down hard on Hermione's bed. "That thing with Keisha, that was a setup, wasn't it? The whole thing. You and her on the floor hugging and crying. No wonder it all seemed so fake. Like TV instead of real life."

"No," I said, crossing the floor to sit beside him. "I had no idea what she called us over there for."

"Let me tell you something, Aria. Let me tell you something about me. I want a family. A regular family. Even when I had Trey, we weren't a family. I want a kid that can call me Daddy. When I call Trey on the phone, you know what he says? He says, 'What's up, Dwayne?' I want a kid that can call me Daddy."

"It would be the same," I said. "We would raise this

baby in our house, with us." I reached for his hand; he let me hold it, but didn't squeeze mine back.

"You are not hearing me, Aria. I don't want no half this, half that. I don't want no complicated mess in my family. It's not just having a child that counts. It's having a child that belongs to me, that belongs to my wife. I don't want technology. I don't want Hermione's egg or Keisha's baby."

"What *do* you want?" I asked him. "Tell me what you want. If I can get it, you can have it. Just tell me that what you want is something I have."

Dwayne didn't answer, only shook his head with his lips folded between his teeth.

"We don't have to have kids," I said. "It can just be me and you. We'll be Link's favorite uncle and aunt, spoil him to death." By now I was holding on to Dwayne's forearm with both my hands. He looked at my fingers digging into his skin and I let him go.

Just like that, I let him go.

"I don't want to be married to somebody who would look me in the face and lie to me. Somebody who will let everybody in town know what's up except for me. I wasn't raised like that."

"I'm sorry," I said. "I'm very sorry."

He wiped his mouth with the back of his hand. "So what are you going to do about it? Untell the lies? Un-sign the papers for me to get my boy back?"

I could have cried then, using my tears to show the breadth of my regret. But the sight of my remorse spilling down my face would provide no comfort for Dwayne, no relief for me.

"I'm sorry," I said again.

"So what?" Dwayne stood up with a sigh of box springs and headed toward the door.

I can imagine Dwayne leaving 739 Willow Street, snagging his foot on the roots of the hickory tree dominating the front yard. In my mind I see him starting the Crown Vic, looking at his own face in the rearview mirror, switching on the headlights before pulling away.

In my old bedroom I pulled back the plaid spread on my childhood bed, covering myself with those familiar sheets.

Chapter Sixteen

Rochelle eloped in the middle of August, on a Wednesday afternoon. "The ritual has obscured the meaning," she explained to me that morning, without hinting of her plans. At lunchtime on the very same day, Rochelle floated into my office smelling of hot weather. "I love my mom, you know I do. But she is driving me crazy. If Rod and I do not get married right now, *today*, I will never speak to my mother again." I was sitting at my desk, quietly eating bread and a slice of cheese.

I didn't interrupt her as she spoke, spilling her rationale. This was how I was these days, more quiet, trying to listen to people when they talk. I hope that if I listen closely, someone will say something to me that will make the world easier to understand. I'm not depressed, as I had to explain to Rochelle. I'm just quiet.

Of course I agreed to be a witness, signed my name on the important line, used my best penmanship. The bride and groom wore what they had worn to work that day. Rod in his dentist's scrubs, Rochelle in a knee-length denim skirt and canvas tennis shoes. The judge, young and worried-looking, assumed that I, wearing my linen dress and matching jacket, was the bride. After a few awkward seconds, he figured out who was who and proceeded to marry them. I took my role very seriously; I was there to *witness*.

I watched Rochelle answer all the judge's questions with a sincere "I will." I believed her, I loved her, and I envied her.

On the ride home she was reflective. "You know," she said, "everything that seemed so crucial, so huge, so *decisive*, the dress, the guest list. None of that seems important anymore."

Rod concurred, thoughtfully stroking his chin as he navigated through downtown traffic. "I agree completely. But I am not going to be the one to tell your mother."

In the backseat I didn't comment, but I was reflective as well. It would be easy to get married in tennis shoes when you knew you had seventeen yards of hand-beaded Chinese silk hanging in your closet. But I didn't say anything. I am learning to listen more these days.

But Rochelle, being herself, and having the spooky ability to see into my heart, left two gifts for me. I know that I was supposed to give presents to the newlyweds, but she deleted all her registries, insisting that she needed nothing. She bequeathed to me Kitten and all of his toys and gadgets. This, she made in an official presentation after the movers had hauled all of her things to Rod's home. The second gift I found later that evening, when I was alone in the house, so lonely that I could taste her absence.

Hanging in my closet, near the back, beside my winter coat, was Rochelle's extravagant wedding gown with all its careful beadwork and brocade. She had used a seam ripper to remove Rod's initials from the train. Tiny snippets of threads, like silken stubble, showed where his name used to be. Shoving all of my clothes to one side of the closet, I gave the gown room to breathe.

Keisha had her baby in October. A little boy, named Wellington, but everyone calls him Peanut. He's hers, all eight and a half pounds of him. And she didn't lie. He is a very good baby. She often brings him by LARC to visit us. He is a cute kid, all shining eyes and dark curls. Rochelle, Lawrence, and I take turns holding him over our shoulders and clapping his back. Lawrence whispers to the baby as he takes slow paces across the room.

Keisha herself is doing all right, working more and sleeping less. She seems older now, not in an old and haggard kind of way, just more adult. I do my best to help out. I've promised to look after Peanut on Wednesday evenings while Keisha sits in on Rochelle's GED prep seminar. She will retake the exam just after Labor Day.

When I went to her house to tell her that I couldn't adopt the baby, Keisha hadn't been home. Her mother,

Mary, had answered the door, had let me into the living room, where I took a place on the sofa. I stumbled around telling her how honored I was to have been asked. How very much I wanted a family.

"You're not going to take the baby, are you?" Mary said.

"No, ma'am, I can't."

She crossed her legs and shook her head. "I told Keisha it wasn't going to fly. I took one look at your boyfriend's face and I knew it wasn't going to fly. Keisha said she wasn't asking Dwayne to take the baby as much as she was asking you. But I told her that if your man wasn't having it, you wasn't having it." She raised her eyebrows, daring me to contradict her.

"I guess that's what happened. But it's more complicated than that."

"Not for Keisha, it's not." She stood up. "I'll give her your message."

I didn't stand up. "I want to tell her myself. I want her to know how sorry I am."

Mary sat back down too. "Child," she said, "Keisha has been the blessing and the burden of my life. She was premature, you know, tubes in her ears and everything. It was her idea to give this baby up for adoption. I agreed with the first one, she was too young. But this baby might be what she needs. Slow her down a little bit. Help her grow up some. She'll be disappointed when I tell her that you won't help her. But she'll get over it. Don't worry about Keisha."

But of course I worried about her. I worry about her now. Mary was right. Peanut has slowed her down. I think I am the only one that's not sure if this is a good thing or not.

Dwayne and I have been in touch, to handle practical matters such as his recouping of the engagement ring. We keep things friendly, talking about the things you talk about when you don't want to hurt each other. It is uncomfortable to talk like this to someone that I have loved. Although I have never returned to our old house on Bunnybrooke Drive, I think that it might feel the same way, visiting a place where you lived only to find that the furniture has been all rearranged, that your bedroom is now a solarium or something like that.

I guess this is how love is when it comes undone. No matter how tight you knit the stitches, a sharp tug on a loose thread will transform your warm sweater into a mangled heap of yarn that you can't reuse or repair. I have been making a point not to think about it. "Don't get philosophical," Hermione says. Dwelling on pain, spending too much time immersed in it, tasting its flavors, fingering its textures—this makes it only more potent.

Saturday is my mother's birthday. She will be fifty-four; even if she lives to be one hundred, her life is more than half gone. I have not been to her house since Link's party. The recent sadness coupled with the history of the house, the history of our family, the history of us, has been too much for me. But I will go visit on her birthday, and I will take her flowers, peace lilies tied with simple twine. I will present these blossoms to my mother, kissing her face to feel the warmth of her blood beneath her skin. Dwayne is right: blood does call to blood. I was always waiting for hers to beckon to mine, but I never considered that it would be my blood that would call upon hers.

Epilogue

I think about the dogwoods all the time. It's winter now; without their leaves, they stand in the front yard short-trunked and twisted. Although I've known for years that Hermione was right, that the dogwood was never as tall or as mighty as the pine, there was a part of me that believed what my Sunday school teacher said, that the dogwood grows small and gnarled because its wood was used to make the cross. I understood a world in which there was no way for this tree to straighten itself, and it seemed fitting that even its blooms are marked with four-pointed stigmata so that no one could ever forget what this tree has done.

Just this morning, I walked into my front yard wearing only my nightgown to put my hand on the cold twisted branch of a dogwood tree. The street was quiet. Cynthia vanished weeks ago. As the cold moist ground

soaked the soles of my slippers and wet the cotton hem
of my gown, I wondered about my neighbor, hoping she
was alive and understanding that I would never see her
again.

Tomorrow, while the dogwoods are still honest and
bare, before they hide their bent trunks with oval leaves,
I will find Dwayne and tell him everything. By nightfall
he will know what I told my mother and my sister, how
I failed to deliver comfort to the dying. I will use my
words to show him Eloise, the way she was then, and
Genevieve, the baby she held too close to her heart.

Dwayne doesn't understand what happened to him
and me; he says he can't see why I didn't "just" tell the
truth. But the truth is denser than he can imagine, yet it's
more delicate than my body; it's more complicated than
any love that ever passed between the two of us.

At the end of the summer, before the dogwood trees
blazed with red leaves, I returned Dwayne's ring, snug
again in its velvet box. I offered it to him through a hole
in the screen door. Taking it without brushing my fingers with his own, Dwayne slid it into his roomy pocket,
asking just one question: "Why?" As he stumbled down
the crumbling porch steps, I moved my lips, shaping the
empty air, my words clotted in my throat.

Now the engagement ring is there in the shoebox
where he stores all his disappointments, high on a closet
shelf. Dwayne suspects that this is all there is. Maybe he
believes that he will have occasion to touch the ring
again, to tell someone else what he understands of his
aunt Iola and of me, women frightened by the noise of

the truth. But I am different now; today nothing scares me more than the hollow clatter of secrets.

There is balm in the telling, and in the hearing too. These words, these truths, will ride on the air like a ragged scrap of song. With every lamp burning I will speak while Dwayne touches my hands and listens. I will ask him what he knows about the dogwoods, crooked and ashamed, their stained petals an annual remembrance.

Although Hermione is right about a great many things, she was wrong about the nature of things gone by. This is what I have come to know: Our past is never passed and there is no such thing as moving on. But there is this telling and there is such a thing as passing through.